Eagerly Thomas began to stammer out about seeing the rainbow but he heard the door of the bedroom open and Sandy's footsteps coming through to the kitchen. Trying to hurry out the words before 'himself' appeared, Thomas was reduced to jerky inarticulateness. Frustrated, he described with his hands the extent of the arc of the rainbow, and from his gestures and the one or two intelligible words he had managed to utter, Mairi was quick to deduce what he was trying to convey.

'You've already seen a rainbow? My! My! Thomas, then I think that must have been a special one come just to welcome you to Corrie.' She spoke with a lilting confidence. 'Do you not think that is so?' she appealed to Sandy as he came into the room.

'Aye, indeed,' Sandy supported obligingly. He slanted a flinty smile at Thomas, but Thomas was looking down at his feet and did not see it.

LILLIAN BECKWITH

A Shine of Rainbows

Illustrated by Douglas Hall

THE SHERIDAN
BOOK COMPANY

This edition published in 1994 by
The Sheridan Book Company

First published by Hutchinson 1984
Random House, 20 Vauxhall Bridge Road, London SW1V 2SA
Arrow edition 1985

Printed and bound in Great Britain by
Cox & Wyman Ltd, Reading, Berkshire

ISBN 1–85501–493–9

For Robert

1

Big Sandy plunged his spade deep into the moist, black earth of his potato plot, holding it there lightly with one hand as he flexed his broad shoulders. Looking up, he scanned with narrowed eyes the distant outline of the road, so faintly etched against the rumpled hillside as to be barely identifiable save to the practised observer and then only by virtue of the telegraph poles which, like

7

marker stakes against the vast background, irregularly picked out its route. After a few seconds he bent again to his task.

Several times during the past hour he had paused thus in a manner which, to an onlooker, would have suggested anticipation or even a degree of impatience. Yet, despite the seclusion of the croft and despite being unobserved except by Ben, his sheepdog, Sandy's habitually sphinx-like expression remained unchanged, revealing no trace of what thoughts might be passing through his mind.

Ben, nevertheless, had caught a suspicion of excitement. Lying at one end of the plot near Sandy's discarded jacket, he waited and watched, his body taut, ready for instant command; his vigilant eyes straying from his master's face only to flick a baleful glance at a lone gull which, gliding low overhead, broke the afternoon quiet with a few chattered comments before turning to swoop towards the shingle shore where the boundary of the croft met the restless jostlings of the sea.

Sandy had chosen this particular time of day to begin digging the ground ready for his potatoes because of the situation of the plot. From here, where he worked, he would be able to catch the first glimpse of the mail bus as it emerged from a narrow cleft in the hills to begin its meandering descent into the glen and round the shores of the loch. The moment the bus should come into view, Sandy had judged, would be the moment for him to abandon his digging for the day and return to the cottage. There he would blow up the smouldering peat fire into a cosy glow before hooking the kettle on its chain, all ready to welcome Mairi, his wife, who had been for two weeks in the city staying with her friend Buddy and was now coming home on the bus.

His watching was necessary since the bus ran to only a rough schedule, its primary function being not the carrying of passengers but the collection and transportation of mails to and from the mainland. There being much scope for contingencies at every stage of the journey, first by train, then by ferry and finally by bus, it was rarely possible to guess within an hour or so when it and its cargo of mails and passengers would eventually reach the village.

Sandy continued digging, steadily turning over the ground where, if the weather held, he and Mairi would soon be dibbling in their potatoes. The day was by no means warm; his movements were the easy practised ones of a man who has worked the land all his life but the weathered skin of his face glistened with sweat and there was a recurring dryness in his throat which had the effect of making him frequently want to swallow. With his foot poised on the spade, he turned and tried unsuccessfully to clear the dryness, at the same time taking the opportunity to make a more intense scrutiny of the road. Pushing back his cloth cap as if it interfered with his vision, he flung it so it landed on his jacket. Ben stood up, sniffed at the cap and then lay down again. Sandy wiped his sleeve over his brow and, rubbing his knuckles hard into the thatch of his black hair, allowed the cool breeze to freshen his scalp. Reflectively he assessed the area of turned earth before grasping his spade and resuming his digging.

He had completed the digging of two more furrows the full length of the plot before the bus came into view, crawling like a tiny explorative beetle along the intricacies of the road. As if reluctant to keep to his self-imposed plan, Sandy did not cease work immediately but turned over several more spadefuls of earth before finally wiping his spade on a tussock of sedge. Putting on his jacket, he made with purposeful strides towards the cottage.

The hens, clustered importunately around the door, scattered with wild shrieks and stray feathers as Ben,

unbidden, chased them away. It was time for their evening feed but Sandy was indifferent to their pestering.
Before she had gone away Mairi had pleaded, 'Unless the
bus is fearfully late will you leave feeding the hens the
evening I get back? He'll maybe like to help me to do that
. . . and Sandy,' she had coaxed with a diffident smile, 'see
there are a few eggs in the nestboxes for him to collect.
Perhaps put some there if the hens haven't laid. Town
children love to gather eggs.' Her lovely eyes had searched
his face, anxious for his cooperation. Looking down at her,
his grim expression had relaxed as his own eyes had
humoured her with the tenderly indulgent smile only she
ever saw.

When the peats were ablaze under the kettle he went
over to the henhouse and with a slight sense of dis-
comfiture checked that there were eggs in the nestboxes.
Six altogether. That would be plenty, he told himself.
Back at the cottage he poured rainwater into a bowl and
washed his hands and face, afterwards tipping the water
into a pail in which he dipped the stiff yardbrush and
cleaned the worst of the mud from his boots. Finally he
swept the kitchen floor. He was not a domesticated man.
Indeed, Mairi would not have wished her man to be so,
but he wanted to ensure that he had left no avoidable
untidiness that might, even fractionally, mar the pleasure
of her homecoming. For a few moments he surveyed the
room and then, almost as if he had been denying the urge
to do so, he went through into the narrow passageway
which led to the back bedroom. Opening the door, he
stood, letting his glance travel from the bed with its
patchwork quilt made from knitted squares of wool that
had come from their own sheep, to the curtains of home-
spun tweed which draped but did not screen the small
window; from the shiny new linoleum which covered the
floor to the low shelves beside the bed which Mairi had

cajoled him into making and fixing. It was the first time he had seen the room all prepared and ready for occupancy and he found himself needing to take a deep slow breath as if to reassure himself. As he closed the door and the dryness again returned to his throat, he recognized and acknowledged the apprehension that had been dogging him for the past few months.

Going back into the kitchen and seeing the kettle already steaming, he swung it to one side and topped the glowing peats with still more peats to temporarily dampen down the flames. After a slight hesitation, as if secretly abashed at what he was about to do, he opened a drawer in the dresser and, taking out a blue and yellow patterned tablecloth, spread it over the shiny waxcloth which covered the bare wood of the table.

When they had first married Sandy had regarded with wry amusement Mairi's insistence on regularly covering the table with a cloth at mealtimes. In his own home even a covering of waxcloth had been regarded as a luxury. Admittedly his mother had possessed a tablecloth, but that had been of a sad brown colour which had been used only on Sabbath evenings when, with an air of reverence, it had been spread over the table, masking its workaday purpose and providing a more fitting resting place for the big Bible from which his father, until his death, and then his mother had read long passages aloud to the family. The ritual over, both cloth and Bible had been put away.

Such cloths as Mairi used would have been regarded as sinful frivolities by his parents' generation. Sandy himself recalled feeling slightly uneasy when Mairi had first produced one of her bright-coloured cloths, but he had understood that, having been used to being in service in big houses, Mairi naturally accepted the laying of a cloth as a prerequisite to any meal. He had doubted then that the habit would continue for long after she came to live on

11

a croft that was without piped water and electricity and where ironing meant heating an old-fashioned box iron. The extra labour involved in laundering unnecessary tablecloths would, he reckoned, soon make her dispense with them. But he had been wrong. In the ten years they had been married not once had she set food before him without first covering the table with a prettily coloured cloth. She possessed a dozen or more of them, proudly bringing them back like trophies whenever she visited the mainland; even buying them from the heterogeneous bundles displayed by visiting tinkers. While she had been away Sandy had not thought to use a tablecloth, but now she was coming home he wanted the place to look as much like her home as he could and, as he smoothed down the cloth, he had to admit to himself that the kitchen was a livelier place for it, making the room look as if it too was eagerly awaiting the return of its mistress.

Had he not been a man, Sandy thought, he would have contemplated having ready for his wife the kind of repast she would have prepared for him had it been himself returning home after two weeks in the city. There would likely have been a chicken and vegetables in the pot, fresh bannocks and oatcakes kept warm by the hob, crowdie and butter, all of her own making; for though Mairi had come from the city she had soon adapted to being a crofter's wife and had become proud of her skills. She had filled the girnel before going to stay with her friend in the city but there was nothing home-baked in it now. Sandy did not reproach himself. In the Islands the demarcation line was strict. It was still 'man for the land and woman for the hearth'. The man of the house provided the food but it was the woman's task to prepare it and no one would have been more ashamed than Mairi had she allowed her man to turn his hand to the chores that were considered hers. Sandy had done as much as he could. The fish he had caught that day now lay filleted and sprinkled with salt on the slab in the larder. The potatoes were washed and ready for the pot. There were jugs of good fresh milk; there were eggs and there was still butter in the keg Mairi had salted down when there was a more than plenteous supply of cream. They would fare handsomely enough, thought Sandy, even without taking into account the extras Mairi would surely be bringing home from the mainland.

Pulling the door tight shut so as to prevent the hens from invading the kitchen while Ben was not there to harass them, Sandy strode easily, hands in pockets, along the narrow sheeptrack that wound between the rocky outcrops of the croft and led to the steps in the drystone wall near which the bus would deposit his wife. Just a few yards the croft side of the steps there was a high jutting slab of rock which in wild weather provided shelter for anyone, even a man of Sandy's height, while waiting for the bus. As the sound of the approaching bus grew louder a sudden impulse made Sandy seek the concealment of the rock and call Ben peremptorily to heel. He discovered he was sweating and was tempted to remove his jacket, but the cursed dryness was there again in his throat reminding him that it would very likely be futile to do so. His perspiration was not caused by the weather. Peering round the edge of the rock, Sandy watched the bus slow to a halt and as the door slid noisily back and his wife alighted he experienced the familiar leap of delight which the sight of her always brought him.

Ben rushed forward excitedly to greet Mairi, his barked welcome mixing with the called farewells of the passengers remaining on the bus. Sandy, on the point of emerging from his concealment as if he had in fact only that moment reached the spot, stood stock still. Dear God! No! No! The silent protest lodged in his chest and a gout of dismay rushed through him. As if stunned by a sudden blow, his eyes stayed fixed on the thin, frail-looking, be-spectacled young boy who, as soon as all Mairi's bags and parcels had been unloaded, had come half stumbling down the steps of the bus to stand, head hanging dejectedly, beside her. Surely not! Sandy's mind resisted the evidence of his eyes. There must have been some mistake, surely? Mairi would never have deceived him in this way; never have intended to lumber him with a burden such as this? The door of the bus slammed shut; the driver put the engine into gear. Sandy was swept by an overwhelming sense of betrayal. He felt a desire to stay hidden a little longer but already Mairi was looking around with puzzled expectancy, obviously wondering why he was not close behind Ben. With an air of complete composure he strode forward, remembering to salute the passengers on the departing bus as he did so, deliberately keeping his eyes averted from the unattractive child who stood beside his wife.

'Sandy!' She spoke his name joyously but the moment their eyes met he knew she had been expecting his disappointment and was now pleading mutely for his understanding. 'Dear,' she said, and as she drew the boy forward with a gentle hand on his arm, Sandy got the impression that she had rehearsed this meeting many times. 'Dear, this is Thomas. Thomas this is himself, my husband. I think you've been told a lot more about him than he's been told about you.'

'How do you do, Thomas.' Sandy did his best to infuse some warmth into his voice as he held out a steady hand. 'Welcome to Corrie.'

Mairi smiled at him gratefully but Thomas seemed uncertain for a moment whether or not he should make a reciprocal gesture. When his small pale hand did touch Sandy's he withdrew it instantly as if pricked by a thistle. Furtively he glanced up and immediately looked down again, either too shy or too miserable to venture a smile or a word. Mairi, aware of the bleakness of Sandy's expression, said hurriedly, 'Oh, but we've had such a journey with one thing and then another. We'll both be glad to get a nice cup of tea inside us, is that not so, Thomas?'

Sandy thought he detected the boy's head move slightly in response to her words. 'Right then,' he said. 'Let's get you back to the cottage.' He picked up the two suitcases. 'Leave the rest of your parcels and I'll come back for them later on.' His voice was terse, making plain his impatience to get moving.

'Oh, no,' Mairi insisted. 'The rest of the bags aren't heavy at all and Thomas and I are quite strong enough to carry them ourselves, aren't we, Thomas?' She smiled encouragingly at the boy. 'But first Thomas must say a proper how do you do to Ben.' She called to Ben, who had already started to follow his master but who, at her summons, bounded back happily to be fussed over. 'You and Ben will soon be good friends, I'm sure,' Mairi said.

Glancing back, Sandy saw Thomas's stiff reaction to Ben's vigorous welcome. His mouth twitched cynically. The boy looks as if he'd be scared of a wee spider never mind a great lump of a sheepdog, he thought.

Arriving first at the cottage, Sandy took the larger of the two suitcases into his and Mairi's bedroom where he left it on the bed ready for her to unpack. The smaller one he placed on the bed in the back room.

'There now!' Mairi smiled warmly at her husband as she came into the kitchen. 'Just look at that, Thomas! A lovely fire and a singing kettle to welcome us home. Is that not good to see?' So far as Sandy could make out she was still getting no perceptible response from the boy but undeterred she went on, 'I will take off my hat and coat now and put on my gumboots. You come through into your bedroom and do the same. And put on that jacket you got from Andy. We must hurry if we're going to feed the hens before they get tired of waiting and go off to their roosts for the night without any supper. And we'll look to see if they've laid any eggs for our breakfast in the morning, like I promised you.' She turned to dart a questioningly conspiratorial glance at Sandy before taking Thomas off to his bedroom. When she returned she was carrying the small suitcase. 'Oh, Sandy,' she called as he was about to go outside, 'it's the big suitcase that is to go into Thomas's room. This small one has my own things in it.'

Sandy took the larger suitcase through to the back room where Thomas was standing looking out of the window. 'That's yours, I believe,' he said. 'Will I put it on the bed?'

Thomas nodded spectrally.

'He seems to be well provided for if he's needing a suitcase that heavy for his things,' Sandy observed to Mairi as he closed the door of the passageway behind him.

'That's because he's had so many things given to him,' she explained. Seeing his brows lift uncomprehendingly, she went on, 'While I was telling Buddy I would need to get Thomas some good weatherproof clothes, seeing he'd only thin ones suited to city life, Buddy's neighbour came in. A few minutes after she'd gone she was back again with a big parcel of clothes her own son had grown out of. Good ones they were too, and she was so pleased at being able to pass them on to someone she knew, I hadn't the heart to refuse them.' She caught her husband's glance of annoyance. 'I insisted on giving her something for them, of course,' she placated him, 'but it was nothing like they would have cost new.'

Sandy seemed unappeased. 'Surely, Mairi, you knew I would not have begrudged having to spend on new clothes for the boy,' he reproved her. His pride was hurt. Although he had not her interest in the boy he was willing to accept it as his duty to provide for him as lavishly as she thought needful.

She came and leaned against him and as her hand went up to caress his cheek his arms closed round her. 'Dear,' she explained, 'it's not just as simple as that. When you've been in an orphanage you kind of get used to hand-me-downs. You long for new clothes, of course, but I can still remember how strange it felt when I was given a complete brand new outfit to wear. The prospect was exciting and I felt as proud as a peacock, and yet there was this strangeness because not one of the things I was wearing had belonged to any of the bigger girls before me. They hadn't the right feel to them somehow. I suppose it's a little like getting into a bed and lying beside someone who's already taken the chill off it, rather than getting into a cold empty one and warming it yourself.' Her lips curved in a small, nostalgic smile. 'The strangeness didn't last long because I was staying on at the orphanage then, but remembering it made me realize that leaving the orphanage and coming to live here with us is such a tremendously new experience for Thomas. To be dressed in all new clothes, I thought, might accentuate the feeling of unfamiliarity.' She shrugged, keeping her shoulders lifted as she went on. 'It's not easy to explain but I feel strongly that we must try not to thrust too many new experiences on him too suddenly. I think he should be gentled into his new life.' She waited, looking up at him as if wanting his approval. 'You see, he'd already met Andy and obviously he admired him a lot so I think he was quite thrilled to be presented with the clothes Andy had grown out of. Maybe he thought they'd help him to grow more like Andy.'

Sandy nodded slowly, accepting her reasoning though only half appreciating it. As so often happened, he felt humbled by her perception and understanding. Swiftly he lifted her until her face was level with his. 'Glad to have me back again are you?' she murmured, her cheek against his.

'Would you believe me if I said I wasn't,' he teased, his hard mouth softening as it moved over her fair hair. Abruptly he set her down. 'Go and feed your hens, woman,' he bade her, though his strong hands made no effort to relax their grip on her shoulders. His eyes dwelt on the sweet curve of her lips as she smiled at him provocatively. He knew himself to be a stern man – stern even with his own emotions – but this small shining woman he held imprisoned in his grasp could so easily shatter his composure. His voice rasped in his throat. 'Go now, while I can still let you go,' he told her.

Laughingly she broke away from him. 'Aye, and if you don't get out and see to your sheep, you'll need to be chasing them with a lamp,' she warned him.

He lifted the smaller suitcase from the table where she had put it and took it through to their bedroom. As he stood recovering from the effect of her nearness he heard her calling Thomas. Returning to the kitchen, he was in time to see them both go past the window on their way to feed the hens.

2

At the edge of the moor where the land began to rear
steeply to merge with the hills, Sandy leaned on his crook,
watching his flock of sheep, many of them still heavy in
lamb, grazing their leisurely way towards the sheltered
corrie where they would spend the night. Ben stood beside
him, quiveringly eager for the command to herd them.
But the command did not come. The sheep were moving

19

placidly, not bunching together as they would if there was a suspicion of danger and Sandy, seeing no reason to harry them unnecessarily, spoke a monosyllabic veto to Ben and turned back in the direction of his croft. Almost argumentatively Ben stood for a moment looking from his master to the sheep before giving in and following to heel.

The gathering dusk was being thickened now by a thin drizzle of chill rain and as Sandy retraced his path he could see two faint glimmers of lamplight from the windows of the cottage. He was used to seeing only the lighted window of the kitchen at this hour, but he remembered that Mairi would no doubt be in their bedroom taking the opportunity to unpack her suitcase and put away her city clothes.

By the time he reached the cobbled path that led to the door of the house the drizzle had developed into a heavy downpour. Ben, preceding him now in his anxiety for the meal that would be awaiting him, became suddenly alert and then, to Sandy's surprise, made as if to go round to the back of the house. Sandy, suspecting the dog had picked up the track of some predator intent on pillaging Mairi's henhouse, made to follow, but at the corner of the house Ben halted and began whining a greeting.

The dark figure which stood close against the wall of the house bent forward to pat Ben briefly before retreating again into the shadows. All Sandy could be sure he was seeing was a pale face uplifted to the rain. Thomas! Astonished, Sandy almost spoke the name aloud. What was the boy doing standing out there in the darkness and getting soaked by the chill rain? Had Thomas been a crofter child he would have thought nothing of his being there since crofter children seemed from birth to be weather-resistant. But this delicate city child? He wondered at Mairi allowing him to be out there; wondered if indeed she knew he was there; wondered why the boy was

standing so strangely still; and then, with a stab of com-
punction, he wondered if Thomas's face was uplifted to
the rain so it might wash away the evidence of tears.
Momentarily nonplussed as to how he should react,
Sandy limited himself to calling a banal comment on the
weather. There was no audible reply and with a sense of
having been rebuffed Sandy turned and went into the
cottage.

In the kitchen Mairi was humming to herself as she
lifted fresh-baked scones from the girdle and wrapped
them in a clean teatowel.

'The rain is on again,' he remarked, thinking that if she
knew Thomas was out there she would immediately call
him inside.

'Indeed I saw that,' she replied. 'Weren't we lucky it
waited until we got home?' Sandy shot her a veiled glance
but her attention was on her baking. She made no allusion
to Thomas.

Pulling a sack from the pile behind the door, Sandy
rubbed the worst of the wet from Ben's shaggy coat before
he himself sat down and pulled off his boots. 'You've
gotten yourself busy already,' he observed to Mairi. 'I was
thinking you would be after bringing back fancy breads
from the city for us to eat tonight.'

'And so I did.' Mairi flashed him a warm, teasing smile.
'But tell me now, who would be content to eat city food
when he could be eating fresh scones from the girdle? Not
you, Sandy MacDonald. Not you, indeed.'

The creases at the corners of Sandy's eyes deepened in
acknowledgement of her banter. 'I would have eaten it
though and saved you having to start baking the minute
you got indoors,' he rejoined.

'Ach, it's just that I cannot help spoiling you, fool that I
am,' she returned lightly. Her voice grew soft. 'It's what I
miss doing when I'm away from you, so I'm glad to be

21

starting again.' She was brushing the flour from the girdle into the fire and her back was towards him, so she missed seeing the depth of tenderness in the look he gave her. But she knew instinctively that it would be there; guessed that he would be covertly watching her as she put away the girdle and spread yet another bright new cloth on the table. She herself was wearing an apron which she had also brought back from the city. Darting a quick, mischievous look at him she caught him unawares as he watched her.

'How do you like my new apron?' she asked, smiling archly at him as she saw the faint flush that always touched his cheekbones when he was embarrassed.

'I was thinking what a swank you're looking tonight,' he said as he bent to put on the slippers she had placed in readiness under his chair. There was a flurry of rain against the window and the catch of the outer door rattled. Mairi glanced at the door.

'The wind's getting up again,' she commented.

'Aye.' Reaching out an arm, Sandy picked up the newspaper she had brought for him. 'I take it you know the boy is out there in the rain?' he said with forced nonchalance.

'I do indeed.' Mairi sounded a trifle piqued by his question. 'Did you think I wouldn't be knowing where he is and him only a couple of hours hardly in the house?'

'I was surprised to see him,' he admitted. 'It's pretty wet out there and he looks kind of frail to be getting a drenching. It's not a thing he can be used to, I reckon.'

Mairi moved over to sit on his knee. 'That's just it,' she told him. 'He's certainly not used to it. Someone would have got into trouble for allowing him to do it. I'm thinking maybe he's out there because that's one of the things he's always wanted to do.' Sandy cocked an eyebrow. 'Yes,' she went on, 'just that. To stand out in the rain and let it soak through his clothes. I'm not going to call him in. Not for a whiley, anyway.' Sandy rested an arm lightly around her as she made herself more comfortable on his lap. 'You know, kids do have secret longings to do what seem to adults to be the silliest and simplest things.' She sighed reflectively. 'We used to confess our secret longings to one another sometimes after lights out at night. You know, the sort of things we'd seen or read about other children doing but which we never seemed to get the chance to do because we were in a home. I remember one girl saying the thing she most wanted to do was to walk with one foot on the pavement and one in the gutter so that she bobbed along as if she had a peg leg. We all thought that was terribly funny. Another wanted to sit on a kitchen table and swing her legs while she stuffed cakes fresh from the oven. That was her idea of having a real home. Yet another longed to swing on an iron gate, letting it clang shut again and again.' Mairi gazed up at the ceiling as if abstracting memories from the air. 'They were such trivial things, mostly. Little mind pictures that we yearned to make come true just once in a while.' She shrugged. 'But we were too well disciplined.' She felt Sandy's arm tighten around her. 'Not cruelly so, of course, but enough to have to subdue our little yearnings.'

'And what was your own secret longing?' Sandy asked.

'Oh, I was so greedy. I had lots, but the one I best remember is wanting to put orange peel in a puddle and then tread it down with my boot heel so the oil squeezed out and made little swirlies of colour which floated on the water. I'd seen a girl do it once, but I wasn't allowed to get my boots wet.' She smiled reminiscently. 'The first chance I got I did it, but it was a fearful disappointment. Perhaps I'd got too old by then to enjoy it the same.' She chuckled. 'Or perhaps it was the orange that was too old because there seemed to be no oil in the skin to squeeze out.'

She sprang up from his knee at the sound of the door opening. Thomas came in. His hair was plastered down with rain and he was having to screw up his eyes against the light, but he looked strangely elated.

'Goodness me, Thomas, but how wet you are. Give me your jacket to dry it and then you go through to your bedroom and change into dry clothes.' The trace of scolding in her voice was deliberate, Sandy suspected, more to reassure the boy than to scold him. He watched obliquely as Thomas took his spectacles out of his jacket pocket and laid them on the table. 'They'll be all misted up with the rain,' Mairi said, picking up the spectacles and polishing them on her apron. Thomas peered at her shortsightedly as she handed them back to him. 'Now away to your room and get into some dry clothes. And be quick because your food will be waiting for you. I'm ready for putting it out right now, so see you don't leave it till it gets cold.' Thomas scurried away obediently.

Sandy pulled a chair up to the table and sat waiting. 'The boy looks as if he's needing a good feeding,' he commented as Mairi ladled fish and potatoes onto his plate. 'I reckon they don't get overfed in these homes.'

'Oh, that's not true,' Mairi denied. 'Not these days. There was always plenty at our orphanage and I dare say that's true of the rest. But it's institution food. Sometimes we liked it, sometimes we didn't. Never anything different to look forward to, though. You know what I mean. But then, I suppose,' she added thoughtfully, 'it must be difficult to please so many children and it stands to reason they couldn't encourage faddiness. If you didn't like what was there you just had to go without or fill up with bread and what passed for butter. There was always plenty of that.'

'And will you be encouraging faddiness?' Sandy asked.

She put food on Thomas's plate and on her own plate

and sat down at the table before replying. Aware that Sandy was still regarding her quizzically, she rested her chin on her hands. 'I might, just to begin with,' she conceded.

'Is it not best to start the way you mean to go on?' he cautioned. 'It will likely be easier for you in the long run.'

'There's not such a lot of variety for him to be choosy about, is there?' she riposted.

Thomas came into the kitchen. He had changed into dry clothes and had rubbed his hair into tousled dryness.

'There now,' Mairi smiled at him. 'Come and sit you down and himself will say Grace.' They bowed their heads.

Later in the evening, when a tired Thomas had taken his candle and gone to bed, there was an unusually long silence between Mairi and Sandy.

'Well,' Mairi said at last with a note of challenge in her voice, 'what have you to say to me, Sandy MacDonald?' She had taken up her knitting and Sandy, having filled and lit the one pipeful of tobacco he allowed himself of an evening, had settled himself in his chair with the newspaper, his long legs stretched towards the hearth.

'I was thinking of asking you if you'd enjoyed your stay with Buddy and Dr Nigel,' he replied.

'Indeed I did so,' she told him. 'And both of them were on at me again to persuade you to leave this backwards place and go to live near them. We'd be able to have a nice house with electricity and a bathroom and the shops handy. Nigel has a busy practice and he's on several committees so he has plenty of influence. He reckons he could arrange for a good job to be waiting for you to step into.' She avoided looking at him while she was speaking.

'Is that so?' Sandy's voice and attitude were expressive of the total disinterest of a man accustomed to being

25

teased on the subject. He continued reading his paper and while she studied his profile Mairi's lips tilted in a fond smile. She had been teasing him, of course. She invariably teased him so when she returned from the city, passing on, in some measure, the teasing she got from friends about burying herself in the country. There were times when she allowed herself to ponder over whether, were she seriously to demand it of him, his devotion to her would lead him to renounce this place and the life he loved to become a city dweller, no matter how repellent the prospect. She suspected he might be prepared to make even that sacrifice. But she knew, beyond all doubt, that she would never ask it of him. Though she herself had grown up against a city background, she had become more than content with the crofting life she shared with him. She enjoyed a visit to the city on occasion – even indulged herself by envying the relative ease of the city housewife's life – but so completely had she succumbed to the beauty of the island with its gaunt hills and wide skies, its seascapes and sunsets, its patchwork of crofts, its clean, so clean rain and soft mists through which rainbows frequently danced and shimmered against the mosaic of the moors, that she could recall no single moment of nostalgia for the city. Despite the toil entailed by lack of amenities, she knew, and she guessed her husband also knew, that should he ever propose their moving to the city it would be she herself who would resist.

The wall clock ticked on hollowly; Ben snored behind Sandy's chair; the rain driven by the rapidly rising wind spattered like hail against the window. Sandy, aware that Mairi was directing anxious glances towards him, waited for her to speak. When she did she put to him the question he had been dreading.

'You aren't very pleased with me for bringing Thomas here, are you, Sandy?'

'I agreed to it,' he countered flatly.

'Yes, I know you did. But you hadn't seen him then. Now that you have seen him you're disappointed, aren't you?' Her troubled eyes were wide above the spectacles she wore perched on the end of her nose whenever she was knitting some intricate pattern. She saw her husband's jaw tighten for an instant before he replied.

'I'll not deny I'd expected you'd choose a boy that had the making of a man in him. Someone that looked stronger and healthier altogether. I'll feel ashamed. . . .' He stopped short, realizing how much his words were upsetting her.

'You were expecting someone bonnier altogether,' she pressed him.

'What man wouldn't?' Her hurt expression stung him but he could not hide the truth of what he felt. His voice became resentful. 'I cannot understand why you'd choose such a shrimp of a lad, Mairi.' He nodded towards the door that led to Thomas's bedroom. 'He looks as if the first gale of wind will wither him.' Half turning towards her, he saw the tenseness of her attitude. Uneasily he went on, 'He's not right for either of us, Mairi. You'll soon see the life here will be too tough for him and then what will happen? He'll be wanting back to where he came from and your heart will be full of new grief.' He paused and after he had cleared his throat his voice became gentler. 'It's you I'm thinking of, Mairi.'

Mairi's hands rested on the knitting in her lap. 'Dear, he won't want back,' she said confidently. 'Not if we can give him a loving home. Nothing else will matter.' Her voice was full of appeal. 'And though he looks frail enough now, what better place than this can there be for helping him grow big and strong? Only try to make him welcome, dear. Please do try, for my sake.'

The tears glistening in her eyes discomfited Sandy.

'You know I will. You know fine I'll do just that, seeing you're so keen to have him here,' he confirmed emphatically. 'But he's not helping me much when all I've got when I've spoken to him is a bare nod. I've not heard the poor creature speak a single word either to you or myself since he got here,' he defended himself indignantly.

'Yes, dear, I know. But it's so difficult for him,' Mairi explained. 'You see, dear, he stammers very badly and it gets much worse when he's nervous, which he naturally would be meeting you for the first time.' There was an anxious frown on her brow. 'He's not backward,' she was quick to assure him. 'He knows what he wants to say but when he tries to speak, the words just won't come. It makes him so ashamed he just hangs his head and tries not to look at anyone.'

Oh, God! No! Sandy felt a new sense of outrage. A nervous, sickly looking creature with bad eyesight was surely burden enough for them to take on, but now, to learn that a bad stammer was yet another of his handicaps! What next would he discover? He stared morosely into the fire, fearing to look in his wife's direction lest his expression should betray the depth of his disillusionment.

'He'll get better, I'm sure,' Mairi was saying. 'But you see, dear, you're very big and strong and you have such a grim expression always that you can be quite frightening to anyone who doesn't know you. Especially to a youngster. Once he gets used to you, I'm certain you'll get on just fine together. Be patient, dear. I do so want the three of us to be happy.' Sandy gave a resigned nod.

After a few minutes of silence Mairi yawned and, putting down her knitting, got up from her chair. 'There's such a lot I have to put to rights before I can go to my bed,' she said and went through to the bedroom where he heard her opening and closing drawers.

Contrary to his usual habit, Sandy relit his pipe and settled back in his chair. He still held the newspaper in front of him but his mind was ranging back over the years since he had met and married Mairi, recalling the sequence of events which had begun three years ago and which had now led to the presence of Thomas in their home.

3

Three times in the first five years of their marriage Mairi had become pregnant, yet she had never succeeded in bearing a child. She had so much wanted a family that it had come as a crushing blow when, her third miscarriage having put her own life at risk, the doctors had made it impossible for her to conceive again.

She had struggled hard not to inflict her grief on Sandy,

but he, knowing how much she had yearned for a child and with what joy she had spoken of the prospect, felt stricken whenever he saw the secret anguish which showed in her hollowed, dark-shadowed eyes. There were times when her suffering made him feel traitorous, his own sorrow being relatively shallow when contrasted with his unbounding relief that Mairi had been spared to him. There were times when he felt shamed by the inadequacy of his efforts to comfort her.

It was not only the loss of the babies that had kept her spirits low. 'Folks in these parts think little of a woman who cannot bear her man a child,' she had sobbed. And he, all too aware of the truth of her assertion, could only offer the solace of a dismissive epithet on their stupidity.

But with time Mairi had recovered well enough to conceal all signs that she might be grieving still over her childlessness. And then about three years ago the postman had brought her a letter which, though neither she nor Sandy could have known it at the time, was radically to affect their lives.

The letter was from a girl with whom Mairi had been friendly when they had been children together at the orphanage. 'She'd been christened Rosebud,' Mairi had told him, her voice teetering on a giggle. 'That's the name she was known by at the home and she hated it. She used to shrivel every time she heard it.' Mairi's giggle broke into a laugh. 'She always said she knew perfectly well she never had and never would look like a rosebud. More like a warty carrot, she used to say, because her hair was red. Actually I remember her as being quite attractive. Just a bit big for her age and a bit bumpy in shape, and she used to get pimples on her face quite a lot,' Mairi reminisced. 'I nicknamed her Buddy and she liked that much better. We soon found we laughed at the same things and dreamed much the same dreams, so in spite of the difference in size

– I was a shrimp then – we got on well together. I missed
her a lot when the time came for her to leave.' A small
frown appeared between Mairi's eyes as if she was having
difficulty in remembering. 'She left about six months
before I did and she took up nursing. I had one letter from
her telling me she was enjoying her job and I replied
telling her I was going into service. It was years before I
heard from her again and that letter came from Canada
where she'd taken a temporary job. By that time I was
working here at the Laird's house.' She looked at Sandy
and her face creased into a roguish smile. 'D'you know, I
distinctly remember writing and telling her about the big
handsome man who used to bring lobsters for the Laird. I
said all the maids were in love with him but that I found
him a bit scary and had christened him The Sphinx
because no one ever saw him smile. I wonder if she'll
remember my telling her that?' Her laughter pealed out.
'What fun it's going to be to write and tell her I married
my Sphinx.'

Buddy had written to say she was now married to a
doctor and was living in the city; that they had two
children; that if her letter ever reached Mairi, she would
very much like her to get in touch and perhaps pay them a
visit if she felt so inclined.

'Oh, I'd dearly love to see her again,' Mairi had cried
enthusiastically, and Sandy, always anxious for her happiness, had given his encouragement. Mairi's stay had
lasted three weeks. She had come back much refreshed
and with an invitation from Buddy and her husband to
visit them again the following year. It had been subse-
quent to this second visit that Mairi had put to him the
suggestion that they might consider fostering a child. 'Not
a wee bairn,' she had hastened to stress. 'I reckon I'd be
considered too old for that now – but perhaps one of school
age or thereabouts.'

Her suggestion had so thrown Sandy that his impassivity had given way to a moment of sharp surprise. Mairi's clear grey eyes had regarded him steadily. 'The ache hasn't gone altogether,' she had explained simply.

'No!' His tone was stilted, as if the word had been wrung out of him. Objections chased one another through his mind but he baulked at voicing them.

'Why so, all of a sudden?' he found himself saying.

'Oh, it's not sudden at all, dear,' she had surprised him by saying. 'It's an idea that's been plaguing the back of my mind for a whiley now. I don't know . . . perhaps ever since . . . ' She broke off, shaking her head as if confused by her own thoughts. 'I didn't speak of it to you because I kept telling myself I wasn't being fair to you even thinking of it.'

'Mairi!' There was reproof in his voice.

'Oh, Sandy! But a man wants his own. Any woman knows that.' She was standing by the table and he saw her fingers clench and unclench as she held the edge of it. 'I cannot give you your own, that's why I felt it wasn't fair. But then, the first time I went to stay with Buddy, she took me with her on a visit to the local orphanage – or children's home as they're known nowadays. Being a nurse and a doctor's wife as well as having been reared in an orphanage, she feels well qualified to keep an eye on things so she visits regularly. I went several times while I was there. It was a happy enough place but we both remembered the little things that don't show no matter how much they hurt: the emptiness one felt when one of the children went for adoption and you wondered why they'd been chosen and not you. That in itself made you feel unattractive. Then there was the criticism if you were a bit rebellious sometimes or if you were slow in being grateful even for something you didn't want or particularly like. Kids can be damned unhappy without showing it.' Her eyes had grown shadowed with remembered sadness and it was several seconds before she spoke again. 'Buddy and Nigel have adopted two children since my first visit,' she said, 'a boy and a girl about the same ages as her own two and they're settled as though they've always belonged there.' Her eyes glowed softly as though she was seeing the four children playing together. 'I'd kind of like to do that for a child,' she said.

To Sandy's relief she had not pursued the subject at the time but, as he knew she would, she had touched on the subject at intervals, not pressing him for a decision but leaving him in no doubt that she was not going to give up the idea easily. He had proffered reasons against her proposal. Might not the taking of a child into their home reawaken past grief? Might it not disrupt their life together, bringing regret rather than happiness? It was not unknown for such things to happen. She had listened to him gravely, her own reasoning blunting his objections. He was still loath to take a strange child into his home, but he knew, despite all his misgivings, he would yield to her entreaties. She had always given him so much and asked so little in return, he could refuse her nothing that would add to her happiness. If fostering a child would help assuage the ache that lingered in her heart, he must be willing not only to accept his share of the responsibility but also to try to warm to the prospect.

'There's so much love we have here in this cottage, dear,' she had whispered when she was finally assured of his acquiescence. 'There's surely some we could spare for a child who has maybe never had very much.' She had been standing behind his chair then, her arms warm around his neck and, inclining his head, he had rubbed his chin against the smooth skin of her hand. 'Buddy wants me to go and stay again before the end of next month because they're all going off to the States for a whole year.

Nigel is going to do some research there, it seems. That means I shan't see them until the following year if I don't go soon.'

'So?' His tone had been one of lenient surprise.

'Well, if you agree, I'd like to bring a child back with me. It would be only on a trial basis to see if he likes it here. We'd have to get all sorts of papers signed before we could officially adopt him.'

She felt him stiffen slightly. 'Him? You already have a child in mind, then?'

'Yes,' she acknowledged. He had noticed the slight catch in her breath. 'His name is Thomas and he's eight years old.'

'Next month seems kind of soon,' Sandy prevaricated.

'Towards the end of next month,' she had pointed out. 'Nigel will arrange it all, seeing he's on the committee and seeing it was he who put forward the idea in the first place.' She paused. 'The doctor here and the nurse and the minister will vouch for you if it's needed, surely.' She paused again. 'I really would like to bring him then.'

'Why not?' The disquiet he felt at the imminent sharing of his home had not been detectable in his voice.

'Dear!' Coming round to the front of his chair, Mairi had dropped a soothing kiss on his brow.

She had been happily painting in the spare bedroom one day in preparation for the new arrival when Sandy had come in. 'My, but that looks fine,' he had observed. 'He'll be greatly taken with all you're doing for him, I'm thinking.'

'I hope he will be.' She had not looked up from her painting. 'You haven't asked me much about Thomas, have you?' she had reproached him. 'Aren't you at all curious to know if he has dark or fair hair; whether it's curly or straight; whether he's short and chubby or whether he's tall for his age? If it had been you who had done the choosing, I would have been bursting with questions as to what he looked like.'

'That's because you're a woman,' he had parried. 'Anyway, have I not always trusted your judgement?'

All he had known about Thomas at that stage was that his mother had died while he was still an infant; that he had then been looked after by his granny until her death when he was only five years old; and that since then he had been cared for at the orphanage where Mairi had found him. For Sandy that much knowledge had sufficed. His mind had shaped no image of the boy they might expect. Boys were boys; some quiet; some mischievous; some wily. Mairi would have chosen well, he had no doubt, nor had he any doubt that in time they would all grow accustomed to one another. He had seen no reason for probing further.

Moving furniture into the back bedroom in readiness, laying new linoleum and constructing shelves had succeeded, as Mairi had hoped, in tempering Sandy's misgivings with interest. There had even been moments – though quickly banished – when he had suspected himself of actually looking forward to having a youngster about the place. A boy he might teach to row and to fish; to set creels; in time to involve himself with the work of the croft. But his first meeting with Thomas had instantly dispelled the interest that had begun to flicker within him. He knew that for Mairi's sake he must make allowances for the boy; that he must fight his disappointment and try his best to take to him. But in his own mind he knew that even if Thomas should want to settle permanently with Mairi and himself, he would never measure up to his own idea of what a boy should be.

He was staring morosely into the fire when Mairi came back into the kitchen. He noticed she was carrying her nightdress over her arm. As she draped it over a stool to

36

warm in front of the fire Sandy raised a quizzical brow. It was unusual for her to warm her nightdress except in the coldest of weather. 'I'm feeling the cold something terrible tonight,' she told him with a little shiver.

Sandy, his own body almost feverish with desire for her, spoke with concern. 'I hope that doesn't mean you've caught a chill?'

'No, I think I just got a wee bit cold on the ferry coming over,' she yawned.

He gave her a meaningful glance. 'You'll soon be warm enough,' he told her.

She smiled vaguely and went back into the bedroom from whence she returned carrying a small flat box. 'You'll be wanting to see the birthday present you're to give me,' she said, handing it to him.

Birthdays went unobserved in crofting communities, and Mairi's insistence on presents whenever either of their birthdays came round was yet another of the innovations Sandy had come to accept. But since he left the island rarely, and then only to attend cattle or sheep sales which were held well on the outskirts of even the smallest towns, he had to give Mairi the money to buy whatever she fancied as her present from him. Opening the box, he saw it contained an arrangement of embroidered handkerchieves. 'Nice,' he commented, giving the box back to her. It pleased him more and more to know that she liked pretty things.

'They're special,' she said, and added with a chuckle, 'The Dear knows if I shall ever get round to wiping my nose on one.'

She went into the larder and returned carrying a pan half full of milk which she set on the hob beside the fire. From the dresser cupboard she took out a glass and a bottle of whisky which she set on the table within Sandy's reach. When the milk was hot she filled a mug and sat sleepily sipping while her husband, after knocking out his pipe, poured whisky into his glass.

Mairi yawned again. 'Indeed, I'm as tired as an old dog,' she said. 'I can never remember being as tired as I am this night.' She finished her milk and picked up her nightie, hugging its warmth against her bosom. 'I'll not wait for you tonight, dear,' she said.

Sandy drained his glass. 'I'm coming too,' he said, getting up and preparing to extinguish the lamp.

'Sandy, please,' she whispered, putting out a hand as if to restrain him. 'I'm so very tired. Tomorrow night . . . ? Please?' she entreated.

She saw the swift look of chagrin and disappointment that crossed his face as he stared at her. His lips tightened and, turning from her, he poured himself more whisky, tossing it back as if it had been a mere sip.

'If that's the way you want it,' he said resignedly.

Instead of following her through to the bedroom he opened the door of the cottage and stood for some minutes peering out into the wind-hustled darkness. Already, so it seemed to him, the presence of the boy Thomas had begun to come between him and Mairi.

4

Thomas woke early, screwing up his eyes against a shaft of steel-bright sunshine which had been newly released from a canopy of morning mist. Drawing up the sheet so as to shut out the brightness, he lay for some minutes wondering a little nervously what he could expect to happen on this first day of his new life. When he had been shown his bedroom the previous evening, his apprehension had been much relieved by its smallness. When he had come to bed, the golden glow of candlelight coupled with the curiously friendly smell of melting wax had helped chase away the last straggling fears of the unknown. When he had got into bed and pulled up the bedclothes, the scent of bog myrtle, which Mairi always used among her stored bedding, had struck him as oddly pleasing, so different from the nondescript smell of his bed at the orphanage that he had soon breathed himself into smiling drowsiness. When Mairi had looked in to dout the candle, he had been fast asleep.

The shaft of sunlight faded and Thomas sat up, appreciating the slowly mounting thrill of finding himself alone. Swinging his legs from under the bedclothes, he let his feet snug into the curly sheepskin as he sat on the edge of the bed, savouring the knowledge that this was the first morning he could recall being wakened by the sun shining on him from between undrawn curtains. At the orphanage it had always been noises which had awakened him: doors slamming; footsteps thumping on the stairs and along the corridors; voices, sometimes querulous, sometimes demanding; bells. As he surveyed his room, he was again conscious of how differently it smelled from the rooms and corridors of the Home. Deciding that he liked it, he told himself it must be the smell of cosiness as opposed to emptiness. He swung his legs back onto the bed and sat cuddling his knees. This was his own room! His and no one else's. Mrs Mairi, as he still called her, had promised him that, and he knew that, more than anything else, he wanted to believe she would keep any promise she made him. Cautiously he tried bouncing on the bed. It creaked a little but it seemed to Thomas that they were creaks of acceptance rather than protest.

He pulled the clothes round him again, reminding himself Mrs Mairi had told him he needn't get up until he wanted to. Not until he started school. His spirits plummeted momentarily at the thought of school, but he pushed it to the back of his mind. Discovering he was eager to get up, he pushed back the bedclothes and slid his feet into the slippers which had been placed handily beside the bed. 'I will have no bare feet in my dormitory,' the remembered voice of authority assailed him as he looked down at his feet. The slippers were orphanage slippers and smacked of orders. Defiantly Thomas kicked them off and padded barefoot over the linoleum to stand in front of the window.

The cottage was of the type usually described as a 'but and ben': squat and single-storeyed and comprising only a kitchen and a bedroom, between which there was a small hallway where gumboots and oilskins could be left to dry. Soon after Sandy and Mairi had married they had, in expectation of the family they planned, built onto the back of the house to provide a small extra bedroom and also a pantry, the two divided by a passageway which led from the kitchen. The windows of the two front rooms of the house gave a wide view of the croft and beyond that of the sea, but the back bedroom which was now Thomas's looked out onto an area of spare grass and dark, almost black, earth, pitted with the hoof marks of cattle and now, after the rain of the previous night, shining moistly in the patchy morning sunlight. The area was bounded by a low, drystone wall within which stood the cow byre, a windowless drystone building, roofed with black felt and breached by a single door, near which there reposed a sizeable dung heap. Sheltered by the nearer gable of the byre stood a couple of dumpy haystacks weighted down by boulders and covered with tarpaulins. Beyond the boundary wall Thomas could see that the land rose steeply as the rough grass gave way to heather clumps, the heather to crags of grey rock which looked as if they had long ago rolled there after breaking away from the distant hills, the shapes of which were still obscured by the swirling mist.

What would have seemed to many to be a cheerless view did not disappoint Thomas. 'Wildness and wet you must expect, Thomas,' Mairi had stressed, not wanting him to have any illusions about the place he was coming to. Wildness and wet there was indeed, Thomas thought, but was it not proof that he could rely on Mrs Mairi to tell him the truth? There would be howling gales to contend with too, she had told him. Gales that could blow a man's feet from under him and drive the rain so hard you felt as if you were being hit by pellets from a gun. 'But on calm days,' Thomas remembered how her voice had deepened with enthusiasm as she spoke . . . 'on calm days there are wide, wide skies such as you've never before thought possible anywhere in the world. And the clouds can smile as well as weep; the sea can whisper as well as roar. And you will see rainbows, Thomas. Such rainbows! Until you've seen a Corrie rainbow, you haven't seen one that's worth a second look. So many there are, I think sometimes how deserted the sky can look when it's not tied with a rainbow.'

Standing there by the window, Thomas caught his breath incredulously. Even as he watched, a rainbow began to emerge from the mist, reticently at first and then more decisively, until it had formed an arc of such vividness that its shimmering splendour appeared to imprint a secondary arc, only a fraction less brilliant, on the sombre slopes of the hills. Thomas, enraptured by the sight, could hardly breathe. He could see one end of the rainbow and, pressing his face against the windowpane, he strained to see if he could see the other end, but the window was too small. Although he had seen rainbows before, they had been rare sights and pallid in contrast. Never had he seen or dreamed of seeing a rainbow which seemed to dominate the sky with its brilliance and looked sturdy enough for him to climb, had he really wanted to. He ran quickly to the door of his room, intent on dashing outside to try and chase the rainbow, but remembering he was not dressed, not even wearing the hitherto compulsory slippers, he shuffled his feet into them. He knew he ought to dress but there was no time and Mrs Mairi would surely understand the urgency, he told himself. She would be eager for him to see such a sight. But as his hand grasped the latch his resolve faltered. Supposing he should encounter 'himself' there in the kitchen and not Mrs Mairi? Thomas's brow puckered with doubt. 'Himself' seemed so stiff and unyielding Thomas thought he would be unlikely to understand the magic of rainbows and how compelling was the impulse to rush outside so as to see it in its complete glory. He stood for a few frustrated seconds, torn between the desire to rush out as he was and risk 'himself's' displeasure, or waste precious time dressing. Mrs Mairi had assured him that 'himself's' forbidding expression concealed a warm and gentle nature, and though Thomas believed her, he was fearful of putting his belief to the test so soon. Releasing the latch, he sped back to the window. The rainbow was still visible but much of its brilliance had paled; the encroaching mist tore it into segments and within seconds it had disappeared.

Still exhilarated by what he had seen, Thomas crossed to the washstand where he poured peaty brown water from an ivy-patterned ewer into a similarly ivy-patterned bowl. He planned to wash quickly, but when he felt the unaccustomed softness of the water against his skin and saw the copiousness of the soap lather, he dawdled, swirling the water into thick suds until it looked as if the bowl was filled with melting snow.

When he had dressed he went quietly through to the kitchen. There was no one there, but the moment he closed the door behind him he heard the sound of Ben's tail thumping against the floor behind Sandy's chair. Lazily Ben rose, stretched and offered himself for a fussing, after which he returned to his place behind the chair. Thomas saw that the grate was full of peat ash which seemed to indicate that neither Mairi nor 'himself' were up, but as he was debating whether he should return to his own room and wait until he heard someone stirring, Mairi came through into the kitchen, fully dressed but still engaged in tying the strings of her apron.

'Why, Thomas!' she exclaimed with a broad smile. 'You're up and about awful early. I was thinking you would be staying in your bed just to celebrate not having to get up.'

Eagerly Thomas began to stammer out about seeing the rainbow but he heard the door of the bedroom open and Sandy's footsteps coming through to the kitchen. Trying to hurry out the words before 'himself' appeared, Thomas was reduced to jerky inarticulateness. Frustrated, he described with his hands the extent of the arc of the rainbow, and from his gestures and the one or two intelligible words he had managed to utter, Mairi was quick to deduce what he was trying to convey.

'You've already seen a rainbow? My! My! Thomas, then I think that must have been a special one come just to welcome you to Corrie.' She spoke with a lilting confidence. 'Do you not think that is so?' she appealed to Sandy as he came into the room.

'Aye, indeed,' Sandy supported obligingly. He slanted a flinty smile at Thomas, but Thomas was looking down at his feet and did not see it.

'Doesn't that just go to bear out what I have been telling you about this place, Thomas? This is surely rainbow land and just now is rainbow weather when the mist and the showers and the sunshine all want to take their turn at outdoing one another,' she continued. 'And if there's a pot of gold at the end of every rainbow as the Irish believe, I'm thinking Corrie must be near sinking under the weight of it all.'

Thomas watched her poke dry twigs among the peat ash in the grate. Almost immediately smoke rose from them and with a pair of bellows she blew the smoke into flame before building dry peats expertly around them.

'There now,' she said when, having checked the kettle was full, she hung it over the fire. 'We will go now and let out the hens, Thomas. The earlier they're about in the mornings, the more inclined they are to lay. Go and put on your gumboots. The ground is terrible boggy after all the rain we've had, so I doubt you'll need to be taking them off again until you're ready for your bed.'

When they opened the door to go outside they saw there was still a fine drizzle of rain. Mairi, picking up a couple of hessian sacks from a rack behind the porch door, draped one around her own shoulders and, handing the other to Thomas, bade him to do likewise. 'It will keep this bit of rain off you well enough,' she told him. More than anything she had said up to now, her calm instruction made Thomas feel that, so far as she was concerned, he had already slipped into place in the household.

Before he had left the orphanage it had been made clear to Thomas that his stay at Corrie was to be for a trial period. Only then, if he felt he could be happy with Mairi and Sandy and they with him, would the arrangement be finalized. Despite the aloofness of 'himself', it took Thomas less than a month to make up his mind that he wanted to stay with Mairi for ever at Corrie.

But it was not just his feeling for Mairi that accounted for his wish to stay. The wish was compounded of delight in the privacy that having his own bedroom gave him; of the relative freedom of life on the croft and the discovery that each day was likely to bring some new experience – an experience which, if he felt so inclined, he could probe further without fear of fuss or reprimand. Accustomed in the past to rising early at the start of a disciplined day, he still woke early, but now waking was tinged with expectation. Everything was different. Just the act of getting up was different. Now, instead of dressing immediately, he went first to look out of his bedroom window, hoping to catch a glimpse of some creature of the early dawn. Already he had been rewarded by the sight of a buzzard being mobbed by ravens; of a hedgehog snuffling around the haystacks; of a weasel sinuously exploring its way along the drystone wall; of a cat, far too large, he was sure, to be any domestic cat, streaking away up the croft in the direction of the moors.

He wanted to stay at Corrie. Of that there was no shadow of doubt in Thomas's mind. He could not bear to think that he might some day have to return to the orphanage. What he must hope for now, he told himself, was that Mairi and 'himself' should want him to stay with them. Mairi made no secret of her affection for him and of her joy in having him share her home. But 'himself' remained taciturn. Although Thomas sensed his kindness and longed to respond, Sandy so rarely spoke to him directly that when he did so, Thomas, caught offguard, became tongue-tied, too ashamed even to look up. The fear of incurring 'himself''s' displeasure was a constant tremor at the back of his mind and, miserably wrestling with the problem, Thomas could think of only one solution and that was to make himself so useful around the place that 'himself' would agree to him staying for that reason alone.

5

On the first day of the new term Mairi accompanied
Thomas to the village school, where he was enrolled
among the dozen or so scholars. Not having met any of the
village children, Thomas had been dreading this day and
as a consequence was stiff with nerves and stammering
uncontrollably. The orphanage school had taught him
how cruel children can be towards affliction and he had

suffered much from the persistent, though necessarily covert, mockery and mimicry of some of the pupils. But, to his bewilderment and relief, he discovered that the Corrie children were shy of him as a stranger in their midst. Once over their shyness, they showed plainly that their interest was in himself, as a city boy, not in his affliction. Far from mocking him, they tried hard to understand him, framing their questions so a nod or a gesture was sufficient reply. When he had to struggle for speech they waited with patient understanding, displaying neither irritation nor turning away before he could complete what he was trying to say.

At the orphanage school Thomas had sought every opportunity to isolate himself from the other pupils, but here at Corrie he allowed himself to show a reciprocal interest, and the shared curiosity led to a gradual shedding of reluctance to mix with them. As he grew more relaxed in their company he found his throat muscles more yielding to his will. His stammer began to ease, giving him the hope that the day would come when he would be able to speak as fluently as they.

But it was Mairi and the seals who most helped him to overcome his stammer.

Every day, except in the stormiest weather, Mairi made a point of going down to the shore, and whenever he could Thomas liked to accompany her. Mairi seemed to regard the shore much as a supplementary store cupboard and there, in their season, she and Thomas would gather winkles to boil and eat; dulse to make soup, and carragheen for puddings. There they collected driftwood, carrying it home in rope-tied bundles or, if it was too heavy, dragging it up above high-tide line for Sandy to collect later. Sometimes they just wandered over the shingle picking up attractively coloured stones or interesting pieces of flotsam and jetsam. Other times they simply made for their favourite vantage point, a large boulder, black and shiny as a wet oilskin, which Mairi called Rabbit Rock because it resembled the shape of a crouched rabbit. There they would sit, watching and listening to the sounds of the sea and the gulls, while at the same time keeping their eyes open for the occasional school of porpoises or lone basking shark or for the more common sight of bobbing seals.

They were sitting on the Rabbit Rock one day when two young seals rose out of the water, obviously disputing the right to a large salmon which one of them held in its jaws. The dispute settled, the seals submerged. After a few minutes Mairi said, 'Let's try calling them back, shall we, Thomas?' Thomas smiled, suspecting her of joking. 'Yes, I can call seals,' she confirmed. 'Would you like to hear how I do it?' He nodded, still smiling tentatively. 'Listen then, and keep watch,' she told him. Putting her hands to her mouth and lifting her normally soft voice, she startled Thomas by sending out a loud ululating cry, amplifying and directing the sound by the movement of her fingers. Repeatedly she called, and Thomas, scrutinizing every joggle of a wave, perceived at last the shiny, dark blob of a seal's head emerge from the water. Thomas turned to gape at Mairi in surprise and delight. She continued to call and soon the head of a second seal appeared close to the first one.

'They've seen us,' Mairi cried. The seals seemed to be watching them curiously. 'Now, Thomas, see if you can imitate me and call them in closer.'

Irresolutely Thomas put his hands up to his mouth. 'Go on!' Mairi urged. 'Take a deep, deep breath and then push it out with all your strength.' Thomas did as she said but his call came out feebly. 'Louder!' commanded Mairi. She put a fist on his abdomen. 'A great big breath now,' she instructed. Thomas breathed deeply and felt a kind of hiccough in his chest as his throat swelled and the sound he was striving to make burst freely from his mouth. Immediately his hands dropped loosely as if the effort had weakened him. The seals stayed where they were, watching them but not coming any closer inshore. 'Try again!' Mairi could not disguise the satisfaction in her voice. When for a second time Thomas's call boomed out, the seals submerged, but just as he was beginning to feel disappointed, they bobbed up again, discernibly nearer the shore.

'No, not again!' Mairi said as Thomas, with growing confidence, was about to put his hands again to his mouth. 'The tide's going out so they won't come in closer for fear of getting stranded.'

The seals were still visible, bobbing up and submerging as they ranged along the coast, when Mairi decided it was time to return to the cottage. The third time Thomas turned to look over his shoulder towards the sea Mairi said, 'Did you know that some folks believe you should always tell your sorrows and joys to the seals?' Thomas shook his head. 'They do indeed. They say the seals take messages to the seal king. If you tell them good news there's a great rejoicing among seals everywhere.' Mairi paused. Thomas looked up at her inquiringly. 'And if it's sad news,' she went on, 'the seals ask the seal king to help you. And they say he does; that the very next seal you see will bring you a sense of great comfort. That's why you should always tell the seals when someone you love has died because the seals are supposed to keep in touch with the spirits of those who have passed on and can give them messages about things you'd like them to know about.'

Thomas regarded her gravely. 'D'-d'-you b-believe these things?' he asked.

'Yes, I think I do,' Mairi replied with equal gravity, though she was careful to keep her fingers crossed. 'I believe if you were to ask the seals to help you get rid of your stammer then they would.'

Since she had come to live in Corrie, Mairi had heard many stories of people who were reputed not only to be able to call seals but also to communicate with them. She had heard about seals taking human shapes; of women having seal lovers and being carried off to sea. They were part of the folklore of Corrie along with the stories of 'wee folk' and 'water horses'. By this time Thomas had probably heard them too, but when she had told him she herself could call seals, her claim had been the result of a sudden impulse which itself had sprung from a desire to find some way of helping Thomas combat his stammer. She was familiar with seal noises as groups of them frequently hauled out on the skerries beyond the bay where they conferred and grumbled as they jockeyed for the best positions on the rocks. All she had to do was to try to imitate them. When the first seal had appeared she had been even more surprised than Thomas. She knew it was no more than coincidence, but all the same, when the second seal bobbed up she wondered if her mimicry was being successful.

When Thomas had summoned his own throat to produce the sound, she had been so overjoyed that on the spur of the moment she had invented the story of the seal king and seal messengers, hoping that if she could encourage him to use his voice to call regularly to the seals, he might find it easier to control his stammering. To her delight the strategy appeared to work. Often, after he had come home from school, Thomas, without saying where he was going, would disappear for half an hour and would come back bringing the smell of the sea with him. One evening when he returned he confided stumblingly, 'The seals c-came. I asked th-them t-to tell my G-Gran how happy I w-was here.' He and Mairi exchanged a shy conspiratorial glance and Mairi exonerated herself from any vestige of guilt over her deception.

Gran was the only mother Thomas had ever known, his real mother having died before he was three months old. That much Mairi had learned from the orphanage records, but when she and Thomas were alone together, and as his speech improved, she had, by reminiscing about her own orphanage experiences, gently drawn him into recalling memories of his own childhood. The memories had come fitfully, usually sparked off by something she had said, but from them she had pieced together a fairly complete story.

He appeared to have had a happy if fairly repressed childhood, his Gran having been a loving but often irritable and sharp-voiced guardian, not much given to any display of affection. When he had discovered that other children of his age had someone they called their 'Mum' and he had asked why he couldn't call her 'Mum' instead of 'Gran', she had explained that she was not his 'Mum' and had told him gently enough about his mother. The same had not happened when he had asked why he had no one to call 'Dad'. Then the snapped reply had been, 'He was a bad man. I will not speak of him!' With timid persistence strengthened by yearning, Thomas had pursued his questioning, wanting to know how bad his father had been, but his Gran had glared at him, angrier than he had ever seen her. 'He didn't want your mother and he didn't want you when you were born,' she had told him and Thomas, cringing at the terrible disclosure, had never again felt tempted to ask about his father.

Shortly after his fifth birthday and only two days before he was looking forward to hanging up his stocking for Santa Claus to fill, Thomas had been wakened by hearing his Gran's voice calling to him from across the narrow landing that divided their bedrooms. Running quickly into the old lady's room, he had found her fighting for breath and, between gasps, trying to tell him to run and get the next-door neighbour. As soon as the neighbour had arrived she had sent Thomas to call yet another neighbour and shortly afterwards the nurse had arrived. Thomas remembered being worried, but since he had been told he must stay downstairs he had sat in the Christmas-garlanded kitchen trying to give all his attention to his toys. He was there to see the doctor arrive and to see him leave a few minutes later. Thomas's worry eased. A doctor would have to stay a long time with someone who was really ill, he had reasoned. The fact that the doctor had left so soon after arriving meant that Gran was going to be all right again. He had worked out in his own mind what must have happened. His Gran had been doing the Christmas baking the previous evening and she was always popping bits of whatever she was mixing into her mouth as she worked. She must have got one of the bits stuck in her throat, he reckoned, and that was why she had been gasping so much. Now the doctor had been able to remove whatever it had been and she would soon be well again. He could imagine how she would chide herself for having been so careless. Except for low murmurings and soft treads upstairs, the house had settled back into its usual quiet, which seemed to Thomas to bear out his theory. Any minute now he expected to be told he could now go upstairs and see his Gran. But the first neighbour had come down and explained that Gran was sleeping and the doctor had said she mustn't be disturbed. Shortly afterwards the second neighbour and the nurse had come down, and the second neighbour had taken him to have dinner with herself and her two children who, though they sometimes bullied him, he counted among his playmates.

He had stayed on for tea but he had begun to worry again about his Gran. He told his neighbour he must go back to the house, but she had said no, not yet; Gran would still be sleeping. After her own two children had been told to go to bed she had drawn him to her gently and told him that he would have to stay for a few more days because his Gran had died and was now on her way to Heaven.

Thomas hadn't believed her. At that age his ideas about death had been misty and confused. People who died vanished so you never saw them again. Thomas was quite sure his Gran hadn't vanished. Gran was asleep in her own bed in her own bedroom. Death happened to people who had accidents or who had been taken to hospital because they were poorly. His Gran hadn't had an accident and only last night she had been teaching him to sing 'Good King Wenceslaus' while she baked mince pies. He hadn't been able to believe that someone could bake mince pies one night and then die the very next morning. Somebody had made a mistake. Gran would wake up again soon and tell everybody off for being such fusspots. But all the same, he wanted to run back to the house just to make sure. Again the neighbour had restrained him. Granny's house was now locked up. He would not be able to get inside. He remembered he had cried then, not because he had come to believe his Granny was dead but because he knew it was expected of him.

Still only half convinced that Gran would not appear and briskly take him back home with her, he went numbly through the Christmas celebrations. But then, two days after Christmas, the elder of his two playmates had confided that while Thomas had been taken shopping he had seen a van arrive at his Gran's house and some men had carried away his Granny in a big black box. Thomas admitted to having started to scream out loud then, partly because of the dreadful image that formed in his mind, partly because he now knew that what everyone had been telling him was true. He was never going to see his Gran again.

His next memory was of the minister, a restless little man, a bit like a blackbird, Thomas recalled, who had set him on his lap telling him he must try not to be sad any more because his Gran was now resting safely in the arms of a loving Jesus. Thomas's pale cheeks had reddened with shame as he confessed to Mairi how he had turned on the minister, pummelling at his face and crying that Jesus couldn't be loving like people said. That he must be cruel because he wanted people packed in big black boxes before they were sent to him.

When he had been told he was soon going to live in a big house where there would be lots of other children for him to play with, his first idea had been to get into his Gran's house some way or other and barricade himself in so that no one could take him away. He described the old house vividly. His own little bedroom with the peg rug Gran had made; the kitchen with its big range; the sturdy wooden table on which he could spread out his drawing books when Gran wasn't using it for baking or under which he could take his toys and pretend he was in a castle or in a tent in the desert. He spoke fondly of the red paisley-cushioned sofa which always seemed to be holding out its arms invitingly; he remembered the rows of plates, shining like friendly faces on the shelves of the big dresser which Gran had always kept so well polished it seemed every firelight flame was reflected by the dark wood.

His playmate, eager to be first with the information, had told him, 'It's not really a big house you're going to at all. It's an orphanage.' He had spoken the word gloatingly, Thomas said, as if it was the only three-syllabled word he knew. 'Children who haven't got mums and dads are sent to orphanages when nobody else wants them.'

Until that moment Thomas had been wanting to get

away from his temporary home as soon as he could, but anyone's home was then, it seemed to him, better than an orphanage. He remembered working up the courage to ask if he could stay on but there had been so many reasons against it, it was plain even to him that they simply didn't want him. The neighbour had cried a little but it hadn't convinced Thomas. He knew it was because he didn't belong. Remembering about his father, it seemed that there was no one to want him now that his Gran was dead.

The morning the car had come to collect him he had noticed a furniture van outside his Gran's house and some men loading the big dresser into the van. He told Mairi he had thought then that Gran must be missing her dresser so much she had asked Jesus if it could go to Heaven with her. He'd wondered if he could hide inside it and go and be with Gran again. But they were sure to see him and prevent him, he'd thought. Resolving to be brave and not watch any more, he was turning away but just then he caught sight of two more men carrying out the paisley-patterned sofa. He'd felt a sudden urge to take a last look at it before it was taken away and ducking from his escort he had started to run towards the van. A shout of laughter made him pull up short and to his horror he had seen that one of the arms of the sofa had been broken off. The man who was laughing was waving it about for his mate to see. 'The old sofa's no more than firewood,' he had called as he tossed the arm into the back of the van. Someone had come and led Thomas back to the car then – the car that was going to take him to what he thought of as yet another place of 'not belonging'.

Of his life at the orphanage Thomas spoke little. He remembered being ill shortly after he arrived there and he thought the illness had been quite a serious one because afterwards he'd been sent for a time to a convalescent home near the sea. He thought he must always have had a tendency to stammer because Gran had sometimes reproved him about it, but he seemed to think it had got much worse as a result of his illness. He couldn't remember having been teased about stammering before, but as soon as he returned to the orphanage and had begun to attend the orphanage school the teasing and the taunting had begun, so much so that he had come to dread having to speak at all. It had been decided he must wear spectacles too and he'd hated that. They made him clumsy, he said, because they never stayed in place on his nose. He appeared to retain no pleasant memories of his life at the orphanage save of a brief friendship with a girl of his own age who had also stammered but who all too soon had been whisked away by adoptive parents.

Mairi, who, throughout her own childhood and adolescence, had known at first hand the difficulties some children faced in adjusting to communal life, was deeply touched. Sometimes, when Thomas had broken off suddenly in the middle of retailing some memory, as if he found it too painful to recall, she longed for his further confidence. But at no time did she press him. As much as he told her, she felt, he needed to tell someone. It was as if he wanted the telling to ease the lacerating awareness of being unwanted which was still gnawing at his young mind. Mairi, sensing it was also, however unwittingly, an appeal against further hurt, yearned to reassure him but she knew from experience that children who have been badly hurt do not easily accept such assurances. She could only wait to convince him until he had absorbed the permanence of Corrie as his home and learned trust in his own way.

Once or twice Thomas asked her about her own life in an orphanage and Mairi had told him that, since she had never known her parents nor any relatives, nor indeed any other life she had been content enough. 'What you've never had you never miss,' she said lightly. But when she had met his puzzled eyes she had admitted to sometimes being aware of a sense of deprivation, as when those children who could recall a pre-orphanage life swapped wistful memories which gave glimpses of what a home might be. She told him how, when she had been very young, one girl had disclosed that whenever one of her teeth came out she would wrap it in a piece of paper and put it under the pillow for the tooth fairy who would then come and take the tooth and leave a sixpence in exchange. Mairi had never heard of such a happening but she remembered when her next tooth came out to pop it under her pillow as the other girl had said. But it seemed tooth fairies didn't visit orphanages because the tooth was still there the next morning and the next and the next until eventually she had thrown it out of the window in a fit of rage and disappointment.

While she talked she was mixing scones in a bowl on the table and when she looked up she saw that Thomas was watching her sombrely.

'Well,' she said as she wiped her floury hands on a cloth, 'that's all I can tell you about my early days for the moment.' She was gathering up the cooking utensils when Thomas said, so quietly that she barely heard him, 'I wish you were really my Mum.'

His words brought such a leap of joy to her heart that for a moment it was she who felt tongue-tied. 'Let's make ourselves believe that's what I am,' she suggested. Her voice shook a little but her smile was steady.

'If I c-could c-call you M-Mum it would be easier to b-believe you really are my M-Mum,' he said diffidently.

The words were so much those she wanted to hear that she feared for an instant she might sound too gushing. 'Then why not call me Mum,' she said. 'I'd like that.'

'Truly?'

She looked directly at him and saw the blush rising to his cheeks. His eyes glowed as his lips began to lift in a smile that spread ecstatically over his face. 'Truly,' she said.

'M-Mum!' He spoke the word tentatively at first. Mairi's smile was encouraging. 'Mum?' he said again as if testing the feel of the word on his tongue.

'It sounds fine, doesn't it?' They looked at each other as if together they had made some precious discovery. Thomas noticed that one of Mairi's hands was on her heart.

'D-Does your heart hurt you?' His voice was anxious.

'Sometimes. But only when I'm happy,' she said.

Thomas stood up and going into the porch opened the outer door and stood looking out at the weather. She heard him pulling on his gumboots and taking down his jacket from the peg. He did not say where he was going and she did not ask him. She guessed he was going to tell the seals.

6

Thomas, zealously carrying out his intention of earning the approval of 'himself', made determined efforts to help whenever he could around the croft and house. He worked willingly beside Mairi at the potato planting, sometimes wondering as he spaced the seed potatoes in the furrows already dug by Sandy whether he would still be at Corrie to help eat the results of his labours. And when he worked at the peats, helping Mairi lift and arrange the cut peats into what she called 'castles' to dry off before being finally built into the large stacks which would stand firm against the winter storms, he let his mind race ahead to create a picture of 'himself' striding down the croft carrying a well-packed creel of the dry peats; of Mairi deftly placing the peats on the fire; of the way the flames immediately ignited the myriad of rough fibres, first nibbling at them and then leaping to devour and transform them into glowing embers that seemed to him to breathe as they burned. He saw himself poking crab claws into the embers to roast for a tasty evening snack.

He volunteered to look after the hens, not just taking over the feeding of them but also the cleaning of their shed, which he did cheerfully and regularly without the need for reminders. Believing Sandy despised him for his puniness, he took upon himself the task of carrying water from the well, struggling sometimes and causing Mairi many a secret but proud smile because in his earnest desire to prove his strength he tended to fill the pails too full.

He learned to milk the cows and when the time came for the first of the season's calvings and he was allowed to be present in the byre, he watched with as much goggle-eyed concern as the cow herself while the calf was born. A few days later he was feeding the calf, offering his fingers as a substitute teat while it drank the warm milk from the pail.

When the sheep-shearing time came he joined the other children, sometimes helping them to keep the sheep from straying out of the fold but more often watching the shearing itself, intrigued by the way the newly shorn-off fleeces stayed sheep-like as if they had a separate life of their own, so much so that he found himself wincing when they were roughly gathered up and kicked and rolled and thumped into bundles ready for dispatch to the mainland mills for spinning into wool.

It seemed to Thomas a little unreal when Mairi later consulted with him over the colour they wanted the wool to be dyed, and when, weeks later, the carrier delivered two sacks of spun wool which Mairi tipped out onto the table he handled the thick skeins, winding them speculatively around his arms and draping them over his shoulders. When, after several periods of busy knitting, Mairi presented him with socks and pullover knitted from that same wool he felt he could truly claim to belong to Corrie.

After school and during the holiday Mairi encouraged Thomas to seek the company of the other children of the village. As a consequence he joined them in their search for gulls' eggs, practising the trick of testing the eggs for freshness in a can of water. At other times they would take him fishing and once he had been initiated into the intricacies of baiting a line he soon became as expert as they at hooking the small brown trout which abounded in quiet pools in the burns and in bringing in the bronze-gold sea wrasse which populated the deep water around the rocks of the shore.

When a hint of autumn brought the promise of ripening nuts and purpling brambles, Thomas was often one of a group of eager children who, armed with stout sticks and with a lunch 'piecey' in their pocket, would go off to spend a day among the random hazel trees and tangle of sprawling brambles which, when contrasted with the barrenness of the moors, could legitimately be described as a wood.

The more he was in the company of the crofter children the more like them he became in appearance. His downcast expression was slowly replaced by one of cheerful alertness; his spindly body began to manifest signs of increasing sturdiness; his hair, no longer cropped by an over-efficient barber but kept trimmed by Mairi's scissors, was now rarely covered and, responding to the challenge of the wind and rain, showed signs of growing as thick and shaggy as that of a highland calf. And almost without his noticing it his eyesight improved.

When Thomas had been at the orphanage the supervisor had insisted on him wearing spectacles at all times, not simply for reading. Puzzled but compliant, Thomas had done so and in time had ceased to remember that until he was made to wear them he'd been just as able as other children to see the whole length of a street and even to see the birds fluttering among the trees across the park. When he began to attend the Corrie school he was sensitive to the fact that he was the only pupil who wore spectacles. Indeed, he soon found that except for Mairi, who needed them when she was doing close work in the lamplight, he was the only person in Corrie who needed spectacles. The fact that he did so impressed the other scholars. Why? they wanted to know, and when he replied that he could not see without them they made no secret of their bafflement. They begged, in turn, to try them on, peering myopically when they did so and exclaiming how blurred everything appeared. Without any intention of making fun of him, they sometimes withheld his spectacles, refusing to give them back until he had managed to identify to their satisfaction objects which they were sure he ought to be able to see. When he had done so, they gave their unanimous opinion that he could see almost as well as they and was therefore stupid to wear them. Anyway, they warned, it wasn't safe for him to wear them when he was out scrambling and climbing because he, like them, often took a tumble. He could easily smash his glasses and perhaps run the risk of blinding himself. So, in their artless way, they reasoned, and Thomas, eager to earn their approval, was tempted to take their advice. There was, however, an even stronger inducement to Thomas to try to manage without his spectacles.

The Corrie climate produced a superabundance of

misty days and when he was outdoors Thomas found he had so often to take off his spectacles and wipe them clear that it became less frustrating for him to leave them off on misty days and try his best to see without them. When he was down at the shore calling and keeping a lookout for seals, it was not just mist but salt spray which coated the lenses, so again he preferred to take them off and concentrate on seeing as much as he could without their aid. The persistent staring into far distances brought noticeable results. His weak sight gradually strengthened; his range of vision stretched, bringing distant images more sharply into focus. Thomas himself was slow to recognize the improvement and sometimes it was not until he put his hand in his pocket and found his spectacles there that he realized he had not been wearing them.

His sight was still less good than that of other children. He could not, like them, easily distinguish the shapes of deer and sheep on the hills, but then, he accepted, he was disadvantaged. As Mairi explained, Corrie children were born with their eyes looking up to the hills; town children with their eyes looking up to the nearest lamppost. Thomas was convinced that if he persevered the day would come when he could dispense with his spectacles completely.

The change in Thomas was not lost on Sandy.

'I wouldn't have believed it possible,' he remarked to Mairi one night after Thomas had gone to bed. She looked at him inquiringly, knowing full well what he meant but nevertheless wanting him to put it into words. 'The boy,' said Sandy. 'You wouldn't know he was the same child that you brought here.'

'Didn't I say that would happen?' she retorted. 'Now you've seen what Corrie has done for him, do you wonder I wanted to bring him here?'

'Is it Corrie that's made him what he is? Had

you nothing to do with it then?' His tone was ironic.

'A little perhaps.' She paused. 'You've noticed he calls me Mum now?'

'I had so.'

'You don't mind?'

'Why should I?' He darted a look at her. 'What does he call me when he speaks of me?'

'Just "himself". I think he knows you wouldn't have wanted him to call you Sandy so he just refers to you as "himself".'

Sandy grunted. 'Good enough,' he said.

Mairi gave him an anxious look. 'Dear,' she began, 'I wish you'd try and talk to Thomas more than you do. Oh, yes, I know,' she forestalled his protest. 'You've said before you can get no response from him but, you see, he's not nearly so nervous now as he used to be. Perhaps if you tried telling him about what sort of day you'd had on the hill or what sort of fishing you'd had; oh, about anything you've seen or heard that might interest him . . . ' Her voice trailed away as if she was daunted by the expression on her husband's face.

'You know fine I've never been one for much talk, Mairi,' he reminded her. There was an edge of finality in his voice which Mairi chose to ignore.

'Yes, I do know,' she replied. 'But what I'm asking is for you to try. Thomas would just love to be able to talk to you, but he can't. You could talk to Thomas if you chose, but you won't.' She made a small gesture of helplessness. 'I believe it would help him a lot if you could get to know each other better. . . . He's not stupid Sandy, dear. Mistress McLeod says he is one of her best scholars.'

'Sharing the same house with him all this time, do I not know him well enough, then?'

'No!' Mairi's voice rose a little. 'You don't know him. You won't either until you learn to share other things with him. Not just a house.' She was leaning towards him earnestly and her knitting slid off her lap. Bending forward to retrieve it, she missed seeing the dismissive twitch of her husband's mouth. He rose and, picking up the half empty peat bucket and the hurricane lamp, went out to the peat shed. As the door closed behind him, Mairi sighed and resumed her knitting.

Sandy topped up the pail with dry peats and then leaned back against the stack, meditating sourly on his wife's request. He had gone along with her idea of taking the strange boy into her home. He had tried, so far as he could, to make the boy feel welcome. He was resolved to continue to wait patiently for the response which Mairi repeatedly assured him would one day come from Thomas, but not even for Mairi would he be able to shed his natural taciturnity. His dour, religious parents, mistrusting what they termed 'a flowing tongue', had suppressed in their children the slightest tendency to talkativeness. 'Wise men think – fools talk,' his father had been fond of quoting and, having absorbed his teaching from earliest childhood, Sandy knew that brevity of speech was too deeply ingrained in him for him to change now. He stayed for some minutes, letting the sounds of the night soothe his disgruntled feelings.

'Indeed, I thought you must have fallen asleep out there,' Mairi reproached him when he got back to the kitchen. She reached for the teapot and poured him a mug of tea.

Sandy put down the pail of peats and blew out the hurricane lamp. As if he had not heard her he said, 'I believe we're in for a fine spell of weather.'

Mairi sipped her tea thoughtfully. 'I was thinking I would go across to the mainland tomorrow,' she said. 'It's keeping calm enough and the bus has been getting back fairly early the last few days.'

'See and don't tire yourself then,' Sandy warned. The last time she had been across to the mainland she had come back pale and exhausted.

'No, I'll not do that but, you see, it is Thomas's birthday shortly and I'm wanting to get him a darra of his own so he can go fishing.' Sandy thought there was a slight note of challenge in her voice.

'It's a wee bit late in the year to be buying tackle, surely,' he pointed out.

'Not too late, though,' she returned. 'Young Shamus was showing Thomas a good lythe he'd caught only the other evening when he was out fishing with his brother. I think Thomas is hoping that if he has tackle of his own Shamus's brother might take him fishing too.'

'Maybe,' said Sandy flatly, aware that she was obliquely censuring him for never having offered to take Thomas fishing himself.

The next morning, after he had seen Mairi away on the bus, Sandy prepared to go and lift his lobster creels. Thomas always took a 'piece' to school for his lunch and since, when he came home from school, he would see to the feeding of the hens, Sandy reckoned that he himself would not need to get back to the cottage much before the time Mairi would be returning. For some time he had been planning to collect a good plank of wood which had been washed ashore in a cove a little way along the coast, but either the weather had been too stormy or else he had been anxious to get back to his sheep. Today the tide and the weather were favourable and he need be in no hurry. On his way back from lifting the creels he would at last be able to pick up the wood. So he had planned, but when he nosed the boat into the cove he saw a young seal pup lying above the tide line. Leaving Ben aboard, he moored the boat and waded ashore. The seal lifted its head, its big eyes following his every movement as he carried the plank down to the tide line and loaded it onto the boat. In general Sandy considered it best to leave any seal pups well alone since the mother seal was likely to be in the offing ready to tend it when she felt it necessary, but there was something about this pup that troubled him. Going back, he circled the seal deliberately, assessing its condition. Approaching closer, he worked his hands under its body, urging it towards the water. Weakly the pup tried to protest at his handling it, but its head sank slowly down to rest on the shingle. Sandy, suspecting it was weak from starvation, went back to the boat thinking he would try catching one or two fish to feed it, but as he started the engine he thought of Thomas. Mairi had confided the story of the seals and of how Thomas went often to call to them and recalling it made him also remember her plea of the previous evening. He looked at the horizon and at the amount of light on the water by which means he judged that Thomas should be home from school. Instead of steering the boat out to where he might find fish, Sandy turned the bow to head homeward.

Thomas, having fed the hens, was trying his hand at building up part of a drystone wall which had collapsed. He had seen 'himself' coming up from the shore but pretended not to notice.

'Thomas!' The stone Thomas was lifting slipped from his hands as he looked apprehensively towards Sandy. 'Come now! There's something you must see.' Incredulously Thomas saw 'himself' beckoning to him before turning back and making in the direction of the shore. Half bemused by what was happening, Thomas followed him.

Out in the bay Sandy caught fish and then turned the boat towards the cove where the seal pup still lay helplessly, but when he offered the fish the pup would not take it.

'Stay there!' he told Thomas and going back to the boat he returned with a pair of thick gloves. Thomas's eyes were wide with inquiry. 'He's not used to feeding himself. We'll need to teach him or he'll starve. You don't want that, do you?' Sandy spoke in clipped sentences. Thomas shook his head. 'Right. Keep a hold of one of those small fish and, when I force his mouth open, ram it in quickly.' Eagerly Thomas grasped a fish and held it ready while 'himself' held the seal's mouth open with a stave of wood. The fish disappeared down the seal's throat and Thomas pushed in another and then another. The seal squirmed as if the food had instantly restored its strength.

'Leave him now and come away home.'

Reluctantly Thomas followed Sandy down to the boat. He wanted to ask if the seal would survive but though the words reached his throat he could not speak them. All he could do was to sit and look miserably back at the seal.

When Mairi came home and Thomas told her what had happened she listened thoughtfully. As soon as Sandy came in she asked, 'Has it a chance, d'you think?'

'Maybe.' He sounded noncommittal. 'Thomas can come with me tomorrow when he gets back from school and we'll try feeding it again.' He was looking at Mairi, so did not see the look of delight that spread over Thomas's face. 'It should soon learn to take the fish from us.'

'I hope the weather stays calm for it,' said Mairi. 'A storm might wash it back to sea.'

'If it starts to look bad, we'll maybe net the pup and bring it back to the shore here so it'll be easier for Thomas to feed it,' Sandy told her.

Thomas stared at Sandy. When they had both bent over the seal pup together Thomas's questioning eyes had seen for the first time the tenderness behind 'himself's' grim expression, but he was still hardly able to believe he was hearing what he thought he heard. He looked at Mairi and then back again at Sandy. But they were looking at each other and in their expressions there was something too deep for Thomas to understand.

They had fed the seal pup for some days, Sandy catching the fish while he was out attending to his lobster creels and leaving enough under the floorboards of the boat to keep fresh, ready to be taken to the cove as soon as Thomas came home from school. The pup quickly learned to recognize them, moving its head curiously from side to side as it watched them wade ashore, squirming and making little noises, like cut-off yawns, as they approached. It was not long before it was taking fish from them without Sandy having first to force open its jaws and when they left to return to the boat it seemed to Thomas, at any rate, that the pup watched their departure forlornly. And then one evening when they arrived at the cove there was no seal there waiting for them.

'Likely it's decided it can fend for itself,' said Sandy briefly and headed the boat back towards the bay.

Thomas was not as dismayed as he might have been over the seal pup's disappearance, Mairi having warned him that as soon as it felt strong enough it would probably make its way back to the sea to join its own kind. He was more dismayed at the thought of there being no more trips with 'himself', for though few words had been exchanged between them while they were together there had been communication of a sort; a kind of swift interpretation of each other's thoughts that was like the beginnings of understanding. Thomas, pondering over it, was even more inclined to believe in 'seal magic'.

7

In Corrie there was no tradition of birthday celebrations; birthday cakes and the giving of presents, even to young children, were alien practices indulged in by the feckless people of the mainland towns and cities. The staid crofters of Corrie were not disposed to waste time and money on observing such useless customs.

Mairi, who during her years in service had often been

involved in such celebrations, gave Thomas his birthday present darra before he left for school that morning. When he came home in the evening it was to see the table spread with Mairi's newest tablecloth in the centre of which there stood a round, pink-iced sponge cake.

Thomas gasped with pleasure at the sight. 'Is that for me, Mum?'

Mairi nodded. 'That's the best I could manage in the way of decorations though,' she told him flippantly. 'No one's ever heard of birthday cake candles in this part of the world.' She laughed.

When she had spoken to the bus driver about the possibility of his getting her some cake candles he had been so mystified by her request that, dubious as to what he might contrive to find for her, she had thought it wiser not to pursue the matter. When she had inquired at the few shops the mainland village boasted she had been met with suspicious refusals. They sold only standard household candles, they told her frostily, implying by their tone that anything other than a plain candle was, in their eyes, associated with papism. Thinking about their attitude as she was returning home on the bus, she wondered wryly how she had ever dared imagine that cheerful baubles like cake candles could have sneaked, however slyly, into such a stronghold of Calvinism.

Not really seeking an alternative but with the thought lingering at the back of her mind, she had spotted in a sheltered patch of the croft a few remaining plumes of bog cotton which had not been shredded by the autumn gales. She had plucked nine of them that morning and had pushed their thin stiff stalks into the cake as a substitute for the candles.

Thomas was still staring at the cake as if he doubted it was real. 'They look m-much nicer than c-candles,' he assured Mairi with such feeling that she had to believe him. 'They look like silver flags around a castle.' The little smile that was always hovering around Mairi's mouth broadened to embrace him in its warmth.

'You do make me feel clever, saying things like that,' she said.

'You are c-clever.' He loved to see her smile at him as she was smiling now. He loved it even more when it was something he had said that caused the smile. 'You're cleverer than all the other women in Corrie,' he declared staunchly and immediately rushed to get on with the task of giving the hens their evening feed.

On his way back he was met by the strong hunger-making smells of toasting flour and roasting meat and entering the kitchen he saw Mairi bending over the range testing the tenderness of a dish of cooked skart before sliding it back into the oven. The smell of the rich gravy filled the kitchen. Thomas almost groaned with the hunger that the combination of smells aroused in him. He fidgeted around for some minutes before settling down with a book, but all the time his ears were alert to catch the sound of 'himself''s' return since not until then would they begin their evening meal.

When Sandy did get back he brought a pail half full of large crab claws. Thomas's eyes gleamed. What a feast! Skart pie, potatoes, birthday cake and now roast crab claws to look forward to! He had his chair drawn up to the table before Sandy had taken off his boots.

The birthday cake was half eaten by the time they got round to roasting the crab claws and while Thomas sat on the hearth rug, having as usual claimed the job of cracking the cooked claws as they came out of the fire, Sandy watched him secretly, contrasting the pale limp-fingered hands of the boy who had first arrived with the firm, tanned hands which now grasped the poker and wielded it with such confidence. His gaze shifted to Mairi. How much she had done for this boy! How sensitive of his needs she had been! How gently she encouraged him! There were times when, acknowledging in his own mind how little he had contributed to Thomas's transformation, he was pricked by uneasiness. True, he had come to accept the boy as a permanent presence in the household, neither criticizing nor interfering with any of the plans Mairi chose to make for him. He had provided for him ungrudgingly, but he knew that everything he had done had been with Mairi's happiness in mind rather than out of concern for the boy. And there was no doubting Mairi's happiness. The coming of Thomas appeared to have driven away any last shreds of grief over her childlessness. Only occasionally did Sandy notice the lines of strain beneath her blithe expression and then he would wonder anxiously whether the responsibility was proving more of a strain than she realized.

The weeks went by and Thomas, impatient to try out his new darra, was constantly thwarted. The short winter days left no light for him to go fishing after he had returned home from school and the weather that winter seemed to reserve most of its savagery for the days when there was no school. He had to console himself by leaning over the dinghies when he was down at the shore, running his hands along their gunwales and imagining how it would feel to row out into the bay, lower his darra over the side and perhaps return home with a string of fresh-caught fish.

Sandy owned three boats: *Mairi*, which was the motor boat he used for lobster fishing and which was moored in a miniature lagoon formed by a narrow indentation of the coast, and two dinghies, *Puffin* and *Beulah*, which he kept on the shore at the bottom of the croft. *Puffin*, which he had recently purchased, was small and light enough for Mairi to be able to manage by herself; *Beulah* was big and husky, needing a man's strength to haul her up and down the shore and to wield the heavy oars.

With the coming of spring there were calmer spells and lighter evenings, but then the work of the croft occupied most of the hours of daylight and Thomas had to accept that not until the interval between the end of spring planting and the beginning of the harvest would Mairi be able to keep her promise to take him fishing.

On one of the first fine evenings, after the spring work was complete and while Sandy was away inspecting the herd of highland cattle which stayed permanently out on the moors, Mairi said, 'I think we should try out your darra this evening, don't you, Thomas?' Quick as a shot Thomas bounded into his bedroom and, returning with his darra neatly rolled, followed Mairi down to the shore. Together they launched *Puffin* and, taking the oars, Mairi rowed out into the bay. They did not go beyond the bay because, as Mairi pointed out, at certain stages of the tide there was a fierce tide rip in which a small boat could easily be caught and swept out to sea unless there was an exceptionally strong rower to pull against it. So they stayed within the stretch of sea that was held protectively by the arms of the bay and, when they reached what Mairi thought was a likely spot for fishing, she rested on her oars and told Thomas to lower his darra. She had chosen well. Thomas felt the darra quiver almost immediately as a fish investigated the coloured feathers on its hooks. He shouted excitedly as the darra became heavier. Telling him to haul it in, Mairi shipped her oars and hurried to help pull in the line, unhooking the fish before their writhing could turn the line into a tangle that would take them the rest of the evening to unravel. Again Thomas lowered the darra, again the fish flung themselves onto the hooks. But when he lowered a third time the line hung limp. Evidently either *Puffin* had drifted off the shoal or else the

75

fish changed direction, since though they continued trying they caught no more fish on the hooks.

'By the time we've gutted all these and filleted those we want to eat, it'll be time for our supper and our beds,' Mairi said, pulling the boat round and rowing slowly towards the shore. 'Anyway, Thomas, d'you realize if we were to go on catching fish at that rate we'd be near enough to sinking poor *Puffin*.'

Thomas looked down at the silvery fish lying in the bottom of the boat. 'I don't think I'm going to be able to eat more than two of them. Leastways not tonight,' he said mournfully.

Mairi chuckled. 'And that's having eyes bigger than your belly,' she teased.

They gutted the fish, standing at the water's edge and flinging the entrails to the hovering gulls, and when they had finished they put aside what fish they wanted for themselves and threw the rest into the big barrel in which Sandy kept his lobster bait.

'Well, Thomas,' said Mairi as they walked back to the cottage. 'Are you happy now you've well and truly christened your darra?'

Thomas beamed at her. Her hand was resting in the region of her heart as she walked and he knew, because she had already told him, that meant she too was very happy.

In the few weeks that followed and whenever it was calm enough to go fishing the pattern of the evening was repeated. Thomas soon learned how to row, first by taking one oar while Mairi took the other and then progressing rapidly under Mairi's coaching until he could take both oars and also backwater and turn as necessary. The fishing was not always so good as it was that first night but when it was slow they simply let *Puffin* drift, moving the oars sporadically to keep her from heading towards the mouth of the bay. And while they drifted they sometimes sang to try to lure back the seals which seemed to have deserted the bay during the warmer months of summer; or they watched the seabirds busy about their own fishing; or, when the beauty of the night tempted them to linger longer than usual, they shielded their eyes from the glow of the fiery sunset so as to peer down into the violet depths of the water.

But inexorably harvest time crept up on them and again the days were filled with the demands of the croft. Thomas enjoyed helping to gather in the sweet-scented hay and the mealy-smelling corn, but since he had discovered the thrill of fishing he tended to resent the fact that Mairi was too tired after her day's work to be beguiled into taking him fishing in the evening. He could understand her tiredness; he was often aware of feeling tired himself after only a few hours of strenuous harvesting, but given the chance to go fishing he would instantly have forgotten his tiredness.

It was on a day towards the end of the harvest and as he was getting ready to go to school that Mairi reminded him that in two weeks' time the officials from the Adoption Society were expected to visit Corrie, bringing with them the necessary documents which when signed would endorse his legal adoption. Thomas had not needed the reminder. She had first mentioned the proposed visit and the purpose of it three months previously, since when he had wakened each morning with the thought of it gladdening his mind. Throwing her a smile over his shoulder, he dashed off to school, warmed by the thought that in fourteen days he would belong to his Corrie home as securely as other Corrie children belonged to theirs. In fourteen days' time 'himself' would become legally his 'Dad', but Thomas wondered more wishfully than hopefully if the day would come when he would be encouraged to address Sandy as such.

77

The day was grey and by the time school was over lowering cloud had wreathed the land with a drearily persistent drizzle. As the pupils dashed off towards their homes, one of them stopped to observe, 'Ach, I believe it would be good fishing this evening and seeing the day's not been fit for any work in the harvest he'll maybe fancy going fishing.' He darted off purposefully and Thomas, grasping the reason, also hared home, rejoicing that Mairi, likewise having been prevented by the weather from working in the hay, would probably not say no to an evening's fishing. The days were shortening rapidly but if he hurried there would still be time before it got too dark, he told himself. He was breathless with haste as he burst into the kitchen, the suggestion that they go fishing ready to leap from his tongue.

'Mum!' he began. But the woman who was bending over the range was not Mairi. Thomas stopped short, staring in consternation at the district nurse in her blue dress and white apron. He was used to seeing the nurse at the cottage. After she had paid her monthly visit to the school she usually called to have a cup of tea and a chat with Mairi. But now there were no cups or scones on the table and the nurse was in the act of moving a steaming kettle over to the hob. She turned and nodded at Thomas affirmatively as if he had asked a question.

'Your mother is not well,' she told him. 'She is away to her bed.'

The nurse's uniform coupled with her sharp voice brought back memories of an almost forgotten authority. 'Is Mum ill?' he asked timidly. In his mind there could be a big difference between being 'away to her bed' and being ill. He glanced at the bedroom door and then back again at the nurse.

'She's ill enough not to be bothered by anyone,' the nurse replied meaningly. 'Now drink this tea I've made

78

for you and get yourself a piece of whatever you have with it. Then you'd best try and see what you can do to help.'

Thomas drank the tea obediently but there was a tightness somewhere in his stomach that blocked any desire for food. He went outside. It was too early to feed the hens but noticing that the peat pails had not been filled he carried them over to the peat shed.

When he returned with the full pails he asked the nurse, 'Is "himself" here?'

'Mr MacDonald is not here yet, no. I should think he will not be long. No doubt he will be getting a lift with the doctor when he comes.'

The doctor? Thomas experienced a cold tremor of fright. The doctor didn't come all the way out to Corrie unless there was something seriously wrong. He stood irresolutely by the door, wanting to ask more questions but, discouraged by the nurse's manner, he watched silently as she poured hot water from the kettle into a bowl, cooled it with water from the pail and then washed her hands. He was still watching her when they both heard footsteps outside.

'That will be the doctor and Mr MacDonald now,' said the nurse, drying her hands and preparing to follow the doctor into Mairi's room.

Thomas looked up. He had never seen 'himself' look so stonily grim-faced as when he entered the kitchen. Just looking at him brought back so much of his earlier fear that he could not stop himself from trembling. Sandy looked through him and, turning his back, stood staring out of the window, not moving until the nurse came out of Mairi's room.

'Away to your room for a wee whiley till I have a word with Mr MacDonald,' the nurse commanded Thomas. Reluctantly he went towards the passage but with his hand on the doorknob he paused and looked back. 'Himself' had turned to face the nurse and the way the nurse was looking up at him without speaking made Thomas wonder if she too found 'himself' frightening. Catching sight of Thomas still lingering by the door, she gestured him impatiently away. Thomas closed the door behind him and went slowly through to his own room. He heard the doctor leave and assumed the nurse had also left but, on his way out through the kitchen, he noticed her outdoor clothes were still draped over a chair and wondered fretfully how much longer she was going to stay? How much longer she intended to keep him away from his mum?

When he had seen to the hens he looked around for other jobs to do. He built up the fire and refilled the kettle; scrubbed the potatoes for their meal and set them on the fire. He lit the lamp and prepared Ben's meal and last of all he put 'himself''s' slippers beside his chair. He was sitting beside the fire when 'himself' came back into the kitchen. Thomas waited tensely.

'You can go through now, boy,' he said. Thomas jumped up but the nurse was there in the doorway ready to restrain him.

'Now you must be very quiet and sit still. Mr Mac-Donald is seeing me to my car so you're in charge, but only until he gets back. Don't forget now,' she bade him. Torch in hand she followed Sandy out into the darkness.

Very gently Thomas opened the door of Mairi's bedroom. The lamp had been turned low but he could see her lying back against the pillows.

'Mum!' he called softly.

'Thomas!' Thomas had to check himself from rushing towards the bed so relieved was he to hear her speak. As he drew closer he saw she was smiling at him and holding out her hands. When he bent over her, she cupped his face in her hands tenderly. 'Oh, Thomas, did you get a fright

80

coming home and finding me in bed?' she asked. 'Oh, I'm sorry,' she added seeing his miserable expression.

'Are you feeling b-better now, Mum?'

'Lots better,' she told him. 'I'll be perfectly all right soon but the doctor says I'm to go into hospital for a few days just to make sure I have a good rest,' she added.

'Hospital?' There was panic in Thomas's voice.

'Just for a few days. It's silly really but the doctor thinks I won't get proper rest if I stay here.' She put a finger under his chin. 'Don't look so glum about it,' she said.

'It was awful coming home and you not there smiling at me.' His teeth were pulling at his bottom lip and in the lamplight his eyes were shiny with tears. 'If I had to go from here I'd miss your smile more than anything else in the world,' he told her.

'Oh, Thomas,' she said, her eyes caressing him.

They talked quietly until Sandy came back and said the nurse's instructions were that her patient must now settle down for the night. Thomas made no attempt to prolong his time in the bedroom because, even while they had been talking to each other, he had noticed her eyelids fluttering as if sleep had begun to press them down.

The nurse was back at the cottage when Thomas woke up the next morning. 'Get your breakfast and make yourself useful as you can,' she told Thomas. 'There's plenty to do.' She bustled back to the bedroom.

Thomas, resenting her tone and the implication that he would not be making himself useful, went sulkily about his morning tasks. The next time he saw her he said, 'Can I go in to see Mum before I go to school?'

The nurse's voice lost its sharpness. 'Aye, you can do that, laddie. She's been looking for you to go already.'

She was sitting up when the nurse ushered him into the bedroom and in the daylight Thomas thought she looked strangely pale and tired. But she had not lost her smile.

81

'Thomas,' she said, indicating the chest of drawers which stood beneath the window, 'in that top drawer you will find a thin flat cardboard box. Will you get it and bring it to me, please?' He found the box and took it to her and when she opened it he saw it was a box neatly packed with embroidered handkerchiefs.

'This was a present from my husband for my birthday,' she told Thomas. 'I haven't used one of them yet but I will be taking them to hospital when I go so I shall have something pretty to wipe my nose on in front of all the other patients.' She chuckled faintly. 'But this one,' she took out one of the handkerchiefs and unfolded it. 'This one is for you and d'you know what I'm going to do with it first?' Thomas gave her a puzzled smile. 'You remember you said you'd miss something more than anything in the world?' Thomas nodded. 'Well, I'm going to wrap one of my smiles in this for you to keep while I'm away.' She held the handkerchief over her face and above it her eyes glinted with fun. 'There!' She folded it quickly back into shape and put it into his hand. 'Keep it safe and don't waste it,' she cautioned. They grinned at each other intimately.

The nurse opened the door. 'Time's up,' she announced. 'And it's past time you were on your way to school, laddie,' she added.

He wanted to ask his mum if it wouldn't be wiser for him to stay at home but something told him he must not bother her with questions which needed a decisive answer. He knew he ought to ask 'himself', but 'himself', the nurse told Thomas, was up on the croft keeping a lookout for the ambulance. Thomas went dolefully to school.

8

The thought of his mum in hospital had been pressing heavily on Thomas's mind all day, and after school the sight of a disconsolate Ben emphasized the fact that she would not be there to greet him when he entered the kitchen.

Mrs McAlister, Shamus's mother, stood in the doorway. 'You will be staying with myself and Shamus while

83

Mairi is away in hospital,' she told Thomas. 'Sandy will likely stay by her a good part of the time so he says for you to see to Ben.'

Thomas gaped at her. 'I don't need to stay anywhere but here,' he protested. 'Mum taught me how to cook and I'd sooner sleep here. I'll be all right with Ben for company.' Mrs McAlister was looking at him shrewdly. 'I want to stay here, truly. I can do most of the jobs myself now.'

Mrs McAlister was in some way relieved though she did not show it. 'You will come for your evening meal,' she insisted serenely. 'For the rest, I dare say you're as well able to look after yourself as any other body that's lived on a croft. Very well, I will tell that to Sandy myself when I see him next.'

Ben, obviously lost without his master, followed Thomas to school next morning and was there waiting for him outside the school in the evening. It was the same the next day. He slept in Thomas's bedroom at night and when the weekend came the boy and the dog were inseparable. Thomas carried on with as much work as he could around the croft, leaving the cottage only to go to school and to Mrs McAlister's for a meal. He didn't think much of Mrs McAlister's cooking, but Mr McAlister, who was keeping an eye on everything during Sandy's absence, went up to the post office every day to telephone through for news of Mairi. The news he was given did not greatly increase Thomas's worry. She was still tired was all Mr McAlister told him; she still needed rest.

'Tell her to get better as quickly as she can and tell her I'm managing fine by myself,' he said to Mr McAlister, though there was a note of wistful uncertainty in his voice. But when, after a day or two there was still no news of her coming home, he asked Mrs McAlister, 'If she's not coming home soon, d'you think they'll let me go and see her?'

'Indeed, I'm sure they'll do just that,' replied Mrs McAlister. 'Maybe in a day or two.'

The following day was the start of the half-term holiday, so Thomas was at home getting on with his self-appointed chores. He was in the peat shed, the door propped open to give some light while he filled the peat pails, when Ben started to bark suddenly. Thomas heard a strident female voice and looking out saw an enormously fat tinker woman with her almost equally enormous bundle slung over her shoulder. She was standing in a rather proprietary way in front of the open door of the cottage.

'Where is the lady of the house?' she demanded to know.

'She is away from home,' Thomas called back mistrustfully.

'Oh, my! Then is there not a body here that would be wanting to see the fine things I have in my pack?' she responded plaintively. 'What about yourself, now? Would not a young man such as yourself be wanting a wee thing for his mother or his sister?' She set her pack down in the doorway and began untying it.

Thomas was for a moment troubled by her persistency but then a thought came to him. It would be his mum's birthday the following Thursday and for weeks, in the hope of being able to get across to the mainland to buy her a present, he had been saving up his pocket money. He knew there was no likelihood of making such a trip while she was in hospital, so approaching the tinker he asked hesitantly if there were any aprons in her bundle. 'P-pretty c-coloured ones, I mean,' he stressed.

'Indeed I have so,' the woman assured him, juggling through the contents of her bundle and offering several aprons for inspection. Thomas thought them all inexpressibly drab, as indeed appeared to be everything else she offered. He shook his head but the tinker woman

85

doubled her persuasion, tipping up the whole bundle in her enthusiasm. Glimpsing an edge of colour among the pile, Thomas pointed to it.

'What's that?' he asked.

With a flourish the woman extracted and held up a tablecloth, stretching her arms wide to display it fully. The cloth was bright yellow with a deep blue border and a centrepiece of red flowers. Thomas knew it was exactly right. The bargain was completed and the tinker woman departed. Thomas, taking the cloth through to his bedroom, hid it in a drawer and for the rest of the day went about his work more cheerfully than he had since Mairi had gone to hospital.

Two days later when he was at the McAlisters' he had a message that he was to catch the bus next morning and go to the hospital. So she was getting better at last! Thomas felt an overwhelming sense of relief. Tomorrow would be Wednesday and he debated with himself whether or not he should take the tablecloth with him so she would have it to look at on her birthday the next day, but he decided against it. Much better now to wait until she arrived home and then spread the new cloth on the table all ready for her.

A woman he had never met before was waiting by the bus stop.

'You will be the Corrie laddie?' she greeted him. She took him to the hospital and as they entered she bade him fussily, 'Quiet now. Don't make a noise.'

The warning was scarcely necessary. Thomas was too subdued by the smell and the orderliness of the hospital even to whisper.

A door opened and a nurse came out of one of the rooms along the corridor. The woman urged Thomas forward and then left. As the nurse stood aside to let him enter the room, Thomas was aware of 'himself' sitting in a chair between the bed and the window. Thomas tiptoed across the room, coming to a stricken halt beside the bed with his eyes fixed on the face, so thin it could have been that of a stranger; so pale had it not been for the frame of golden hair it would have merged into the whiteness of the pillow.

Thomas saw 'himself' bend over the bed. 'It's the boy come to see you, Mairi. Thomas.' He indicated to Thomas that he should come closer.

'Hello, Mum!' Thomas's voice seemed to tie itself into such a tight knot that even he thought his greeting must have been barely distinguishable. But he saw the eyelids lift fractionally, giving him a fleeting glimpse of grey before they fluttered and closed again. The fingers of the strangely thin hand on the counterpane flexed weakly and though Thomas longed to touch her he was loath to do so for fear his own hand, now so rough in contrast, might chafe the paper-thin skin.

'Mum!' he whispered again. 'Mum!' he pleaded, his eyes searching for some further sign that she heard him. The eyelids fluttered again and he thought he heard her give a faint sigh.

It seemed to Thomas less than a minute before the nurse was back and touching him lightly on the shoulder. 'Say goodbye, now,' she said. 'We mustn't tire her any more.'

He looked helplessly at Sandy but Sandy was looking at his wife. He had to kneel on a chair to reach over and kiss her pale cheeks and as his lips touched her he was swept by the frightening conviction that his mum had already gone too far away to respond to him; too far ever to return. As the nurse led him out of the room he turned to look back, but 'himself' was still bending over the bed so he could not see the mingled anguish and entreaty in the glance Thomas directed at him.

He followed the nurse along the shiny, bare hospital

87

corridor and with every step the certainty that his mum was going to be taken away from him for ever, just as his granny had been taken away, seemed to rise up and strike him. It bore pitilessly into his mind, making him clench his jaws to stop them trembling. And then anger came; a smouldering deep-down anger that in some way helped to neutralize the soreness of grief. He was angry with the doctor who had sent her to hospital; angry with the hospital for not making her better; angry with God and Jesus and Heaven and the angels. But he let no one detect his anger, hiding it from the nurses who tried to be kind; hiding it from the white-coated doctors who did not try to be anything. It was with him as he walked beside yet another stranger who had been deputed to see him on the bus; it enclosed him as the bus jogged its way back along the Corrie road; and even when he found Mr McAlister had brought Ben to meet him at the end of the journey, his anger abated only enough for him to give them a stilted greeting.

Mr McAlister stayed late that night. How late Thomas did not know because he himself went to bed early, taking his anger with him and nursing it until it was temporarily swamped by tears. But the next morning he rescued his anger to use it like a bandage over his hurt so it would not be so easily discernible.

When he was at the McAlisters' the next day they told him with what he knew was false cheerfulness that the news was a little better that morning. But again, when evening came, Mr McAlister called and stayed late, and Thomas, finding his presence strangely comforting, went early to bed. He had lain awake for a long time staring at the ceiling which in the lamplight alternately gleamed and dulled as fragments of feebly nourished hope chased great clods of despair through his mind. It seemed to him he had been asleep only for a few minutes when he was wakened by Ben's whining and the sound of footsteps outside; slow heavy footsteps which did not sound at all like 'himself's' footsteps though Thomas knew, from Ben's excited reaction, that it could be no one else. He heard the low disjointed mumble of talk in the kitchen. He heard Mr McAlister depart without any called farewell. And as he lit the lamp he knew with a final dreadful certainty that his mum was dead.

With uneasy yearning he allowed himself to wonder if, on seeing the light, 'himself' might come to his bedroom and share the terrible news with him, but though he listened intently there came no further sound from the kitchen; no footsteps in the passageway.

From the moment he had heard his master return, Ben had been snuffling along the bottom of the door of the bedroom, whining imploringly and scratching. Thomas got up and opened the door. The kitchen door was closed but Ben ran to it and whined again more urgently. Thomas hesitated. There was a rim of light showing beneath the door so, surely, if 'himself' was in the room, he would hear Ben and let him through? But though Ben's scratching became more persistent there was no sound of movement. Thomas forced himself to go forward and gingerly open the door.

Sandy, still wearing his outdoor clothes, was sitting in his chair beside the cold range, staring bleakly into space. Only when Ben pushed his attention on him did he stir and look across at Thomas who was standing mutely still, holding the doorhandle and shivering with cold and dread. Sandy's gaze shifted from him and for a few moments he did not speak. Then in a flat, distant voice he said, 'She is gone.' Thomas made no sound or movement. Hearing the words spoken seemed to him to wound even deeper than the knowledge. 'She is dead, d'you hear me?' Sandy's voice was now harsh and thick. Except for the dry sobs that heaved at his chest Thomas still did not move. Sandy brushed a hand across his brow. 'Go, try and get some sleep, boy,' he bade, striving to soften his voice, but the need to be alone was so overpowering that when Thomas made no move to go his tone became peremptory. 'Go now.' As if he had been struck, Thomas closed the door and rushed blindly to his bedroom.

The faintly familiar smell of burning wick made him realize his lamp must be running dry and he turned it out and lay down, pulling the bedclothes around him. Not welcoming sleep, he stared into the darkness, shivering still even beneath the bedclothes. Without Mairi what was going to happen to him? He moaned into his pillow and the anger that had throbbed inside him since his visit to the hospital slowly drained away; the sharpness of his grief became blunted and as the cold gradually released its grip on his body he was conscious only of a feeling of utter desolation.

9

Thomas woke to the white light of snow reflected from the thinly clad hills and, in the misty seconds before the ache of sorrow reasserted itself, his mind ran through the routine he had established while he had been coping alone. Rekindle the fire; make the porridge; milk the cow and put her out to graze; feed the hens. . . . No doubt now 'himself' was home he would be taking over some of the morning work but, for today at any rate, Thomas was

91

eager to carry on as he had been. Entering the kitchen, he was disconcerted to see the fire already brightly ablaze and the porridge pan keeping warm on the hob. Going into the larder to get the milking pail he found the pail already full of fresh milk. 'Himself' must have got up early and done the chores, Thomas realized. But where was he now? He listened for noises that would indicate that 'himself' was still busy about the cottage, but hearing none, he wondered if he had gone back to bed. But no, for then Ben would have been left in the kitchen and there was no sign of Ben anywhere. Had 'himself' already gone off to the hill or out to his creels, leaving him alone? Slowly the awesome silence of the room closed in on him. He had been on his own here much of the time Mairi had been in hospital without being afraid, but now, though death had not entered the cottage, the pervasiveness of death pressed all around him. Trying to brace himself against mounting trepidation, he rushed to the door and stood there staring at the sleety rain while telling himself that to be afraid in the cottage now was almost like being a traitor to Mairi. But his mind refused to accept that the unnerving silence of the kitchen was in any way connected with Mairi. It was the aura of death that was frightening and to Thomas death seemed an entirely separate and daunting thing. His glance strayed to the henhouse and with a spark of relief he saw that the hens had not yet been let out and fed. As he poured corn into a bowl to take to them he recognized with relief that the aura of death in the cottage was not solely responsible for his uneasiness; a portion of it had been caused by the despairing suspicion that 'himself', having resolved to send him back to the orphanage, was intending to lose no time in assuming responsibility for all the work of the croft, including that of feeding the hens which for so long now Thomas had come to regard as a task that was his alone.

He had no appetite for breakfast but, because Mairi would have urged him to do so, he ladled porridge into a bowl, sluiced it with milk and ate it, standing by the open door rather than in the kitchen. He wished fervently for 'himself' to appear. 'Himself' would bring his own silence but his presence there would leave no room for ghosts.

He considered what he should do with his day. Whether or not he should go to school; whether he dared go to school for though he now felt emptied of weeping he was uncertain if he could trust himself not to break down in front of the other children. His mind switched to wondering about 'himself'; whether, when he came back to the cottage, he would expect to find Thomas there; whether, on the other hand, 'himself' would be cross if he found he had absented himself from school. Had the day been less discouraging, he would have chosen to go down to the shore and there, safe in his regular hideout, try calling to the seals, which had now returned to frequent the bay, and, in the belief that they would bring him comfort, tell them the extent of his wretchedness. But the day was sleety and cold and the rapidly rising wind, which had already churned the waters of the bay too fiercely for any seal to be visible from the shore, would, with the flowing tide, soon be sending lashings of spray to flood every nook and cranny of the rocks.

Unable to thrust down his fear of being alone in the cottage, Thomas set out for school, his feet growing more leaden with every step he took. Once there, the unspoken compassion of his schoolmates came near to tearing down the flimsy shutters with which he had tried to cover his heartache and he longed for the time of release. Shamus whispered a message that the arrangement for him to take his meals with the family was to continue for the time being and that until after the funeral was over he was also to sleep there. Thomas did not demur. The memory of losing his granny had almost vanished from his mind, but he had seen Corrie's dreary and neglected burial ground and the thought of Mairi being lowered into a wet, dark hole and left there was like a physical pain, and he was grateful that there was to be a friendly place to which he could withdraw until it was all over.

Though he suspected that without Mairi the cottage would be little more than a hollow replica of the home he had known, he still felt possessive about it and was eager to return to it. He could think of no other place where he belonged more, but in the meantime he was relieved to submit himself to the kindly supervision of the McAlisters who were companionable rather than tight-lipped and whose home was quiet rather than silent.

He did not forsake the cottage while he was with the McAlisters but trekked twice daily across the stretch of moor that divided the two crofts to feed and water the hens. At first he had worried lest he should arrive to find them already attended to, but as if by tacit agreement 'himself' continued to leave the task for Thomas. While he was there he made himself go into the cottage and check that the water pails were full and that there was dry peats for the fire ready for when 'himself' came home of an evening, but he never stayed longer than was necessary for him to carry out his tasks. Although he could not identify in his mind the recent ghosts, they seemed to have claimed possession of the cottage, making him recoil from being there alone. It would be different when 'himself' was there too, he thought. There would be memories then but no ghosts, and even if he and 'himself' were unable to communicate sufficiently to share the memories, their love for Mairi must surely bring them to some sort of alliance. Thomas buoyed up his hopes by recalling how, when they had worked together to rescue the young seal, they had

94

seemed to teeter on the edge of an unspoken understanding. Recognizing that they each, for different reasons, suffered from a lack of communicativeness, he wondered if, now they were to be on their own in the cottage, they might at some time achieve a kind of dour companionship.

The day following the funeral Thomas was fully expecting to be told he would now be returning to live in the cottage, but when he asked Mrs McAlister she appeared to become a little embarrassed. 'Give it a day or two yet, laddie,' she told him. The awful suspicion that 'himself' did not want him back at the cottage, that now Mairi was dead he was to be sent back to the orphanage without having the chance to plead to be allowed to stay, began to plague Thomas. He began to fear that the adoption papers might never be signed. He tried sounding Mrs McAlister as to whether 'himself' had spoken of any plans for his future.

'No, indeed. But hasn't the poor man enough to worry him. But he's a good, kind man and you can be sure whatever he decides it will be because he believes it will be the best for you.' She shook her head sadly.

Thomas was in no way reassured by her reply. 'Mum would have wanted him to keep me here,' he claimed.

'Aye, indeed,' Mrs McAlister agreed.

Three days passed. Three days and nights of miserable conjecture for Thomas as suspicion became conviction. And then on the fourth evening when he was trying to concentrate on playing a game of cards with Shamus he heard Mrs McAlister blandly telling her husband that she would be going over to the cottage the next morning to help get it 'sorted' ready for Thomas's return. A throb of relief lightened his gloom and for a moment there was a mist in front of his eyes so he could not see the cards. So he was to return! He was concerned as to why the cottage had to be 'sorted' before he could return to it but his main

concern was to get back and immediately become so
involved in the work of the croft that 'himself' would come
to think of him as being indispensable.

It was not until Mrs McAlister was in the midst of
preparations for their meal the next evening that she
calmly informed Thomas he was to return to the cottage
as soon as the meal was over. Thomas caught his breath.
Now that the time had come he found he was neither
elated nor cast down by the news. It was not going to be
the same going back with no Mairi calling out her cheery
greeting; her voice trilled through his memory: 'There's
yourself now, is it, Thomas?' And on she would go, telling
him of incidents that had happened during the day or
questioning him about his own day. All the time she had
been in hospital he had been saving up things to tell her,
but who would want to hear them now? Not 'himself'.
Even if 'himself' decided to let him remain at Corrie,
Thomas doubted if their relationship would progress far
enough for 'himself' to pretend an interest in him.

Mr McAlister came in, stamping his feet in the doorway. 'My, but that last shower has brought the dark
almost on top of us,' he commented.

Thomas glanced at the uncurtained window, opaque
now against the gathering darkness. By the time they had
eaten their meal the night would be pitch black. Getting
up, he went to the door and looked anxiously at the sky,
willing the daylight to drag its feet until he could get back.
He considered telling Mrs McAlister he was feeling
unwell and didn't want anything to eat so he could set out
right away and reach the cottage before it got too dark, but
he guessed she would find some reason for not allowing
him to rush off so quickly. He closed the door and sat
down again, though his glance went again and again from
the blackening square of the window to the range where
Mrs McAlister was shuffling cooking pots about. Franti-

cally his mind urged her to hurry. At last the food was ready. He gulped it down.

'There now, Thomas. Seeing you will be back sleeping in your own bed tonight, you should gather up what you have to take with you, now,' Mrs McAlister said when the meal was over.

With his bag under his arm Thomas asked diffidently, 'C-can I b-borrow a lantern?' His stammer returned as his agitation increased.

Mr McAlister got up from his chair and looked outside but any hopes that Thomas may have had that he would offer to accompany him were quickly dashed. 'There's a good half of a moon up there will give you more light than a lantern,' he said.

Thomas fidgeted around, taking out and then replacing the contents of his bag, the urge to plead to be escorted warring with the shame he would feel at having to do so. He gritted his teeth. He must find the courage to go alone.

He picked up his bag and at the same moment there came the sound of a foot scraping against the step outside. The door opened and 'himself' stood in the doorway with Ben at his heels.

'So there you are,' Mrs McAlister greeted him as if she had been expecting him. 'And here's Thomas been waiting for you for this past half hour just,' she added.

Sagging with relief, Thomas looked up at him. It was the first time he had seen 'himself' since the night Mairi died. One small tear formed in the corner of each eye as he recalled the scene.

'Aye, well, Thomas. If you're ready, we'll be getting ourselves back now.' His tone sounded more lenient, more gentle than Thomas had ever heard it.

'Surely you will stay and take a wee strupak with us now you're here?' coaxed Mrs McAlister.

'No, indeed. We'd best get back. There's a good frost

on, I'm thinking, and the longer we leave it the worse the going will be.' He turned and opened the door. 'Are you ready, Thomas?'

As he walked confidently beside 'himself' over the crisp heather, the moon shadows which would have pursued Thomas had he been on his own now held no menace. A comforting sensation of warmth began to seep through his body, combating not just the coldness of the night but driving out the chill of fear which had been steadily building up inside him for the past hour or more.

The cottage window, aglow with lamplight, was so expected and familiar that, in a moment of fantasy, Thomas bounded forward. An instant later he had recovered himself. She wouldn't be there. 'Himself' must have lit the lamp before he had come to meet him. The moment lacerated him and as he opened the door the knowledge that she would never be there again seemed to rush at him, making him cower back. 'Himself' was close behind him.

'Well, Thomas,' he said. 'Likely you could do with a cup of tea to warm you after being out in the cold.' He swung the kettle over the fire. Thomas noticed 'himself' did not take tea but instead got out the whisky bottle and a glass which he filled to the brim.

'G-good night!' Thomas said when he had finished his tea. He got a nod in reply.

Before he got into bed he took out the handkerchief Mairi had given him and put it under his pillow.

10

Gusts of wind were thumping against the corner of the house; rain and hail were rattling against the bedroom window, and to Thomas the morning seemed to be even darker than the night had been. Lighting the candle, he dressed quickly and went through to the still, dark kitchen where, reassuringly, Ben stirred and came to greet him. He lit the lamp and, with the intention of having breakfast

99

all prepared for when 'himself' appeared, hurriedly laid dry peats among the hot embers of the fire and, with the bellows, blew them into a blaze.

While the porridge was cooking he went to get a table-cloth from the drawer in the dresser. With a slight start he drew back as his hand found only emptiness. Surmising that Mrs McAlister must have moved the tablecloths to a different drawer during her 'sorting' at the cottage, he opened another drawer, and then another. There were no tablecloths in any of them. Troubled by their disappearance and with mounting resentment against Mrs McAlister for interfering with the way things had always been, he opened cupboard after cupboard seeking the tablecloths among the crockery and the food stores, but without result. The thought struck him suddenly that Mairi had kept her clean aprons in one of the dresser drawers and yet he had seen no aprons either. With growing uneasiness he let his eyes travel slowly around the kitchen looking for other signs of change.

When he had arrived at the cottage with 'himself' the previous evening one change had forced itself upon his attention, that being that Mairi's chair which, during the day, was usually pushed back against the wall so as to allow for easier access to the range, had not been pulled up to the fire opposite 'himself's' chair as was customary in the evenings. The empty space where he had expected her chair to be so sharply emphasized her absence that Thomas had tried to keep his eyes averted from that corner of the room, so he had missed seeing then what he was seeing all too plainly now, that her workbag in which she had kept her knitting and her spectacles, and which had always hung from the arm of her chair as if its handle had taken root, was no longer there. He moved over to the chair, running his hands tremulously along the arms as if it were Mairi herself he was touching. As he turned away yet another implication of death scratched remorselessly at his mind.

He set two porridge bowls and two mugs on the bare table and, when the porridge was ready, ladled a portion into his own bowl. Mairi had always insisted that porridge in a morning gave people strength to face the day, so he managed to eat a few spoonfuls. So far there had been no sound of movement from the other bedroom and, since the morning was growing lighter, Thomas put on his oilskins and gumboots and went out to feed the hens and milk the cow. 'Himself' was putting on oilskins ready to go outside when Thomas returned.

'There was no need for that,' he said, glancing at the full milk pail. 'I will myself see to the milking.' The flat firm voice brooked no contradiction, but Thomas surprised himself by finding his own voice.

'I c-can d-do it. I'd like t-to,' he argued timidly.

'You can get yourself away to school. I am away myself now but I will be back before dark.' The tone was still unyielding, but Thomas's lurking fear that he might be left alone there at night was allayed. He carried the milk pail into the larder and as he was pouring it into the setting bowls he heard 'himself' whistle Ben and the door closing behind them. When he returned to the kitchen he was disappointed to see the other porridge bowl and mug had not been used. He washed his own breakfast dishes, leaving the others in case 'himself' came back and then he sat for a few minutes in 'himself's' chair, his hands gripping the wooden arms and the tears squeezing under his eyelids as he wondered what it was like to be big and strong and seemingly little affected by death.

His thoughts returned to the missing tablecloths and aprons and, curious to know what had happened to them, he plucked up courage to go into the other bedroom. Opening the door cautiously, as if he suspected he might be confronted by some presence, he stepped inside, catching his breath as he saw the rumpled, unmade bed, bare now of the valance and coloured bedspread he remembered. The chest of drawers, the top of which had served Mairi as a dressing table, was also bare, as was the top of the bedside chest where there had stood a framed photograph of herself and 'himself' on their wedding day. Thomas stared and the bareness seemed to stare back at him as if proclaiming the end of Mairi's occupancy. He had intended peeping into the drawers to see if the tablecloths and aprons were hidden away there, but the cold colourlessness of the room unnerved him, making him loath to touch anything. Closing the door quietly, he returned to the kitchen where he made himself a lunch 'piecey' before getting into his oilskins again ready to go to school.

When he came home from school Ben was waiting to greet him so Thomas knew 'himself' could not be far away. Eager to please, he got some potatoes from the shed and was scrubbing them ready for the cooking pot when 'himself' returned carrying the full milk pail.

'You can feed that to the hens,' he told Thomas, nodding towards the pail.

Thomas did not feed the milk to the hens. Instead he took it to the larder where, again, he poured it into setting bowls with the intention of proving his usefulness by skimming it to make butter as Mairi had taught him. After he had finished his outside chores he put the pan of potatoes on the fire to cook while he looked in the larder for fish or meat. His eye was caught by two freshly skinned and paunched rabbits which hung from a hook near the window. On the stone shelf beside them stood a plate of fresh filleted fish. Thomas preferred the fish but hearing 'himself' moving in the kitchen he took down one of the rabbits and carrying the rabbit in one hand and the plate of fish in the other he proffered them inquiringly.

'Anything you've a mind for, boy,' Sandy snapped, and turned away as if irritated by the sight of food.

Undeterred, Thomas carried on preparing a meal sufficient for the two of them, but to his dismay when it was ready 'himself' disappeared into his bedroom where he stayed until after Thomas had gone to bed.

It was the same the next day and the next, but still Thomas refused to be discouraged. Each morning he got up in time to cook the porridge and when he came home from school he started to prepare the evening meal. 'Himself' seemed to accept that despite his age Thomas had learned to cook well enough and there was always meat or fish in the larder, but he never showed any inclination to join Thomas at the table nor indeed to show any interest in food. Thomas began to doubt whether 'himself' ate anything at all. He never saw him eat breakfast, but he reasoned that 'himself' must have eaten after he had left for school because when he came home from school the pan and dishes were always clean and back in their places. However, when the weekend came and he made the porridge as usual and, as usual, left it on the hob, he found it still there hours later, the smooth surface of the thickened meal undisturbed by the imprint of a ladle. Eventually he tipped it into the hen pail to be mixed with the mash and if 'himself' noticed it he made no comment.

It was much the same in the evenings. When the meal was ready, 'himself' always declined it, muttering something about eating later. But when morning came, though the pan and the dishes would have been washed and put away, more often than not when Thomas went to mix the hen mash he would find 'himself's' share of the meal he had cooked in the hen pail.

Where and what and when 'himself' ate became for Thomas a matter of increasing puzzlement. He wondered if he was buying food from the weekly grocery van and taking it to eat alone in some secret place such as the shepherd's bothy away up in the hills. He wondered if his cooking was spurned because it tasted less good than Mairi's cooking, and then again he wondered a little forlornly if 'himself' so strongly disapproved of his own presence in the cottage that any food he cooked had to be rejected.

Thomas wished fervently that he could speak of his worries, but 'himself's' reserve allowed neither comment nor question. The fact that he was not left alone in the cottage at night was a source of comfort to Thomas, but though they shared a kitchen there was no companionship between them. Evening after evening 'himself' either went to his bedroom or else sat in his chair with a book held in front of him but looking so stiff that it seemed as if he was adopting an attitude rather than reading. Thomas sat in his chair trying to read or to concentrate on some school work, but a strained silence separated them, pressing on Thomas his yearning for Mairi until his stretched nerves came near to goading him into shouted protestation. All too soon he would become aware of a growing restlessness and, apprehensive that it might bring a rebuke from 'himself', he would say goodnight and go to his room where, snugged up in bed against the cold, he would either read or make candle pictures the way Mairi had shown him.

Thomas was in no doubt that 'himself' was eager enough for him to say good night and go to bed. Indeed, his relief was almost as palpable as a firm push on the door closing behind him. He had little doubt as to the reason for it.

Except for the first evening back at the cottage after Mairi's death, 'himself' had avoided drinking in Thomas's presence, but Thomas knew only too well from the smell of whisky lingering in the kitchen when he got up in the morning that the abstinence ceased as soon as he had left the kitchen. The knowledge distressed him, adding to his worries. At the orphanage he had heard many tales of children being abandoned by drunken parents, even ill-treated by them, but though he had no fear that 'himself' would ever hurt him physically he did have a recurring fear that in a moment of drunken indifference he might temporarily forget how useful Thomas had become and might make an irreversible decision to send him back to the orphanage.

The extra work he had taken on gave Thomas little time for brooding during the day, but at night when he was in bed despondency sometimes ensnared him like a net from which he had to struggle to escape. Then he would convince himself that he had detected signs of preparations to send him away from Corrie. Even to send him back to the orphanage. When he woke in the mornings the weight of his imaginings would still be with him and all day he would be impatient for school to end so he could rush down to the shore and shout his fears to the seals. And after telling the seals, he would wander back up the croft thinking how terrible it would be if he had to leave Corrie and questioning how the hens and the cows would manage without him. If 'himself' was not in the byre he would go in there, letting his feet sink into the soft bedding of rushes as he talked to the cows and leaned on their warm gurgling bodies while they blew their strong breath over him. Oh, they were his! They were his! he cried silently. Had he not struggled to help harvest and carry the hay they were eating? Had he not helped to gather the rushes for their bedding? Surely no one would be cruel enough to part him from everything Mairi had taught him to help and to love? He felt that Corrie possessed him and he in turn felt possessive of everything that was Corrie. Not just the cottage and buildings, nor even the animals, but the croft and the crops it yielded; the hills, the burns, the lochs; the rain and the wind and the sea. So well he knew the different winds now and the way the sea shaped itself to meet them. If the door of the byre rattled, he knew the wind was westerly and the seas would be rolling towards the far shore and crashing against the point. If the hens hid themselves against the dyke, the wind had north in it and the breakers would be shorn so the spray plumed and raced along their length like the steam from an engine speeding through a deep cutting. The rain hitting his bedroom window meant it was driven by a southerly wind and the sea would be piling great breakers which reared and broke on the rocks immediately below the croft. When the wind whined around the house, the sea was mostly calm except for little frills of white that danced across the bay. All these things had inscribed themselves on his affections and he told himself he could never be happy away from them.

It was following upon one such spell of gloom, when he was wandering around the wilder parts of the croft half heartedly looking for traces of rabbit runs, that his eye was caught by a dark patch in a hollow that divided two outcrops of rock and, being familiar with every inch of the croft, he knew the patch had appeared since he was last there shortly before Mairi had died. Wondering if 'himself' had been working at something there, he went towards it. From the distance the ground looked as if there had been a fire there and he was puzzled because the regular place for burning rubbish was in a cleft of rock down by the shore. Closer investigation showed it to be a sodden pile of ash and charred shreds of material and, assuming that some tinkers must have stopped by and burned some of their rubbish where the fire would be screened from the cottage, he kicked distastefully at the pile. The next moment he was down on his knees, staring horror-stricken at what his foot had uncovered. The spectacles lay half buried among the ashes and though the lenses had gone and the metal frames were distorted Thomas recognized them beyond all doubt. They were Mairi's – his mum's spectacles which she had always worn when doing close work. The poignancy of the discovery made him cry out sharply; his chest began to heave as if his breath was being punched out of him. His uncertain fingers probed among the ash and, retrieving what was left of the spectacles, he raced back to the cottage, too confused in his mind to know why he was doing so. As he reached the cobbled path, 'himself' appeared in the doorway of the house. He waited, his eyes expressionless, his mouth a thin, inflexible line. Thomas, speechless and panting for breath, came to a halt in front of him and almost without realizing what he was doing he held out the spectacles. As his eyes lifted to 'himself's' face and he saw the grimness freeze swiftly into a stony greyness like a cloud shadow passing over a frost-coated hillside, his hand dropped weakly to his side and he shuddered at what he had done.

'Take those back to where you got them and never interfere again.' There was such steel in 'himself's' voice that Thomas felt the words striking him like spear thrusts. With a stifled sob he turned and fled back up the croft where he reburied the spectacles under the ashes.

It did not occur to him for some time that the charred shreds of material he had seen could have been anything but the rags he had assumed them to be, but it came to him later that they might have been the remains of the missing tablecloths and aprons. The realization brought with it a desperate longing for communication and understanding. He resolved to confide in Mrs McAlister, telling her not only about the discovery of the spectacles and 'himself''s' reaction, but about his whisky drinking and also about his own suspicions that 'himself' was not eating anything at all.

She was sympathetic but she did not seem to be unduly perturbed. 'Aye, but a deep wound must be well cleaned before it can start to heal, laddie,' she said by way of explanation, and when she saw he only vaguely understood, she added, 'You will no doubt come to know these things better when you are a man yourself.'

Thomas tried to understand. He continued doing his best to help and make himself needed, but at no time was he rewarded by more than a distant nod of acknowledgement from 'himself'. The weeks went by and, there being no noticeable change in the relationship with 'himself', Thomas grew increasingly disconsolate. The winter was in full stride now; the weather at its most savage; the days at their shortest. It was only just light when he set off for school and nearly dusk before he got home at night. The hills were snow-cloaked, their whiteness cleft by narrow burns that raced to pour themselves into rivers that in turn hurled themselves into the sea. Icicles hung like sets of organ pipes from overhanging rocks while rushes stood like grey sentinels guarding the stillness of the frozen lochans.

Despite good fires in the range, a cold austerity which Thomas could do nothing to alleviate seemed to have settled over the kitchen of the cottage and he blamed it on the silence which had supplanted the laughter and talk there had been when Mairi was alive. He wished he was old enough to be more of a companion for 'himself' and the wish reminded him that he would soon be ten.

He recollected his last birthday and the cake Mairi had made and decorated for him. How quickly that had been eaten! How cosy the evening had been, with even 'himself' shedding enough of his reserve to comment on the darra

Mairi had given him for his birthday present. As his thoughts swung back a bold plan began to take shape in his head.

On his birthday Thomas hurried home from school so as to be at the cottage in plenty of time before 'himself' returned. As soon as he had the preparations for the meal well in hand, he went to the drawer where he had hidden the tablecloth he had bought from the tinker and which he had wanted to give Mairi for her birthday present. There had been no tablecloth on the table since Mairi's death and Thomas felt a little nervous as he spread the cloth now. In the centre of the table he placed a dish and on the dish he set a pink-iced cake which Mrs McAlister, at his request, had brought back from the mainland for him the day before. The cake hadn't the nice sweet smell of the one Mairi had baked for him and he had been unable to find any bog cotton to decorate it, but Thomas was pleased enough. He stepped back to admire it. The tablecloth seemed to bring Mairi's presence back into the kitchen and he had a warm feeling that she was near and approving of his plan. When he heard 'himself's' footsteps on the cobbles outside, the cautious optimism he had nursed since he first conceived the idea gradually gave way to doubt. Would 'himself' break his reserve now and wish him a happy birthday? Would he notice the birthday cake and the bright cloth and remember what a happy day it had been last year? Thomas felt his breath grow tight in his chest; his mouth gave a little quiver of anticipation. The door opened.

Sandy stood stiffly, staring at the table as if he could not believe his eyes. Suddenly the stiffness seemed to slacken and striding forward he grabbed at a corner of the cloth as if he was about to tear it off the table. Thomas, fearing for the safety of the cake, jumped up to rescue it, and as he stood clutching the plate, his eyes, dark with anguish and entreaty, were fixed on Sandy. Sandy's fingers released their grip of the cloth.

'You should keep that for yourself,' he said, tight-jawed. Picking up the milk pail, he went out to the byre. It was a long time before he came back and by then Thomas had taken the tablecloth back to his room and hidden it again in the drawer. He had managed to eat a few mouth-fuls of food but he had not touched the cake. Brooding over the failure of his plan, he went early to bed and lay miserably trying to fathom why whatever he did seemed to displease 'himself'.

He slept fitfully and, waking with a dry throat, he lit his candle intending to get a drink of water from the kitchen. The lamp was still burning and Thomas could not decide whether he had not slept as long as he thought or whether he had overslept and 'himself' was already up and about. Stealthily Thomas opened the door. 'Himself' was sitting by the table, his head resting on his arms, and Thomas thought he was snoring. The whisky bottle and glass were beside him. Thomas crept to the water pail, helped him-self to a drink and was creeping back when Ben thumped his tail on the floor and immediately 'himself' raised his head and looked at Thomas.

'I was thirsty,' Thomas mumbled as he hurried back to his room. But he was disturbed by what he had seen. The strange slackness of 'himself''s' shoulders, the drooped head on the arms, the unguarded hopelessness of his expression when he had looked up were all so at odds with the severe, inflexible man of whom he was so much in awe. As he thought over it, Thomas slowly began to grasp how deeply 'himself' had felt the blow of Mairi's death. 'Him-self' had loved Mairi for a long time whereas he, because he had known her only a short time, had loved her only for a short time. He could not accept that he loved her less but a new feeling of tenderness towards 'himself' began to work its way into his mind. With sudden resolution he got out of bed again and, convinced that what he was about to do would please Mairi, he reached under his pillow for the handkerchief she had given him and made his way to the kitchen. 'Himself''s' head was back on his arms but Thomas hesitated only for a second before going up to the table and pulling at his sleeve.

'You c-can b-borrow this,' he said when Sandy looked up. 'She g-gave it to me. She wrapped one of her smiles in it for me to k-keep always.' 'Himself' was staring at the handkerchief as if stupefied. 'I put it under my pillow at night and she c-comes and smiles and talks me to sleep.' Thomas paused, and as he looked into the bloodshot eyes that were still staring at him stupidly, Thomas's eyes were soft with pity. 'She'll c-come and talk to you too,' he promised. It seemed to Thomas he was offering the handkerchief for a long time before 'himself' reached out a hand to receive it. As he placed the folded handkerchief in the waiting palm he saw the strong fingers flex. 'D-Don't crush it!' His voice was sharp with alarm. The fingers relaxed. Thomas waited only a moment or two before he backed away from the table and returned to his room.

After the door closed behind Thomas, Sandy continued to stare at the handkerchief. Even through the stupor of drink he was stung by recognition and, turning his hand, he let the handkerchief drop on the table and reached for the whisky bottle. After refilling his glass, he looked at it with a kind of dazed loathing. He was perfectly aware he had already drunk far too much. Striving for forgetfulness, he had drunk too much every evening since Mairi had died. He would have continued his drinking during the day had not Mairi charged him to look after the boy, and for her sake he had done his best, not drinking until after Thomas had gone to bed for fear of becoming negligent.

He filled his glass again and yet again and not until the

lamp ran out of paraffin did he think of going to bed. Picking up the near empty whisky bottle and glass, he lurched through to his bedroom where, after topping up his glass, he put both bottle and glass down on the bedside chest and flung himself onto the bed, but a minute or two later his unsteady hand, groping for the whisky, caught the glass, knocking it over and spilling the contents on the top of the chest. He swore as he heard the liquid dripping onto the floor. His hand was wet from contact with the top of the chest and he wiped it on the bedclothes before rolling over to lie face downwards in the dark, abandoning himself to the drunken sleep he expected to overtake him. But sleep did not come so easily. The memory of the pity in Thomas's eyes when he had offered him the handkerchief would not be banished. Why, when he had reacted so angrily to the sight of the tablecloth and the cake, had the boy responded with pity? Shame and remorse combined to fend off the oblivion he sought. Why? Why? Question after question surfaced above the sluggishness of his brain. What had it cost the boy to offer to share with him what was obviously his most cherished memento of Mairi? Surely he, who had reacted so angrily to the sight of the tablecloth and the cake, might have reacted even more strongly against the sight of the handkerchief? And yet the boy with pity in his eyes had taken that risk. Why? Could it be that he considered him worth the sacrifice? He, who had offered to share nothing? He, who had been so implacable in his own grief that he had ruthlessly disposed of all those things which reminded him too grievously of his wife's death? A feeling of guilt forging its way through the fog of his whisky-befuddled senses reminded him that he had left the handkerchief lying on the table. Whatever his sins, he was not callous enough to leave it there for the boy to find in the morning. Rising from the bed, he lurched back to the kitchen and, picking up the handkerchief, took it to his bedroom. Steadying himself beside the bed, he was about to put the handkerchief on the bedside chest when his brain cleared enough to remind him of the spilled whisky. It would not be right to put the handkerchief down without first wiping the chest dry and he had nothing with which he could wipe it. He looked about dazedly and then, because his eyes would not focus on any place more suitable, he put the handkerchief down beside his pillow and slumped back onto the bed. And sleep came at last – deep sleep, such as he had not known since Mairi's death.

11

During the two weeks before Thomas's birthday the weather had been wild and wet, making it impossible for 'himself' to go to his creels or to catch any fish. However, on the day following his birthday, which was a Saturday, Thomas woke to a cold, crisp morning and a sea so calm it looked as if someone had taken the trouble to polish it to smoothness. After two weeks on a daily diet of salt herring

Thomas was longing for a taste of fresh fish and, convinced that 'himself' would sleep later than usual following his heavy drinking bout of the previous night, he resolved, with great daring, that when he had fed the hens he would take his darra and row out in *Puffin* to try to catch some fish. Ben watched him go but made no attempt to follow him and Thomas, knowing the dog would not move more than a few yards from the house whilst his master was still inside, did not encourage him. He felt more than a prick of conscience as he dragged *Puffin* down the shore, but once in the dinghy with the oars grasped firmly in his hands, he felt only a quickening of confidence. Looking back at the cottage he saw no sign of movement. With any luck, he thought, he might have caught enough fish and be back home before 'himself' was awake. Perhaps then 'himself' would at last be pleased with something he had done.

Despite his excessive drinking of the previous night, Sandy slept only a little later than usual that morning. Calm always awakened him more easily than the noisiest of storms, but since his mind was more crowded with thoughts than it had been for some weeks, he lay for a time letting them rearrange themselves into a sequence he could accept. When he did get up he found he had not bothered to take off his clothes the night before and, with a slight feeling of embarrassment, instead of going into the kitchen where he expected Thomas would be, he went to the door of the house and stood looking out at the tranquil day. It occurred to him that the extra whisky he had drunk must have had some kind of restorative effect since he was aware of a significant lightening of his spirits which could not have been wholly attributable to the freshness of the rapidly brightening day. Going into the kitchen he saw the fire had not been lit; that the porridge pan was still on the shelf and, with a twinge of self-reproach, that the birthday cake was still untouched on the dresser. Assuming Thomas was making the most of not having to get up for school, Sandy lit the fire and made the porridge before going out to milk the cow. On his way to the byre he was surprised to see the hens already fed and out foraging around the croft. So, Thomas was already up, he reflected. After the milking was finished he went back to the house, expecting to see Thomas in the kitchen, but when there was no sign of him he opened the door to the passage and called out. There being no reply, he opened the door of the bedroom. With a kind of mental raising of the eyebrows, he thought that the fine morning had tempted Thomas out early perhaps to set or to inspect his snares. He had intended by way of return for Thomas's offer of the handkerchief to suggest he came out to the lobster creels with him, but if the boy was not back in time that would have to be the end of it. He was conscious of a strange tinge of regret.

While he carried on with the rest of the morning chores he realized he was keeping an eye open for Thomas. He was not worried but the thought of the boy was on his mind, prodding him into examining his own behaviour. To Sandy's way of thinking, he had never rejected Thomas. He had never envisaged, as Thomas had so much feared, returning him to the orphanage, although, because the boy intruded on the dreary solitude he had imposed upon himself since his wife's death, he had thought of sending him away to school. He would be doing the right thing for Thomas, he had told himself, and if they saw each other only during the holidays they would each be better able to come to terms with their grief. But the scene of last night had shaken Sandy. Slowly his mind grasped the fact that it was not separation from each other that he and Thomas needed.

Ben broke into his introspection with a yip of excitement such as he would have made had he seen a stranger approaching or had he heard or scented something that told him all was not well. Sandy's gaze shifted to scan the hillside, but seeing no sign of sheep bunching or being harried in any way, his eyes searched the croft. Again he perceived nothing unusual.

'What is it, Ben?'

Ben's ears were pricked as if he had heard something and he was looking in the direction of the sea. At Sandy's words he began to rear and prance while he yipped insistently.

'Go after it then!' Ben bounded away down the croft and Sandy, knowing now that something was amiss, strode after him. As they neared the shore and Sandy's eyes focused on the small dark shape that was being tossed about in the tide rip, his striding changed to a swift leaping and running. Dragging down *Beulah*, he pulled with swift strong strokes towards the mouth of the bay and as the boat drew closer to *Puffin* he saw that Thomas had only one oar with which he was desperately trying to turn the boat. When they were closing in, Sandy shipped an oar and as the gunwales of the two boats crashed together he leaned over and heaved Thomas into the *Beulah*. The next moment he had hold of *Puffin*'s rope and was towing the dinghy behind. Thomas sat shivering in the stern of the boat, watching 'himself' expertly working *Beulah* out of the tide rip. As soon as they reached calm water he expected to hear the cold, angry·reprimand he knew he deserved.

Beulah was scraping on the shingle of the shore before 'himself' spoke. 'Get you up to the house and get yourself warm and dry!' he commanded. Thomas slid a glance at his face. The flinty expression was as hard as he had ever seen it; the mouth was set firm as a trap.

'I wanted t-t-to see if I c-c-could c-catch us some f-fish,' Thomas stammered through chattering teeth.

'Get you up to the house. And run all the way!' 'himself' reiterated peremptorily. Thomas ran. Sandy paused for a moment to watch the small figure fleeing in the direction of the cottage and a hurried smile flitted across his grim face as if he had been unable to forbid it.

When Sandy got back to the house Thomas was sitting, wrapped in a blanket, beside the blazing fire. His eyes widened as he saw 'himself' put two fish on the table.

'I c-caught three.' Thomas's tone was faintly indignant.

'The gulls, likely, got the other when my back was turned,' 'himself' said. 'Which of us is going to cook them?' Thomas was too surprised to reply. He had been waiting for the backlash of 'himself''s' anger and when it did not come he felt uneasy. He looked blankly.

'Are you dressed and dry under that blanket?' Thomas nodded. 'Right, then I'll do the cooking and you can set out on the table whatever we'll need to eat them.'

Thomas threw off the blanket, took it back to his bedroom and returned to the kitchen.

'Have you ever heard of such things as wedding breakfasts, Thomas?' 'himself' asked.

'Yes.' Thomas looked puzzled.

'Aye, well boy, seeing we'll both be feeling a bit hungry, why don't we have a birthday breakfast?' 'Himself' turned away from the range to glance at Thomas. 'Porridge, fresh-caught fish and birthday cake. How about that?'

Thomas, hardly able to believe his ears, reached for dishes and cutlery from the dresser and began to set them on the table.

'Wait you now!' Surprised, Thomas turned to see 'himself' regarding him with a kind of rueful quizzicalness. 'Haven't you forgotten something?' Thomas watched as Sandy spread his hands in an unmistakable gesture over the table. Thomas's eyebrows shot up in swiftly dawning comprehension. Sandy's eyebrows lifted fractionally in confirmation. As Thomas darted through to his bedroom to get Mairi's birthday present tablecloth, his face lit with smiles.

'Himself' did not wish him a happy birthday as Thomas thought he might and they ate their birthday breakfast along with slices of birthday cake in the silence they had grown accustomed to sharing, but afterwards 'himself' said a little gruffly, 'If you're thinking you're not getting a present for your birthday, you're wrong.'

'A present?' Thomas echoed.

'Aye. From me and Ben. Alistair Ruag's bitch has some puppies. Ben's the father of them. I've spoken to Alistair to keep one for you.' Lying did not come easily to Sandy and he would not look at Thomas. True enough Alistair's bitch had some puppies; true, Ben was the father; but it was not true that he had spoken to Alistair about keeping a puppy. He would do that immediately he left the house. There would be no difficulty in getting one of the puppies for Thomas.

The little breath of caution that always came to tighten Thomas's chest before he could allow himself to accept anything pleasurable prevented him from crying out in delight. 'A pup! Of my own!' he said incredulously.

'Himself' nodded. 'Aye, it'll be ready in a week or two but you can go up and see it any time you have a mind to.'

Sandy rose from the table and went into the bedroom. A moment later he was back in the kitchen. 'You'd best take care of this,' he said, placing the handkerchief carefully on the dresser. Thomas looked up at him as if on the point of asking a question, but 'himself's' expression was so inscrutable the impulse to do so died. He knew he would never ask the question but he knew, or thought he knew, that the sharing of the handkerchief had created some bond between them. He doubted if 'himself' would ever need or accept the loan of the handkerchief again, but if he ever did then Thomas would offer it gladly and the smile would still be there to work its magic.

'Thank you.' Thomas could do little more than breathe the words. 'Oh, and thank you for saving me this morning,' he remembered to add.

'You need more practice in a boat before you go out on your own,' 'himself' told him, and Thomas was relieved that there was only faint censure in his tone. 'I must away to the hill now but not for more than an hour or two. I was thinking you can come out to the creels when I get back. We might catch a fish or two while we're about it.'

Thomas fought down his elation. 'C-can I?'

'Aye. Be ready!'

Thomas became emboldened. 'If I'm to have a puppy, I wouldn't be able to take it with me if you sent me back to the orphanage,' he said.

'You want to go back?' Sandy shot him a quick glance.

'No.'

'Then you'll not go.'

The four words spoken so emphatically seemed to Thomas like being given four more birthday presents. 'Himself' was known as a man who kept his promises. From now on he could cast off all fear of being sent away from Corrie.

'There's just one thing,' Sandy said. 'I had a mind I might send you to a good school.' He saw Thomas's face fall. 'The schoolmistress says you have a good brain and it would be a pity to waste it.'

'I d-don't want to go away to school,' Thomas protested. 'I like being at the Corrie school.'

'Education's a grand thing, boy. You must think what you want to be when you're a grown man. A doctor, maybe, or a minister.'

'I want to be a crofter and work with sheep and fish lobster creels just like you,' Thomas stated flatly.

'Aye, well. I'll leave it to you to tell me if you change your mind. A partner in the boat would be a great help and an extra pair of legs on the hill never comes amiss.' Sandy spoke nonchalantly, but Thomas sat still, letting the thrill of this new relationship between them sink into his mind.

Had it come about as the result of what he was now seeing as his small adventure in *Puffin* that morning? Or hadn't it? His mind grew hazy trying to answer his own question and he gave up. All he knew was that, though there had been a change, he must accept that 'himself' would never change his manner. His dourness had always been and would continue to be part of him and because he was not easy to talk to, theirs would be a taciturn kind of companionship though never a shallow one. But now he knew what was beneath the dourness he would no longer be nervous in his presence.

Sandy was putting on his oilskins in the porch as Thomas approached him. 'If you're going to adopt me will I have to go on calling you Mr MacDonald?' he queried timidly.

Sandy paused. 'It doesn't sound too good, does it?' he conceded. 'What d'you think you should call me?' The door was open and Sandy stood with his back to Thomas, staring up at the rainbow which was beginning to thread itself through the thinning mist.

'I wish I c-could c-call you D-Dad,' responded Thomas, and was surprised at his own temerity.

Sandy did not turn round. 'I doubt you can do that,' he replied. Thomas's heart sank. 'You would only be able to call me D-D-Dad. . . . It would sound a bit daft.'

Thomas detected a teasing note in 'himself''s' voice; the gentle kind of teasing that can draw two people into a

121

deeper understanding of each other. He pretended to be stung by the taunt. 'I c-can. I c-can say it,' he insisted.

'Let's hear you, then.'

'D-D-Dad.' Thomas was furious with himself for stumbling over the word. 'D-Dad,' he tried again.

'I didn't think you could.' The teasing note was less evident but it was still there.

'Dad!' Thomas shouted the word assertively. 'Dad!' he repeated.

Sandy stood stiffly. He had been expecting that some day such a plea might be made and he had resolved in loyalty to Mairi that when it came he would not reject it, but despite that, his stern nature made him resist the sentimentality of the moment. It was several seconds before he could bring himself to speak.

'That sounds all right . . . son,' he said slowly. But still he did not turn to face Thomas. Whistling to Ben, he strode off up the hill.

Thomas moved to stand in the doorway and watch him go. 'Dad!' he whispered, and again, 'Dad!' and as his eyes followed Sandy, he saw the rainbow breaking through the mist to throw a strong arch of colour over the glen. Slowly the sadness that had drawn itself on the young face during the past few weeks was shaded away. The eyes lit with a glint of pride. Thomas found himself almost wishing it was a school day and imagined himself telling the other children, 'My Dad is giving me a puppy for my birthday. My Dad is taking me to the creels this afternoon. My Dad. . . .' He turned to look at the clock. His Dad had said he would be back in not much more than an hour. There would be time, Thomas reckoned.

Cutting himself another slice of the birthday cake, he pulled the door closed behind him and raced off in the direction of the shore, calling out to the seals as he ran and telling them of the new joy that was surging back into his life.

122

M. V. C. JEFFREYS

PERSONAL VALUES IN THE
MODERN WORLD

PENGUIN BOOKS

Penguin Books Ltd, Harmondsworth, Middlesex
U.S.A.: Penguin Books Inc., 3300 Clipper Mill Road, Baltimore 11, Md
AUSTRALIA: Penguin Books Pty Ltd, 762 Whitehorse Road,
Mitcham, Victoria

—

First published 1962
Reprinted 1963

—

Copyright © M. V. C. Jeffreys, 1962

—

Made and printed in Great Britain
by Hazell Watson & Viney Ltd
Aylesbury, Bucks
Set in Linotype Pilgrim

TO J.S.J.

CONTENTS

INTRODUCTION

THE purpose of this book is to examine the educational needs of our time in relation to the character of our contemporary world. The main theme is the self-contradiction of a world which, on the one hand, requires an increasing proportion of intelligently responsible people and, on the other hand, is full of influences hostile to intelligent responsibility.

Maurice Maeterlinck, writing of Henri Fabre's *Souvenirs entomologiques*, says: 'The insect does not belong to our world. ... One would be inclined to say that the insect comes from another planet, more monstrous, more energetic, more insane, more atrocious, more infernal than our own. ... There is, no doubt, in our astonishment and lack of understanding, a certain instinctive and profound uneasiness inspired by those existences incomparably better armed, better equipped than our own, by those creatures made up of a sort of compressed energy and activity in whom we suspect our most mysterious adversaries, our ultimate rivals, and perhaps our successors.'

If we take efficiency, pertinacity, fortitude, dexterity, as the measures of excellence, we cannot claim any natural pre-eminence for man. It is, in fact, not success but failure that marks man off from the insects and, to a lesser extent, from the rest of the animal creation. It is because man is maladjusted that he is unique in Nature. From his maladjustment – evident in the chasm between aspiration and capacity, vision and performance – spring all the distinctively human activities: scientific inquiry, artistic creation, philosophical speculation, and – the supporting condition of them all – historical experience. Historical change – as distinct from the repetitive rhythm of biological process – is peculiar to man, and lifts human life on to a plane of its own. When Caesar landed in Britain, when the Pharaohs built their tombs, when men first learnt to make fire, ants' nests were no worse and no better organized communities than they are now.

Historical experience is at once man's glory and his despair –
his despair because his achievements continually fall short of
his hopes; his glory because his failures prove his possession
of a gift excluded by the very perfection of the insect world –
the power to learn. That is why we are concerned with education, and the insects are not.

Whatever may be the value of intellectual speculation, and
of philosophizing about education in particular, there is no
value in theorizing out of historical context.

Never was it more necessary than it is today to relate our
philosophy to the conditions of a rapidly changing world. And
never was it more necessary to refer our techniques to the
ultimate ends for which they should be used. Shall we be able
to rise to the challenge of our times and will the true nature of
man prevail? Or shall we fall victims of the civilization we
have made and of our own fear of freedom? That is a question
which can be answered only in action. Only history can answer
it – and history as yet unmade at that. But the kind of history
that we make will be influenced by our understanding of the
questions that cry for an answer.

Prologue

PERSONALITY

CHAPTER I

What is a Person?

WHILE social relations are necessary to the very existence of personal values, every form of society offers some kind of threat to these values. In the present age personal values are in special danger; and the future of our civilization depends on the extent to which we are able to rescue and maintain them.

If we are to examine this proposition, we must begin by asking: *What is a person?* Common usage gives us some indications. Advertisements may offer a service or a commodity as being 'personal to yourself'. The fact that what is offered 'to you alone' is simultaneously being offered to millions of other people is neither here nor there. The point is that uniqueness is a characteristic which each one of us believes himself to possess, of which he is proud, and which he expects others to acknowledge.

We may say of an individual: 'He is always fair, but he is so impersonal.' That is to say, he is not responsive to the uniqueness of others. No face-to-face, or person-to-person, relationship occurs in our dealings with him. He deals justly, but he does not appear to take any interest in us as people. A headmaster may be an efficient administrator, and he may know all his boys by name. But still he may convey the impression that he does not *care* about any of them as human beings; all he cares about is an efficiently run school. In that case the school may be efficiently run, but it will be an arid sort of place – which prompts the question whether any administration can be really efficient if it lacks the warmth of personal feeling. The same applies to a class in a school or a 'house' in a boarding school; or to any group of people who can feel themselves to be a community. Many years ago, as a young schoolmaster, I found myself partly in charge of a class which had lost their loved and respected regular master, and felt like sheep without a shepherd. 'What we want', one boy said, 'is someone who will take an interest in us.'

Again, we may say of an organization: 'It's efficient, but quite impersonal.' By that we mean that we are treated as units, not as people with idiosyncrasies. One of the secrets of good hotel-keeping is to treat people as individuals and remember their likes and dislikes. We can hardly expect the Welfare State to be run like a good hotel. But it is certainly true that public administration is sweetened and even redeemed by those public servants who are willing to take the trouble to treat people as people and not as units.

Personal status, then, involves uniqueness and respect for uniqueness in others. But that is not all. In our association with animals we know that, however close our relations with them may be, they have limitations of understanding and of power of communication which assign them to a category less than personal. The relation may be personal on our side, but cannot be fully so on theirs. They can show devotion, great power to adapt their lives to ours and to make us adapt our lives to theirs. But their behaviour is governed by feeling and habit, not by principle. They do not reach beyond the level of response to approval and disapproval. These reflections remind us that personal status involves certain levels of intellectual and moral awareness, and the capacity to organize behaviour at those levels.

The notion of *personality* may be clarified by considering three related concepts.

(a) *Individuality*. In spite of our increased knowledge of the living organism, in its bodily and mental aspects, the identity of the individual remains a mystery. What is it that constitutes and preserves the identity of the individual, notwithstanding the profound changes, both physical and mental, that may take place during the life of the organism? John Smith goes through the seven ages of man, the material of which his body is composed changes completely perhaps ten times, his opinions and attitudes change, he may change his political allegiance and embrace or reject religious belief, he is knocked this way and that by the impact of the world in which he lives. And yet his identity as John Smith is never in doubt. Since experience is the food of growth, it can almost be said that the more he changes the more he is himself.

Although we cannot understand this mystery of identity, we accept it, we expect it and count upon it. Indeed, if the tough cord of continuity is broken, we immediately assume some mental disorder. So fundamental is individual identity – surviving even such grave disturbances as a change of sex – that any disconnexion of identity at once brings the subject of the experience into the field of psychopathology. If one is no longer oneself, one is not someone else; one is mad.

A necessary feature of a person, then, is his identity – a characteristic which he shares with other living organisms. But there is more than that in our notion of a person. At the personal level an individual takes responsibility for what he is and says and does. He is the self-acknowledged author of his behaviour. He puts his signature to his work. He does so whether his achievement is great or small. He does not shelter in anonymity or take refuge behind public opinion; to do so is to behave at a sub-personal level. The truly personal life is not second-hand or reflected; it is original in the sense meant by Thomas Carlyle when he said: 'The essence of originality is not novelty but sincerity.'

To put the same thing differently, the behaviour of a mature person is rational and moral – or at any rate is the behaviour of one who understands the meaning of 'rational' and 'moral'. A mature person has learnt to refer his conduct to values beyond mere social pressures. If he accepts the standards and attitudes of his social group he accepts them because he believes them to be right; he does not believe them to be right because they are the standards and attitudes of a particular social group. Few of us attain to that ideal with any constancy; but at least we recognize it as the ideal towards which it is our true nature to strive.

To have one's own standards, and to adhere to them, is not

easy in a rapidly changing world. In the next chapter there
will be some discussion of the influences which confuse moral
judgement, and particularly of the changed situations in which
moral judgement has to be exercised and the fact that the traditional answers to the traditional moral questions are often no
longer helpful because the questions no longer present themselves in the same forms.

Bewildering as the modern situation is, it has at least this
virtue, that it forces us to distinguish between the dictates of
our own conscience and the prevailing social climate, often
forcing us to choose between the two. In a relatively stagnant
society, where traditional values are accepted as a matter of
course, conformity is taken for granted, and it is not easy for
people to know whether the values that guide their conduct
are their own or merely those of the social group – that is,
whether they are thinking for themselves or merely letting the
environment stamp its pattern on them. A rapidly changing
society, full of strains and contradictions, does at least con-
front the individual with a challenge to think things out.

(b) *Fellowship.* One cannot be a person *in vacuo.* Personality
involves the sharing of personal life with other persons, with
mutual respect for one another's freedom and responsibility.
As Martin Buber puts it, 'All real living is meeting', the communication of person with person : that is to say, communion,
or fellowship. Human relations at a truly personal level are
more possible in a small community than in a large one, since
the larger the community the more difficult it is for the members to know one another as individuals. There was much wisdom in Aristotle's dictum that the State should never consist
of more people than could be taken in at a single view. The
natural and original context for the development of fellowship
is the family.

The respect of persons for one another, which is implied in
fellowship and formulated in Kant's principle that we should
treat other people as ends in themselves and never as means
to our own ends, is the basis of morality. Lying and stealing are
wrong, sexual exploitation is wrong, because these things mean
using other people as means to our own ends. So are violence

and murder wrong, because they seek to incapacitate or eliminate people who get in our way. All these things are offences against the sacredness which belongs to human beings because they *are* human beings; and that is what makes them wrong. If in our morality we do obeisance to the sacredness of personality, so in good manners we doff our caps to it.

Fellowship, however, is not an easy thing to understand or to achieve. Communication at the personal level is altogether different from relations in the mass society, in which it is easy to lose both oneself and other persons in what the existentialists call 'unauthentic existence'. Fellowship (unselfish love) is a complex, contradictory, mysterious thing. There is a necessary tension in close personal relations. Loneliness and friendship are complementary, not opposite, things. Loneliness is not simply the absence of friendship, nor friendship merely the absence of loneliness. In a sense the entry into friendship emphasizes the aloneness of each partner. In Berdyaev's words: 'The person of every other human being must needs remain an impenetrable and untrodden mystery, which even love is unable to fathom.' [1] Love and friendship, just because they mean that so much is shared, emphasize what cannot be shared and cannot be possessed. If love tries to fathom the mystery by force – that is, to subjugate the independent realm of the other personality – it destroys itself. It is against the true nature of love to seek to possess. This is equally true whether the desire to possess springs from ruthless greed or from kindly solicitude. A parent's over-protective attitude towards a child can be as fatal to that child's independent growth as industrial exploitation. An attempt to spare another person the responsibility of making his own choices and living his own life can only injure him. The temptation to be over-protective, however, can be strong, and painful to resist. Since love, by its very nature, involves sacrifice, it is always liable to bring pain to the giver. Yet it is only through loving and being loved in this sense that persons can grow.

It is within the family that we first learn the meaning of personal relations. And it is from our experience in the family

1. *Dream and Reality*, p. 278.

that we can expand our social horizons. Family relations, however, have been changing and in our time are under unaccustomed strains, largely the result of industrial development.

Mechanization and increased production are giving workpeople more purchasing power and more leisure. These things in themselves are potentially good; but there are factors which may complicate their effects. High wages and increased leisure do not necessarily go together. A machine-operator earning £25 or more a week may be working long hours six or even seven days a week to earn that amount. In order that people should learn to use leisure in an intelligent and civilized way, they need both purchasing power and leisure; at present many of the most highly paid manual workers have little opportunity to learn how to use leisure. Again, the manual worker in an industrial society has less room for self-determination, the more he becomes part of a conveyor-belt system. When machines take the place of manual skill, skill often (though perhaps temporarily) suffers a loss of status. The fact that unskilled work is often paid more highly than skilled work again lowers the prestige of skill. If status is lost in the workshop, it is more difficult for the father of a family to maintain the domestic status that he ought to have. In the extreme case, unemployment may hopelessly undermine the status of a father and husband.

The shift system, operating even over the weekend, and the increased mobility of labour, tend to break up the coherence of the family. In the words of the Bishop of Sheffield: 'Full employment and good wages are, of course, an immense boon and blessing; but the price is high if it means a great increase in shift work and in the demand for mobility of labour. The rootlessness of urban and industrial population is a social evil . . .' [1] He goes on to suggest that industry, in its planning, should have some regard for the stability of the family as a unit as well as for economic efficiency.

Another important factor in the disintegration of family relations is the increased gulf between the generations, with the consequent weakening of parental authority. The relatively

1. *The Family in Contemporary Society* (S.P.C.K., 1958).

high wages of young people have given them a new status in the family and in society at large. The teenager today is seriously considered, as never before, as a consumer by industry, publishing firms, film-makers, and television authorities. In a recent address [1] Miss E. G. Malloch quoted Mark Abrams: 'More and more manufacturers, before embarking on production, now consider it necessary to know something about the tastes and spending habits of these young people.' Advertisement is increasingly aimed at those who have money and have not yet fixed tastes: that is to say, to the young who are open to persuasion and have money to burn. In the U.S.A. there has been for some time a cult of 'youth', the effects of which are that the grown-ups never really grow up and the children are never really young. These tendencies do not promote the health of the family as a community.

(c) *The mass.* Reference is made in a later chapter to Dwight Macdonald's analysis of mass culture, especially his emphasis on the phenomenon of 'homogenization', by which the variety of tastes and demands of different classes, nations, and even races tend to be ironed out, and wider and wider publics are offered a common culture – common not in the sense that it is a genuine creation by people sharing a common life, but only in the sense that it is a mass-produced product on sale everywhere.

The effect of this homogenized culture is not to make people more aware of their relations with one another as persons, but less so. Crowds which are assembled to receive the impact of the great mass entertainments are not united to one another as people. The cinema audience has much less sense of corporate unity than an audience at the live theatre. The millions looking-in at the same or similar television shows have no sense of corporate unity at all.[2] This sort of common culture

1. 'Communication and Commitment', *Education for Teaching* (February 1960).

2. It is, however, only fair to acknowledge that the television viewer, although he has no sense of relation with viewers far and wide, may have a more personal sense of intimate relation with the figures on the screen than the members of a cinema audience can have.

does not unite people; it only depersonalizes people – turns them into so much material for receiving impressions. A herd or mass is a very different thing from a community. It dilutes and does not enhance personal relations. It is the great malignant social growth which threatens personal values in the world today.

While we may regret the exposure of people to impersonal social pressures, it is salutary to acknowledge those pressures; and it would be unrealistic not to recognize that their effects are much greater than is commonly supposed. The development of social psychology (especially in America) during the last twenty or thirty years has emphasized the extent to which we are social products. Our attitudes are largely shaped by 'frames of reference' which are unconsciously accepted from the social environment. American studies have shown, for example, that attitudes towards coloured people are determined more by the influence of prevalent attitudes (that is, by what other people mostly think) than by experience of actual contact with coloured people. These 'frames of reference' are stereotypes which influence judgement by imposing a simplified and standardized formula. Thus Negroes are thought to be lazy, Italians to be criminally inclined, just as at one time capitalists were 'bloated'. We are all influenced more than we know by accepted stereotypes of what is beautiful, amusing, reputable, and so on. In the same way the prior acceptance of party labels influences the acceptance or rejection of programmes. It has been shown that programmes are often uncritically accepted because their party labels have already been accepted, and are seldom examined on their own merits.

The fact that most of us are much more socially determined than we realize does not mean, however, that we are of necessity socially determined. We can allow ourselves to be wholly shaped by circumstances. We can allow the most deterministic theory of human behaviour to come true. But we can also make the effort to exercise our autonomous judgement, and we can strengthen our autonomy by exercising it. If we believe that individual responsibility is of our true nature, then we have no excuse for passively allowing our lives to be shaped by social pressures.

All this is not to say that the influence of the social group on the individual is necessarily bad. Man is a social animal and could not be himself without his social relations. He needs the larger society (the nation, for example) as well as the more intimate group. Crude and over-simplified as patriotic loyalty may be, the identification of oneself with the larger community expands and gives status to the self. What is fatal to personal life and growth is to be a mere unit in an impersonal crowd – a member of the television public or the popular newspaper public – and to be little or nothing else. Provided one is an active member of a community or communities intimate enough to foster personal relations and personal values, the significance of intimate group-membership can lend meaning to one's membership of larger and vaguer groups. Affection for one's home, village, or town, will enrich and deepen one's feeling for one's country. It is broadly true to say that group-membership is valuable in proportion as it is personal in quality – that is to say, in proportion as it fosters the respect and consideration of persons for one another. Such group-membership can be therapeutic. Communities of the kind described by David Wills in *The Hawkspur Experiment* and *The Barns Experiment*, and now developed in his special school in Herefordshire, are therapeutic because they are based on respect for human personality and the maintenance of personal values.

This discussion of individuality, fellowship, and the mass may have helped to clarify what we mean by a person.

A person is an individual with unique identity. Personal status moreover implies rational and moral responsibility. A person takes responsibility for what he is and does, as an artist signs his work.

In order to live and grow as a person he needs to be in the kind of association with other persons that has been called fellowship – that is, a relation of mutual respect and responsiveness, or, to give it its shortest and best name, love. Active membership of intimate communities can enrich the meaning of our membership of larger and less personal communities. But, if there is nothing to mediate between the individual and the impersonal herd, the effect of the herd upon him will be to make him less than personal. That is why the disposition to herd-conformity offers the best opportunity to agencies of social pressure (such as propaganda and advertisement) operating at sub-rational and sub-moral levels.

In all our thinking about social relations, government, and education, we must never forget that, as was well said in a recent broadcast discussion, at the end of the day the individual human being must take full responsibility for what he does. We grimly affirmed that principle at Nuremberg, when we hanged people who pleaded that they had been acting under Hitler's orders.

Part I

OUR PRESENT WORLD

CHAPTER 2

A World Difficult to Understand

IF we think of the impact of the contemporary world on ordinary people, and their response to it, we see contradictory tendencies. On the one hand there is a new emergence of the individual, with opportunities for initiative and choice. On the other hand is the absorption, or flattening out, of individuality in the mass, resulting in what Richard Hoggart has called a 'faceless culture'. Put differently, the contradiction is the increasing need for intelligently responsible behaviour in a world that makes responsible behaviour increasingly difficult.

Looked at from one angle, our age is one of unprecedented opportunity for personal development. Material standards of living were never higher. Public services were never so complete and comprehensive. Educational opportunities (and therefore the opportunity to choose one's career) were never so varied and generous. Multitudes today whose great-grandparents, and even grandparents, could virtually exercise no choice at all have a wide range of choice in many fields, from the choice of products on the shelves of a self-service grocery store to the choice of a career.

That, however, is only one side of the picture. Viewed from the opposite side, our world in many ways discourages individual initiative and encourages passivity and conformity. Choice is often more apparent than real. Advertisements try to shout one another down; one detergent is much like another, and the bewildered customer chooses, if at all, for irrelevant reasons. In some fields there is actual restriction of choice; an example is the reduction in the number of newspapers and periodicals and the increased circulation of those that survive – more people are reading the same things.[1]

In higher education, despite increased opportunities, the pressure of competition for places has put a premium on knowledge rather than on thought and understanding. The very completeness of the social services is a temptation to accept passively what the Welfare State hands out. It is, of course, open to the enterprising person to supplement the benefits he receives from the State; but it is no longer a matter of necessity. There is much less incentive to plan ahead than there was in times when the children's future and the care of the aged depended entirely on the efforts of those in the prime of life. There is no need to struggle for things or to fight for things. Poverty is no longer even a major incentive to crime. Everything comes to him who queues. It is interesting to speculate on what the first Elizabethan age would have thought of their descendants, whose civic virtue is the capacity to spend a substantial part of their lives in patient and orderly single file – a docility balanced by outbursts of pathological violence.

1. Writing of the sudden death of the *News Chronicle* in the autumn of 1960, Mr Francis Williams drew attention to the increasing polarization of newspapers. On the one hand are the popular papers with circulations of four million or more. On the other hand are the quality papers, like *The Times* or the *Guardian*, with circulations of perhaps only 200,000, but able to pay their way because they can command quality advertising. There is less and less between these extremes. Unless one wants a quality newspaper one must read what sixteen million other people are reading. More recently there has been the amalgamation of Odhams Press with the Daily Mirror Group, resulting in a near monopoly of women's magazines. A monopoly of this type of magazine is not perhaps very dangerous; but there are important side issues in the field of television. In January 1961 the Prime Minister suggested that the Pilkington Committee should be asked to look into the granting of contracts to programme companies by the I.T.A. In February 1961 *Time and Tide* commented : 'If press amalgamations continue, and there is unfortunately no good reason to hope they will cease, a concentration could begin to build up in television and this would be quite another thing to a monopoly in women's magazines.'

Again, there is the whole field of the mass media of propaganda, advertisement, and entertainment (the distinctions between these functions becoming less and less clear) which, though valuable to those who can use them intelligently and selectively, have an anaesthetic rather than stimulating effect on those who accept them passively and uncritically.

If we try to analyse the reasons why our contemporary world makes responsible choice difficult, we can distinguish ·three main facts about it. The first, with which this chapter is concerned, is that our world is increasingly difficult to understand. The other two, which will be discussed in Chapters 3 and 4, are that our values are confused and that our culture is becoming increasingly standardized.

In these days of universal suffrage, when it is even suggested that the age of enfranchisement should be lowered to eighteen, the citizen is expected to understand (or at least it is implicitly assumed that he can understand) political and economic matters most of which elude the grasp of all but the experts in particular fields – and the experts, because they *are* experts, may not be equipped to relate their specialized knowledge to human life as a whole. It is a matter of speculation to what extent our political and industrial leaders really understand the problems on which they have to make important decisions.

Every day the newspapers report matters on which the reasonably educated and conscientious citizen must find it difficult to have a clear and certain opinion. The ordinary reader often has to choose between two evils – accepting uncritically the views of his favourite newspaper or confessing himself puzzled.

Two or three examples may be taken at random. In March of 1960 occurred the controversy in the Labour Party over Clause Four of the Party's constitution. Historically the party has called itself Labour rather than Socialist, and has never overemphasized public ownership in election campaigns. Clause Four, however, relates to 'the common ownership of the means of production, distribution, and exchange'. After the defeat in the General Election of 1959, Mr Gaitskell decided that it was time to replace Clause Four with something more sedative.

But to the left wing of the party Clause Four was the Ark of the Covenant, and it was clear that it could not be dropped without splitting the party. Mr Gaitskell therefore shifted his ground, decided that Clause Four should remain, but proposed that it should be amended by an 'explanatory note' saying that the Party's ends can be achieved 'only through extension of common ownership *substantial enough* to give the community power over the *commanding heights* of the economy ...' Would Mr Gaitskell accept this description of what happened? What meaning can the ordinary citizen attribute to the compromise formula? And what, moreover, are newspaper-readers to make of the fact that the *Daily Express* announced a Gaitskell victory 'on points', the *News Chronicle* reported a draw, and the *Daily Mail* said that Mr Gaitskell had suffered a severe defeat on a fundamental principle? [1]

About the same time as the controversy over the Labour Party's policy for public control came the Prime Minister's announcement of a small increase in the cost of railway services to the users. Here is one view of the matter. 'Reduced to stark simplicity, the situation is this. The country has a railway system, and wants to go on having one. The whole vast capital value of the thing exists, and the taxpayer is committed to maintaining it. Is it from now on to be positioned to get more and more traffic? Or is it to continue getting less and less traffic, while the toll of death on the roads mounts every day?

'Given the fact of subsidy, the national interest admits of only one answer. It is shocking and alarming to think that the government has not yet perceived this. To justify their subsidy, the railways must be instructed to cut rates and fares in all practical directions so as to secure more traffic. The taxpayer has an interest in subsidizing cheap transport, which will

1. In July 1960 the Labour Party Executive decided to make no change at all in Clause Four. And at the Labour Party Conference at Scarborough in October 1960 Mr Gaitskell got a two to one majority in support of the doctrine that there is room for both private and public ownership in a mixed economy, and that 'further extensions of common ownership should be decided from time to time ... according to circumstances'.

help to cut down internal costs and improve the country's competitive position in export markets; it is fantastic ... that with
this alternative open to him he should be taxed to maintain a
high-cost, under-used, and decaying transport network.

'One cannot imagine Mr Ernest Marples the business man
calling his co-directors together and saying : "Gentlemen, we
are losing business to our competitors. I have a solution to this
problem : we will raise our prices!" ' [1]

On the face of it this comment has the plain common sense
that appeals to the ordinary reader. If it is sound, it would
appear that the government do not know their job. If it is not
sound, the truth is presumably too complicated for the ordinary reader to understand. The example illustrates the (by no
means rare) situation where, to ordinary folk, the action of the
government simply does not make sense. It is one thing to
think the government are wrong, and to be able to say how
and why they are wrong. It is another thing, and much more
demoralizing to the citizen, to be unable to make sense of
government actions.

One more example (of a more momentous problem) may be
taken from the proceedings of the British Association in the
summer of 1959. Sir James Gray, in his presidential address on
2 September,[2] said that the primary objective of scientists
should be to depict man's position in the world of nature as a
source not of fear and doubt but of courage and inspiration.
Man's inventions, he said, had 'not yet' reached the standards
of those produced during the natural course of biological evolu-
tion. For example, it would need a ton of highly complex electronic machinery to do what an animal's brain, weighing a
few grammes, can do.

He went on to say that the future was dark for man unless
he developed and used his full powers. 'The writing on the
wall is tolerably clear : if man behaves like an animal and
allows his population to increase while each nation steadily
increases the complexity and range of its environment, nature
will take her course and the law of the jungle will prevail.'

1. *Time and Tide*, 19 March 1960.
2. *The Times*, 3 September 1959.

The following day Dr Harrison Matthews [1] asked: 'Can it be that the pace of civilization is producing a mass stress syndrome that will bring a catastrophic crash of the populations of America and Europe?' Such a catastrophe was possible 'especially in view of the essentially unsatisfying, aimless, and materialistic outlook on life that is widespread'. Of the 'frightening increase of the human population' Dr Matthews said that, at the present rate of increase, there would be one person to every square yard of the earth's surface in little more than 1,000 years. There were three ways of avoiding the consequences of hopeless over-population: (i) to do nothing and wait for the stress syndrome or some new virus like myxomatosis; (ii) to leave the destruction of civilization to the trigger-happy politician with the largest stock of nuclear weapons; (iii) to devise some method of restricting fertility. This method, it was recognized, would incur opposition from various quarters.

Predictions of gross overcrowding of the planet a thousand years hence may not alarm the man in the street. But he reads and hears enough to make him realize that the problem of over-population will become acute long before that. He realizes too that no very satisfactory solution of the problem is as yet forthcoming. The problem of over-population is only one of a number of problems concerned with the future of our civilization which, if it escapes one of a number of alternative fates, seems likely to fall into one of the others. It is not surprising if people of our generation feel baffled and anxious. Dangers are more demoralizing if we do not understand them.

A hundred years ago large numbers of people in this country did not know where their next meal was coming from. By comparison, our own age is one of unprecedented security at the level of social services. But, whereas our ancestors of a century ago felt confident that they were living in a stable, predictable, and expanding world, in our own day the fate of civilization itself is in jeopardy. A hundred years ago individual calamity was enacted against a background of general optimism. Today the situation is reversed. On the surface we have never had it so good. But beneath that day-to-day security is a

1. *The Times,* 4 September 1959.

gulf of deep insecurity such as the world has not experienced since perhaps the break-up of the Roman Empire. A sense of insecurity at that depth is unnerving even to those who do not deliberately reflect upon it; it infects the least thoughtful of us in the very air we breathe.

Three main reasons why our world is increasingly difficult to understand can be distinguished.

(a) *The vast scale of modern economic and political organization.* It has been held that one of the values of studying the thought and institutions of classical Greece is that by so doing one could see, on a small scale and self-contained, the essential problems of human society. In our own world nothing is self-contained. Things operate on a world scale. Events in one place send ripples round the globe. The controls are remote and concealed. It is difficult to see what makes the whole machine tick.

The medieval village was self-sufficient, except for a few things. There was no mystery about the sources of food and clothing. Every child could see these things produced; and if there was a scarcity, the reason was obvious. A child sent to do the shopping today in a self-service grocery store sees rows of tins and packets. If she is intelligent and reads the labels, she will realize that the things on the shelves have been gathered from all parts of the world.[1] But how the whole system works, how the things are made, packed, and transported, is mysterious and unpredictable. The price of Danish butter may go up. The supply of apples may be interrupted by a dock strike at Liverpool. The ordinary consumer does not reason why, but accepts things as they come.

Political matters are no more intelligible. Do we really understand what is happening in the Congo, Algeria, Indonesia, the Federation of Rhodesia and Nyasaland, the relations between the U.S.S.R. and Communist China? How far do we understand

1. A quick check through the contents of a small larder at the time of writing revealed goods from the U.S.A., Switzerland, Denmark, France, Italy, Portugal, the Netherlands, and four Commonwealth countries.

the issues involved in Britain's entry to the Common Market? It is comparatively easy to discover *what* has happened. But it is a different matter to understand *why* it has happened – what are the underlying forces, who wants what and why? Most of us are lucky if we comprehend enough to enable us to smile at the cartoons in the newspapers.

(b) *The increasing speed of social change*. History moves faster and faster, like the Red Queen. The world changes more rapidly than human power of adjustment, and there is no power to control the rate of change. We hear plenty of comment on the vertiginous speed of political development in Africa, and on its dangers; but there is no suggestion that much can be done about a situation which is open to exploitation but not, apparently, to control. In the field of applied science, technical change threatens to run away with us while our vision of our true destination is blurred by the speed at which we are moving. We are like a motorist who says: 'I don't know where I'm going. But there's 90 m.p.h. on the clock. So what the hell!'

One important social consequence of rapid change is the widening gap between the generations. Two hundred years ago a dress might be passed on from mother to daughter. Fifty years ago a father could still assume that his son would grow up in a world recognizably like his own. Today all stability of values, material and moral, has gone. Children no longer regard their parents' standards and experience as having relevance to, and authority for, their own situations. That is one reason for the present teenage problem. Adolescents in all times have two opposite needs, freedom and security. They are not happy in their freedom unless they have security. Where there is insufficient security, of established attitudes and values, freedom tends to become bravado.

(c) *The 'helplessness of power'*. This phrase has been used to describe the state of affairs in which, owing to the growing complexity of our machines, there is an increasing danger lest the machines should get out of our control, and an increasing risk of chaos if the machines break down.

If my horse goes lame, I can ride him quietly at a walk, or at worst get off and lead him. If my car breaks down, I can prob-

ably do nothing but telephone a garage – assuming the telephone is not out of order. In these days we accept as a matter
of course the fact that we live in the midst of a mechanical
complex on which we become increasingly dependent but
which we ordinary folk can do nothing to repair if it goes
wrong. Our telephones, our escalators and tube trains, our tape-
recorders, our TV sets, our washing machines and electric irons,
are all part of this mechanical web in which our daily life is
caught up. The more control we learn to exercise over our
material environment, the more disconcerting are the effects
of mechanical breakdown. 'All the resources of the Power
Age . . . are available to me, and yet I am more powerless than
the merest savage',[1] because I can do less and less for myself
and am more and more helpless when the machinery goes
wrong. Thirty years ago many car-owners did a good deal of
intelligent tinkering themselves; the modern car is so designed
that it is almost impossible for the owner-driver even to grease
it.

There is also less security in these days. Today a few score
engineers in a great plant can, by striking, put thousands of
other workers out of jobs. In the motor-car industry especially,
the tendency is away from the older practice by which one
firm made the whole car that bore its name. The car-building
firms are increasingly concerned with the assembly of parts
manufactured by other firms for a large number of different
motor-manufacturers. Thus a labour dispute in a factory which
makes speedometers or back-axles for the whole motor industry
can paralyse the whole industry.

There is also the danger of the machines passing beyond the
control even of those whose business it is to control them. In
an age of machines which can translate from one language into
another, or play chess, the problem does not lie in the limitations of the machine, but in the limits of human powers of programming for the machine. The machine can do anything that
we are capable of building into it. In a recent interview,[2]
Professor Norbert Wiener of the Massachusetts Institute of

1. The late W. J. Brown, in *Time and Tide*, 28 November 1959.
2. *Sunday Times*, 28 June 1959.

Technology, a world expert on cybernetics, said that we are passing into a stage when programming for machines is itself being programmed, rather than done by human agency. We are therefore getting machines which are more remote from the people who control them. There is a greater tendency for persons to conform to machines, rather than machines to persons. For example, there is a chess-playing machine whose storage depends not only on what it has played, but also on what its opponent plays. It is therefore more difficult to recognize as a machine, and it can learn to outplay its human opponent. Professor Wiener went on to say that, in industry, it is of the utmost importance to see that the machine's storage includes not only technical efficiency but also social effects. Like the genie of the ring, the machine does what you ask, and upon your own head be it if you ask the wrong thing. If you ask for factory efficiency, you will get it; but do not be surprised if you get unemployment as well. The machine must be integrated into society. Otherwise automation can be a disaster. Such integration is difficult because the advances of the machine are likely to be more rapid than our own adjustment and our rethinking of social purposes. 'The combination of the unmitigated nineteenth-century factory system with automation is devastating.' 'Society at large, and the Government, should be sufficiently informed about its own social purposes to be able to use these new tools for these purposes instead of as purely technical devices.'

That is well said; but it is easier said than done. The problems of what is usually known as automation are very perplexing.

The term automation, though often loosely used 'to cover any situation where a fair amount of automatic working is being carried on ... should strictly incorporate the idea of automatic control; that is, the ability of a system (an industrial process, machine, or even a thermostat-controlled domestic heating system) to regulate itself'.[1] The Moscow Institute of Automation and Telemechanics has produced a device called an optimum controller. 'If, for example, a particular chemical

1. Gerald Segal, 'The Soviet Challenge in Automation', *Daily Telegraph*, 7 September 1960.

reaction is most efficient at maximum temperature, then by suitably adjusting the optimum controller beforehand any changes in the external conditions which might affect the maintenance of maximum temperature are automatically compensated for by the controller.'[1] Automation means the advance from individual machines, each needing human operation or supervision, to a system of transfer machines with complicated forms of integrated processing with electrical controls. For example, a machine can perform 555 distinct machining operations on a cylinder block; cutting tools can be automatically monitored. All kinds of handling operations – pushing, pulling, lifting, feeding from one machine to another – can be performed. There is a smelter where all the materials are drawn off automatically in the exact proportions required, mixed, taken to the furnace, and introduced in a matter of minutes, thus enormously increasing productive capacity. The same principles of using machines to run machines, with sensing devices, can be applied to the processing of data in such businesses as banking and insurance. A computer can digest instructions and then operate machinery. These installations are not necessarily very costly, and are within the reach of small firms, especially when the saving of expense on handling operations is taken into account.

If we ask what are the human effects of these mechanical developments, it is clear that the trend is to reverse the division of labour into repetitive and relatively unskilled operations, and is towards re-integration, creating more responsible jobs which need knowledge, understanding, and decision. Nor is unemployment a necessary consequence; for the resulting increase of productivity could create many more jobs than would be abolished. If fully used, the new techniques could offer this country a once-for-all opportunity to restore the economic power and political prestige which it has been losing since 1900.

The position of this country is indeed becoming critical. 'Britain is moving into the front line of vulnerability to economic attack, inasmuch as both the Americans and the Rus-

1. ibid.

sians, and very shortly the Common Market countries, too, are likely to be ahead of us in the adoption of automation. This vulnerability could prove decisive to our survival as a viable economic power and therefore as a political power.'[1] And it has to be remembered that any diminished likelihood of a hot war means an increased likelihood of economic war, for which the Communist bloc have been preparing for a long time.

There are, however, grave social and educational difficulties. There is, to begin with, the need for many more highly skilled people. The question is whether these people will be forth-coming. Further, there is the problem of what to do with the people who have not the intelligence to do anything but a routine job. The need for highly skilled people does not in itself increase the amount of intelligence in the population. The fact is at present that many manual workers are content with routine jobs, and may prefer them. The development of tech-nology would appear to need a parallel progress in human genetics if we are to have enough people with the capacity to operate the system.

If we could solve the problem of matching human educa-bility to the demands of the technological age, there would still be other, closely related, problems. One, which has already been mentioned, is the need for the programming of machines, and indeed of the whole system, to the end of total human welfare and not only for technical objectives. We are still a long way from appreciating what this means.

An associated problem, or another aspect of the same prob-lem, is that of overcoming various kinds of resistance to the full application of the new methods. To get full effect, auto-mation must be fully applied. Before this can be done, there must be a revolution in the attitudes of all concerned, including the removal of restrictive practices, the traditional opposition of employers and employed, and, in general, the fear of change. In this connexion we have to face the question whether a free economy can adapt itself to the needs of the new situation

1. Léon Bagrit (Deputy Chairman and Managing Director, Elliott Automation, Inc.), 'The Second Industrial Revolution', *Sunday Times*, 1 January 1961.

without a much greater measure of centralized planning than we have yet been willing to accept. 'No machinery exists at present capable of integrating education, scientific research, defence and fiscal policy, towards the objective. Yet it is only by considering all these together that we can make proper use of our resources ... We must beware of doing too little and doing it too late.' [1]

Behind all these more specific questions stands the great question-mark about human adequacy. Can we produce a generation of people with the natural capacity, and the education, to cope with the world of tomorrow?

We do not know the answer to that question. We do know that education is not a magic fluid which, being turned on, can raise the mental level of the population indefinitely. But, equally, we know that we are a long way from discovering the limits of what education can accomplish. In some respects we are only beginning to learn the possibilities of education.

Fortunately for mankind, human achievement is not a simple function of I.Q., but depends at least as much on qualities of character – imagination, unselfishness, courage. There is plenty of evidence that very ordinary people can, when effectively inspired, grow in stature. The future may be obscure, but it is not without opportunity, nor without hope.

1. ibid.

CHAPTER 3

Confusion of Values

PERHAPS the most important consequence of the speeding up of social change is the disturbance of accepted standards of value. Two world wars have brought down the value of money and sent up prices and wages to such an extent that the purchaser has little idea whether he is being charged a fair price. Prices of many things are artificially raised by the use of expendable wrappings and containers; in the United States the cost of packaging is said to add forty per cent to the cost of food. The appearance of new consumer goods, together with the development of social services, has radically changed the priority-scale of family purchasing, and pushed it further in the direction of luxuries. It is no longer necessary to buy education; but it is socially almost imperative to possess a TV set. Desirable things have become much more immediately attainable by means of hire-purchase; people need not wait for a thing until they can afford it.

Not only have material values been disturbed, but moral values also; and the disturbance of moral values is by far the more important. Our world is full of contradictions. If our only problems were technical problems, there would be some reason for believing the millennium to be just round the corner. It is because all our important problems are fundamentally moral problems – and moral problems of which we can for the most part see no clear solution – that life in this age is so puzzling. Material standards of living were never higher, but moral confusion was probably never worse. Housing, however imperfect, has never been better; yet for many people the home has never meant less. We have unprecedented control over our material environment, and at the same time unprecedented anxiety about the possibility of rationally governing human behaviour. Our world offers more opportunity for the exercise of responsible choice than ever before; but it is at the same time demoralizing and frightening, and full of inducements to a flat kind of irresponsible half-life at the receiving end of a system of laid-on services and entertainments. Yet it is a world which, unless our civilization is to fail hopelessly, needs not less but more exercise of responsible choice by more people.

In almost every department of life, traditional moral values are confused. The coming of the Welfare State has thrown into a new perspective the whole problem of making provision for the future, for children, and for aged persons. The traditional virtue of thrift has lost its obvious expediency, and the prudential foundations on which we used to base much of our moral teaching have collapsed. We used to pat the lad on the shoulder and say: 'My boy, if you want to get on, you will practise self-control and self-denial; you will do without things today for the sake of better things tomorrow.' The modern lad knows that, if he has a pound note in his pocket, the one thing he can be sure of is that, if he does not spend it today, it will buy less tomorrow.

As the patterns and techniques of social life change, moral problems change their form so that the conventional answers to the conventional questions no longer fit reality. Sex and war are two important areas of life in which the problems themselves are so different from what they were a hundred, or even fifty, years ago that the traditional formulae no longer apply. The whole problem of war has changed since war ceased to be a limited affair of professional armies and became a peril to whole populations and a menace to civilization. In matters of sex, the fact that things can be done with impunity today which could not be done with impunity two or three generations ago makes people question the traditional taboos.

An interesting example of the way in which technical change can confuse moral judgement is the controversy about A.I.D. (artificial insemination by a donor). The report of the Methodist Conference of 1958 revealed a state of bewilderment on this matter. The problem is this: a woman has a child by a man

who is not her husband; yet she has not committed adultery.
If the woman is married, how does her husband stand in the
rather complex relationship? If she is not married, the moral
issue is clearer, at any rate by traditional standards. After a
good deal of discussion the Methodist Conference of 1958
passed a resolution condemning A.I.D. The Reverend Dr Donald
Soper, however, while acknowledging the difficulties of the
problem, dissented from the majority decision and said that he
did not think we were in a position to declare A.I.D. a sin. In
January 1960 the Archbishop of Canterbury returned to the
subject and condemned A.I.D. When the leaders of the
Churches are so evidently perplexed about the morals of a
matter of this kind, it is not surprising if ordinary folks
have no opinion on the subject, or even dismiss morality as
irrelevant.

The problems of A.I.D., however, are simple compared with
those indicated in the following passage : 'Consider for instance
the strange parentage of certain rabbits which have seen the
light of day and nibbled their lettuce leaves in an embryo-
logical laboratory. The doe which gave them birth was their
mother to a limited extent only, because the ova from which
they were developed had been removed from another doe
(their genetic mother) and transferred to her. Furthermore,
these ova were activated to develop into bunnies not by mating,
not by artificial insemination, but by a short period of chilling
before implantation, and if the baby rabbits had any father at
all it was merely the refrigerator in the corner of the room. I
do not wish to cause either law lords or Church dignitaries to
have sleepless nights, but obviously the problem of A.I.D. is
mere two-times table compared with the intricacies of deciding
the rights and wrongs of such curious parentage when it begins
to occur among humans. For come it most surely will.' [1]

If the authority of parents has been weakened, it is largely
because parents find it increasingly difficult to make up their
own minds what is right and what is wrong, and what standards
to expect of their children. Children need security as well as

1. Roger Pilkington, 'The Stork and the Syringe', *Time and Tide*,
1 February 1958.

freedom, especially the security of parents with definite and coherent beliefs. Children will not necessarily adopt their parents' beliefs; during adolescence they will almost certainly react against them. But they need something definite even to react against. In any case, they stand to gain immensely by growing up with parents who have firm beliefs (whatever those beliefs may be), and whose lives and characters are strengthened by those beliefs. A son may disagree with his father in almost everything, and yet be deeply grateful to him for being a man of positive opinions and steadfast purpose. If parents do not know their own minds, it is not surprising if children drift. It is worth observing that, broadly speaking, neurosis is more likely to result from too little authority than from too much. Dr Charles Newman, Dean of the London Postgraduate Medical School, said not long ago: 'The modern child is brought up by parents who have no idea how to bring up children, or at least they think they have no idea. ... They could probably bring up children perfectly well if only they had the confidence, but everybody has told them a different way of bringing up children, and they do not know where they are, and the children do not know where they are. These poor little blighters and their mothers are suffering from disorders which arise from doubt and uncertainty, which were inflicted on their parents. ... Until we or somebody can implant in parents' minds at any rate some confidence in the bringing up of their children we are going to witness an enormous increase in the number of stress disorders among children.' [1]

In an age of moral confusion and shifting values, the line of least resistance is to have no standards at all – to say that nothing is right or wrong in itself, but only if you think it is. This relativist attitude is often to be found reflected in readers' letters to the press. The following passage is from a letter on the Church's treatment of divorced persons. 'Times change. What was "sinful" even a hundred years ago is today accepted

1. Paper by Dr Charles Newman in *The Nature of Stress Disorder*, a collection of papers read at a conference of the Society for Psychosomatic Research, 1958 (Hutchinson Medical Publications, 1959).

as normal behaviour. In trying to fit man to the structure, instead of the structure to man, the Church endeavours, unavailingly, to hold the clock back.' [1]

It is only too easy to illustrate the lack of moral sensitiveness in our generation. Suzanne Villar wrote recently of the 'cult of cosy sentimental materialism' in women's magazines. 'You can catch your man if you care about personal freshness, keep him by opening the right tins, and make a real home by picking the right brand of carpet.' [2] Not long ago Ivor Brown pointed out the contradiction between the American cult of 'National Projection' and the vogue for fiction and films showing Americans as slobs and sluts. At the same time a review of the film *The Naked and the Dead* (a war film, adapted from an American best-seller, about activities of the American army in a South Pacific island) said that the film 'should never, never have been let loose outside the U.S.', because of the sadistic and power-mad behaviour of the American army as portrayed in it.[3]

Ours is not an age of comfortable moral indifference, but rather of anxious confusion, with a good deal of defensive bravado. Anxiety tries to find consolation in the notion of life as a lottery – the substitution of luck for effort and purpose. The symbols of this superstition are the stars of the entertainment world, whose meteoric rise to fame and wealth appears to be fortuitous. Leo Lowenthal recently compared the biographical articles in the *Saturday Evening Post* for 1901 and 1940–1 respectively. The comparison showed a decline of articles about business, professional, and political characters and a fifty per cent increase of those about entertainers. Moreover, the entertainers chosen for description tend to be of a more frivolous kind than half a century ago. Lowenthal connects the change with the economic depression of 1929, which brought home to the ordinary man the arbitrariness and chaos of capitalism. The masses are invited to console themselves with a dream world in which there are no rules ('So why make efforts?'), and in which chance dominates ('It might have been

1. Letter to the *Birmingham Post*, 10 July 1958.
2. *Time and Tide*, 4 October 1958.   3. ibid.

me!'). The whole of competitive society is presented as a lottery in which a few are winners because they draw the lucky tickets and get the breaks.

A good example of this dream world – and also of another characteristic feature of our society, the serious cult of the teenager as a consumer – is the fairy-tale success story of many pop singers. The fact that the successful stars of light entertainment probably have to work as hard for their success as other musicians or actors is neither here nor there. The delicious illusion is conveyed that, with a little bit of luck, glamour and opulence might be within the reach of any of us. The star is perhaps reputed to earn £1,000 a week. He is for the time being the one pop singer who really knows what teenagers want. Having left behind him his real name and an unromantic job, he may have started singing to a guitar in a nightclub before he was twenty. He has reached the top in two or three years or less, with the help of a shrewd and indefatigable manager and some romantic rumours circulated to build up his reputation. It is said perhaps that he was not happy as a child, not successful at school, and not popular with boys or masters. No doubt he has talent and determination. He always knew that one day he would be big. He is the teenagers' success image.

If the reader should observe that the story of a particular star is quickly out of date, this would only underline another demoralizing feature of contemporary stories of popular success – namely the extreme brevity of fame. An example is the career of James Dean, who died in a car crash in 1955 at the age of twenty-four, after being a teenage idol for a very short time as a film-actor, singer, and car-racer. An only son idolized by his mother who died when he was eight, he turned against the world and typified the 'in love with death' attitude of rebellion against the established order. For two years after his death there was an extraordinary cult of his memory. Warner Brothers received constant applications for his photograph. Girls gave up their boy-friends to mourn before James Dean's photograph in darkened rooms. A Blackpool tradesman did good business selling ivory and gilt James Dean shrines. Two Hamburg girls jumped from the fourteenth floor of a block of flats because they felt Jamie calling them to death. Then the myth suddenly evaporated and James Dean was forgotten. There are always others to follow – but their brilliance tends to be brief. It is worth observing that, at the time of writing (May 1962), swooning – and perhaps jumping from windows – seems to be out of fashion. It is difficult to keep pace with contemporary attitudes.

Reference was made in an earlier chapter to the cult of the teenager. Mr R. C. Bedford, Secretary of the Methodist Association of Youth Clubs, said recently that teenagers 'have become the new rich of our time'.[1] The annual income of teenagers is £900,000,000. 'It gives them pretty well everything except a fair deal. They are being both spoonfed and exploited at the same time. They ... now form the advertisers' paradise. ... Add to all this the fact that they live in a generation in which so many people are willing to call right wrong and wrong right. The teenager feels insecure, because he does not know whom to trust in a warped society. Many of them come from homes which are spiritually bankrupt. Parents today have nothing to hand on to their children.' Mr Bedford went on to say that, in spite of unhelpful backgrounds, teenagers were not nearly as irreligious as they had been painted, and were responsive to the sort of environment in which they could feel at home and secure and knew that nobody would try to get at them.

In an essay on *Plato and Modern Education*, Sir Richard Livingstone writes: 'The main difference between Plato's conception of education and our own is that his concern was to impart values, ours is to impart knowledge and teach people to think.'[2] In another essay he discusses the Greek virtue of *sophrosyne* – moderation, or soundness of spirit – the fourth of Plato's four principal virtues, of which the first three are wisdom, justice, and courage. If we reflect on the Greek view of life, we cannot fail to be struck by the fact that classical Greece was spared one of the most demoralizing temptations of modern life – the possibility of enormous rewards for activities

1. *Birmingham Mail*, 23 May 1960.
2. In *The Rainbow Bridge*, a collection of essays.

which, though perhaps harmless in themselves, are of no great worth. The Greeks did not pay astronomical salaries to their stars of entertainment, and they did not have football pools. They were therefore not exposed to the temptations to put their faith in luck and to see money as the measure of everything.

It is hardly surprising if there is a good deal of disillusionment and cynicism in our generation – a cynicism arising fundamentally from the uncomfortable contradiction between unprecedented security at a superficial level and unprecedented insecurity at a deep level. Richard Hoggart speaks of the 'cynicism which is a nostalgia for belief', and he goes on: 'There is often a shrugging away of authority, not simply of authority of others, but of the authority which is at times required from us – as may be seen in some schoolmasters with their senior forms or evening classes, some adult education tutors, some young dons in seminars. Riddled by a fuzzy form of egalitarianism, ridden with doubt and self-doubt, believing nothing and able to honour almost no one; in such circumstances we stand on nothing and so can stand for nothing.'[1] He points out that the old positive dissent has given way to a negative scepticism – the old nonconformist conscience to no conscience at all. He quotes a statement from the dock by a man accused of murder: 'Oh, no, I'm not particularly moral – but I'm not a murderer'; and comments: 'There are some things one does not do, like committing murder; but the first clause in that statement, "I'm not particularly moral", is not so much an admission of faultiness as an assertion that one belongs with the great big illusionless majority; one is not odd.'

Not long ago Maurice Wiggin wrote a critique of a television programme on venereal disease – Granada's *The Shadow of Ignorance*. The programme was on the whole well done. But some of the people interviewed obviously felt aggrieved. 'This was a symptom of something more disturbing than V.D. The luxurious abdication of personal responsibility, the notion that you can have your cake and eat it, that everybody is entitled as a birthright to happy landings, that the bill is never pre-

1. *The Uses of Literacy*, p. 236.

sented. .... There are too many muddle-headed agencies at work spreading those soppy and dangerous views. Let us by all means do what we can to dispel the shadow of ignorance, discussing everything under the sun fearlessly and openly like grown-up people. But let's not feed the neurotic and delusive myth that in some vague and wonderful way "society" can and should foot the bill for every individual folly.'[1]

Bewilderment and disillusionment undermine national morale. In the United States there is growing discontent with the American way of life – a discontent which is due to other things besides the mortification of seeing Russia take the lead in rockets. Many Americans feel that, in spite of wealth, American life is getting worse and not better. They are sick of civic corruption and crime (especially among juveniles),[2] drug addic-

---

1. *Sunday Times*, 3 April 1960.

2. Whatever may be the cause of crime today in this country and America, it is not poverty. The average prison population of England and Wales in 1958 was 20,000 as compared with 8,000 twenty years earlier. Since the end of the Second World War, the number of young persons under Borstal training has almost doubled. And wages, especially the wages of young people, have been going up all that time. In Derbyshire in 1958 half the detected crimes were committed by young people; and too much pocket-money was suggested as an important contributory factor. Perhaps the most important influence in limiting crime is an effective public opinion. And the lowering of moral standards after two world wars, the weakening of the home as a social unit, and the effect of the Welfare State in encouraging selfishness and removing the necessity to provide for the future have not strengthened the public conscience. The Chief of Los Angeles Police, as reported in the *Sunday Times* of 21 February 1960, gave his opinion that juvenile crime was encouraged by (a) decline of Victorian values in Anglo-American civilization, leaving the individual to mature in a society which establishes no clear definition of right and wrong; (b) direct influence of adult criminality and passive contempt for law and order among large sections of the adult population; (c) increased emphasis on materialism without effort; (d) cultural imbalance between man's advance in technology and no commensurate level of conduct. 'Thus we are attempting to substitute scientific proficiency for social responsibility.'

tion,[1] and TV scandals; they are uneasy about the quality of their education and at the same time are wondering how to pay for the increasing numbers who feel frustrated if they do not go to college.

An interesting symptom of American uneasiness about their educational system is the Report (November 1960) on Education in California, calling for a complete overhaul. The report says that the doctrine of 'education for life in a democracy' has been interpreted in such a way as to 'skimp academic subjects, to lower standards, and to confine and retard the whole educational process'. There is criticism of lax discipline, the games cult, campus beauty queen contests; and there are positive proposals for streaming pupils in ability groups, more thorough teaching of reading (by systematically phonetic methods), more attention to English and mathematics. In short, the report is a plea for the traditional academic curriculum, firmly based on the Three Rs. Subjects like Social Studies should be postponed until proficiency in the Three Rs has been attained. This toughening up of American ideas about education dates notably from the time of the first Russian sputnik, which was a great shock to American confidence. It is interesting to notice that both the U.S.S.R. and the U.S.A. have what we should regard as an exaggerated faith in the power of education to produce types.

Ten years ago the average American still believed his country was superior to all others. 'It was accepted as a truism that the United States drew a secret power from the universe, and that the skyscrapers were symbolic of America's confidential relationship with the Almighty. Today the foundation of this system of beliefs has been almost shattered.'[2] The writer goes on to suggest that the root of the trouble is a lack of any final authority, a refusal to accept discipline, the habit of buck-passing, and the pseudo-democratic attitude that any white man

1. There are 6,000 confirmed dope addicts in Los Angeles County alone, and the number is rapidly increasing. This state of affairs is largely due to the almost wide-open supply of narcotics from over the Mexican border only 150 miles away. In the whole of the U.K. there are 442 registered drug addicts.

2. Unsigned article in *Birmingham Post*, 7 March 1960.

is as good as any other white man and has an equal right (without necessarily doing anything to earn that right) to air his opinions. There is little or no respect in American life, and little privacy. Increasingly the aim of existence is material comfort, and – what is more significant – material comfort with a minimum of effort. Incidentally, the keenest critics of American life are Americans. It is possible to see, in Mr Kennedy's election as President, evidence of a reaction of American opinion against the mass society and its methods. His rival, Mr Nixon, may be considered to have set himself up as representing the mass society.

One of the most recent criticisms of America by an American is Professor Boorstin's *The Image*.[1] This widely travelled writer describes 'how we have used our wealth, our literacy, our technology, and our progress, to create the thicket of unreality which stands between us and the facts of life.' He quotes Max Frisch: 'Technology ... the knack of so arranging the world that we don't have to experience it.' His thesis is that the label on the package becomes more real, more powerful, than the stuff inside the package. Newsmen no longer report events; they create 'pseudo-events'. Because 'images' are simplified and vivid they are more and more acceptable as a substitute for realities in a more and more complicated and baffling world. From the pseudo-event, Professor Boorstin goes on to the pseudo-person. Instead of heroes we have celebrities, who are well-known mainly for being well-known. And they must be on our own level. 'We admire them, not because they reveal God, but because they reveal and elevate themselves.' To talk of 'images' rather than of 'ideals' implies that we can manufacture the very yardstick by which our civilization is measured. God Himself becomes an image – the biggest Celebrity to contain our own emptiness.

It is easy to dismiss a transatlantic trend towards wallowing in comfort, prosperity, and pursuit of the ego as having nothing to do with ourselves. But culturally we have been growing more like America since her entry into the First World War and,

1. Daniel J. Boorstin, *The Image: What Happened to the American Dream* (Weidenfeld & Nicolson, 1961).

given the prosperity, there is no reason to suppose that we should be less inclined to wallow.

In fairness to our transatlantic cousins, however, it should be pointed out that easy generalizations about materialism can be very misleading. American civilization is very complex, and it would be quite wrong to picture the Americans as a people hellbent on material indulgence without any concern for spiritual values or the traditional American virtues. There is, indeed, no simple alternative choice between the material and the spiritual. Many Americans are discovering, through the opportunities of material prosperity, new approaches to beauty in nature and art and new access to intellectual treasures. The travelling salesman who can buy a yacht and take his family for a sail on Lake Michigan is finding new spiritual release. There is a growing market for paperback classics and hi-fi symphonic recordings. The Ford and Rockefeller foundations for some years past have been financing economists, historians, and sociologists to study American society with a view to improving its quality.[1]

Critics of American society should remember that 'since the war the Americans have been way out front in pioneering the techniques of an entirely new kind of human society – in which poverty has been relegated to a marginal problem. Naturally those techniques are spreading to all industrial countries – Britain, Japan, Sweden, even Russia. The mass affluent society brings with it a whole new series of problems – social, psychological, political – that cannot be answered simply by nostalgia for the Middle Ages, or the old Frontier, or even the Village Green. Maybe we are faced with the terrible tyranny of mass-produced mediocrity. But let us, in order to fight it, learn first to admit that in most ways it is better than the tyranny of mass-poverty it is surpassing.'[2]

An attempt has been made in this chapter to illustrate the confusion of values from which the Western world is suffering. In such a condition it is inevitable that large numbers of people

1. cf. P. Worsthorne, 'America at the End of an Era – II', *Daily Telegraph*, 19 August 1960.

2. Christopher Booker, in a review of D. J. Boorstin's *The Image*, *Time & Tide*, 12 April 1962.

will not attempt to cope with life at any depth, but will live in the moment, taking what they can get while they can get it, for the morrow is uncertain enough in all conscience. Thinking, never an easy or congenial activity for the greater part of mankind, is discouraged. The intellectuals take refuge in the cocoons of their specialisms, while the rest of the human larvae are bewildered by perpetual motion.

The intellectuals, incidentally, have their own share of responsibility for the general undermining of standards. The sociologists and social psychologists have not been as careful as they might have been to dispel the notion that our attitudes and behaviour are wholly conditioned and that we cannot help being what we are.[1] And a relativist morality has not been discouraged by the linguistic philosophers. Although Logical Positivism has changed (Professor Ayer no longer says, as he did twenty years ago, that statements of moral judgement are meaningless), the linguistic philosophers still take a subjectivist view of ethics. They allow moral expressions to be persuasive or evaluatory, but they do not recognize the element of *response* to something which is 'there', beyond ourselves.

1. See my *Mystery of Man*, Chapter 6.

CHAPTER 4

Mass Culture

POLITICAL enfranchisement, education, and a raised standard
of living have given the average individual power and responsibility which even half a century ago were enjoyed only by a
few. It is one of the great ironies of history that, in the same
period of time, large-scale economic and social organization, the
extension of State control, and the development of mass media
of communication have largely neutralized the individual's
capacity to use those opportunities.

We live in an age of mass culture which is not only increasingly standardized but also manufactured and synthetic. More
and more we look at the same things, listen to the same
things, think the same things, and passively receive the same
services as they come off the conveyor-belt of the Welfare
State.

Not long ago Mr Christopher Mayhew wrote of TV: '...
minority programmes stand in the way of I.T.A.'s overriding objective, which is to maximize advertising revenue. This can be
achieved only by an endless succession of programmes with the
peculiar characteristic of being addressed to everyone at once.
Programmes which appeal to viewers as individuals, people with
different interests, ages, intellectual levels, sexes, or nationali-
ties, produce less revenue and go to the wall. ... I.T.A. will
never secure justice for minority viewers without a head-on
clash with its powerful programme contractors; and this it has
so far shown itself unwilling to face.'[1] As Oscar Hoffa in Max
Shulman's *Rally Round the Flag, Boys!* said to the playwright
who did not want his play interrupted by commercials: 'In your

1. *Sunday Times*, 28 December 1958.

hat! You get no control over the commercials. We're in business for one reason – and it's not to entertain or enlighten or educate. It's to *sell* – and, buddy, nobody tells us how or when.'

Research on the effects of TV shows that, while TV offers great opportunities to the intelligently selective viewer, most viewers are not intelligently selective. Several years ago an interesting inquiry was sponsored by the *Sunday Times*.[1] At that time TV was installed in rather more than six homes out of ten (that is, three-fifths of the population had TV). Working-class viewers were rapidly catching up and were approaching two-thirds of the whole TV audience. At the time of the inquiry, the BBC estimated the average viewing-time at eleven and a half hours a week, and Television Audience Measurement Ltd put it at fifteen hours a week.

The *Sunday Times* inquiry made an occupational analysis of a typical Sunday evening in winter. Forty-one per cent of English people were watching TV (two-thirds of those owning a set). No other Sunday evening occupation claimed anything like the same allegiance. Two-thirds of church- or chapel-goers came from homes without TV. One in five of people without TV was reading, but only one in fifteen of TV owners. One in five of non-owners went out, but only one in ten of owners.

The most serious effects appeared to be upon those viewers whom the inquiry classed as 'addicts' – that is, those who viewed more than twenty-four hours a week. Addicts, so defined, constituted one-sixth of the total viewing population (sixteen per cent), and were most heavily distributed in the working class, where they amounted to forty-five per cent of TV-owners. They did little else besides working, sleeping, eating, and viewing. Conversation and hobbies were discouraged. Almost the only

1. *Sunday Times*, 13, 20, 27 April, 4 May 1958. The inquiry was carried out by Geoffrey Gorer and the Research Department of Messrs Mather and Crowther Ltd, Advertising Agency. The method of the inquiry was lengthy interviews with selected samples of people aged between sixteen and sixty-five and distributed in areas and social classes in the same proportions as in the last census.

leisure occupations which TV did not seriously interfere with were gardening for men and knitting and other needlework for women.

Nearly one-third of TV owners gave 'relaxation' as the reason for acquiring a set; and no other reason was given by more than one-tenth of the people asked. The 'addicts' often denied that the TV was a time-waster and claimed that they got new ideas from it. But there was little evidence that, for the most part, they did anything but sit in front of it. In their case the TV seemed to act as a mechanical tranquillizer, inducing a mild state of trance.

In general, the inquiry concluded that TV has a low intensity of impact; it is sedative rather than stimulant. 'It strokes rather than prods.' Of 1,246 informants with TV in their homes, only twenty-six could say they had been stimulated to do some reading on a new topic; and only 131 put into practice anything that they had seen demonstrated. It appeared that TV was not successful as a medium of instruction by *words* (that is, as illustrated radio). For example, there was very poor response to requests to identify public characters spoken of on TV, such as Mr Selwyn Lloyd or John Foster Dulles. The efficacy of TV would appear to be almost entirely visual.

One encouraging feature of the inquiry was that it confirmed the fact that young people aged sixteen to twenty-one were the least affected by TV and did not for the most part allow it to interfere with their social activities. TV seemed to have less effect than one might suppose on school children who had homework. Of the 270 children interviewed, 128 lived in houses with a TV set. Less than half the children were able to do their homework in a separate room. But, of the seventy-four who did their homework in the same room as the TV, nearly fifty said either that the TV was never turned on until their homework was finished, or that it was only sometimes turned on. Children who had never known a world without TV seemed to be able to adjust themselves to it. But very young children were at its mercy; it was not uncommon for the baby in its pram to be pushed right up against the screen to keep it quiet. And the poorer the home, the more the child was at the mercy of TV, since there was less escape. The report sums up: 'To have a father or mother who is a television addict is one of the handicaps, and not one of the least serious, which bedevil the careers of bright children who are born of parents who have no fundamental respect for education'; and observes that, although TV may keep children away from bad company, it also keeps them away from good company.

More recent evidence suggests that TV may be losing its grip on the public. Even if the set is less often switched on, however, it does not follow that viewers are becoming more selective. The truth may be that a general saturation-weariness is setting in. Programmes are still available which are too good to miss. But there is a danger, not only that the toy may be losing its novelty for many non-selective viewers, but also that the more intelligently selective viewers may be discouraged by the quantity of indifferent material that is offered. As Walter Ahearn wrote recently: 'The danger is of something happening here which, according to a responsible critic, has happened in America. The type of viewer who thinks before he switches on is neglecting television because so often he does not find it worth watching. The viewing is being left to the switch-it-on-and-leave-it-on types. I am sure it is bad for so wonderful a medium as television to come into contempt. . . .'[1]

In a recent study of the effects of TV on the young, Dr A. N. Oppenheim concluded that 'television is neither the great menace nor the great cultural medium which some have thought'.[2] It was found that most children watch TV for 10–14 hours a week. But there was not more than a quarter of an hour's difference between the bed-times of children who watched TV regularly and of those who did not, and the viewers went to sleep more quickly. As to the effects of TV on children's reading, the indications were that, after a year or so of watching TV, the reading of books increased and became more specialized, because children turned to reference books to check or supplement information picked up from TV pro-

1. *Birmingham Mail*, 3 October 1960.
2. Report published by the Nuffield Foundation, *Times Educational Supplement*, 9 June 1961.

grammes. On balance TV seemed to be more of a loss than a gain to the more intelligent grammar school children, but was on the whole of benefit to the less literate children.[1]

A frivolous but not altogether insignificant example of cultural uniformity is the enormous development, in the U.S.A. and now in this country, of the greeting card for all occasions. Any social or family situation can be met with no use of the brain beyond signing one's name. A recent enterprise in the U.S.A. was to publish cards to be sent to friends or relatives in gaol; 10,000 were immediately sold.

Mass standards, especially when created and maintained by commercial inducements, tend to be materialistic. An American writing recently in *Punch* said that his own countrymen would not know what you meant by 'culture' (except as something relentlessly pursued by their wives), but that they would know what you meant by 'civilization'. And civilization, on both shores of the Atlantic, means mechanical amenities, labour-savers, and entertainments. Not only are the measures of the good life becoming increasingly material, but we are increasingly open to invitations to acquire these good things without effort. We want material things, and we want to get them painlessly as far as possible – from the Welfare State, on the never-never, by some kind of racket, but not, if we can help it, by hard work and self-sacrifice. The prevailing image of the good life has, in fact, no place for self-sacrifice.

That is not to say that the victims of mass culture are uniformly uncritical of what is happening to them. Many Canadians are uneasy about the American penetration of Canada's way of living. What is happening now in Canada may be happening in this country by 1970. More than half Canada's manufacturing industry is foreign-controlled, mainly by America. Canada is a junior partner in North American defence; Ameri-

1. Of television as an educational instrument, rather than as a form of entertainment, it is probably too early to speak. Although a good many educational programmes are available, very little is yet known about the best techniques of presentation. There is room for plenty of useful experiment in this field.

can bases are situated throughout her northland. Canada is flooded with American culture, and the Americans cannot understand why there should be any hesitation about accepting what is offered by the outstretched hand of goodwill. 'The trouble is – there are strings attached to that goodwill. With it comes tyranny – not Communist tyranny, but a tyranny which demands we watch the same mass entertainment, read the same mass-produced international editions of American magazines, subscribe to the same book clubs in order to avoid a personal decision as to what we want to read, drive the same style of motor car, and endure the mass regimentation of best-seller book lists, the Ten Top TV programmes, Madison Avenue advertising, and the ultimate bludgeon in enforcing American conformity – the Gallup Poll. It is, in fact, a tyranny of mediocrity, and many Canadians are frightened of it.' [1]

In his book, *The American Invasion*, Mr Francis Williams records that over £1000 million of American capital is invested in British industry, and every year the amount increases by £150 million. A vast takeover bid is going on, all in the growth industries, from cars to cosmetics. Behind industrial control looms political control, already alarmingly apparent in Canada. Along with the industrial invasion comes the cultural invasion. Other nations must bow to the Golden Image. And the American way of life involves the extravagant instrument of planned obsolescence (wives must be made discontented with what they have so that husbands can find no peace but in buying more), and a mounting prosperity increasingly run on credit. You mortgage your future and your children's future. You borrow more to buy more. In this country, living on credit is still something we keep quiet about; in America it is a sign of status.

An important warning against a self-indulgent materialism has been given by Mr Richard Crossman in the Fabian pamphlet *Labour in the Affluent Society* (June 1960). His analysis of the present situation in this country implies that both Conservative and Labour party leaderships are encouraging the people

1. J. Portman, 'Canada and the Americans', *Time and Tide*, 24 December 1960.

to live in a fool's paradise. His main thesis is that Western capitalism, geared to the satisfaction of mass consumer demands, cannot fail to be overtaken economically by the Soviet system of State planning and control. The future must be considered in relation to the Soviet challenge, and Mr Crossman demands a cold-war economy, in which the State must intervene as it had to in the hot war. If this argument is admitted, we have also to recognize the consequent problem (of which Mr Crossman is fully aware) of how to increase the power of the Executive without plunging our society into totalitarianism. The House of Commons has been progressively deprived of effective authority. Democracy would be lost unless the increased power of the central government were counterbalanced by a revival of the challenge which Parliament used to make to the Executive.

It would not be difficult to multiply illustrations of standardized culture, and many of the examples are comical in themselves. But behind them all is something which is not at all amusing, namely the enormous power of modern means of influencing opinion. No previous civilization has possessed anything like the modern power over the human mind, and for two reasons. The first is the power of the means of communication themselves – the film, radio, television. And we have to remember that kindly pressures may be as bad for the human soul as hostile pressures. Both may be means of exploitation. Indulgence may be more enervating to the human spirit than persecution. As Richard Hoggart has suggested, it is possible to make better citizens and better workers, but worse human beings.

The second reason for the unprecedented power over the human mind is the extreme susceptibility of the human material which is exposed to propaganda and advertisement. The most susceptible victim is the semi-educated person (the well-educated person is forearmed, and the quite uneducated person is comparatively immune); and never before have there been so many semi-educated people in the world – people who are educated enough to be got at, but not educated enough to understand what is being done to them.

In *The Age of Defeat* Colin Wilson[1] argues that people are too much 'other-directed' and not enough 'inner-directed'. His remedy, which (almost inevitably in studies of this kind) is less convincing than his diagnosis, is to seek hope in 'a new existentialism' which must emphasize the primacy of the will and freedom. But he distrusts the hero, and does not sufficiently allow for ordinary people's need for heroes, which will make them choose bad or inadequate ones (like Hitler or the latest pop singer) if they are not offered good ones.

The modern world increasingly needs people with initiative and responsibility. It is the more unfortunate that, in important spheres of life, the individual counts for less and not more, and human values are being lost.

One of the paradoxes of the development of political democracy in the last century or so is the decline in prestige of representative legislatures, including our House of Commons. This decline is mainly the result of the enormous growth of business, which threatens to reduce the House of Commons to impotence. The transaction of Parliamentary business is clogged with trivialities, and Members' time is clogged with (largely trivial) correspondence. Legislation is increasingly done by regulations under the umbrella of widely drawn Acts of Parliament; and in this way the Civil Service increasingly directs and decides matters which ought to be the business of Parliament. Independent Members have virtually disappeared. The rigidity of the party system makes it difficult for Members to take a line of their own.

This hardening of party alignments is apparent in local government as well. In city councils the party line is established outside the council chamber in meetings of the party groups. A matter may be debated for an hour and a half in, say, the City Education Committee, and the voting at the end of that time will be exactly what it would have been if there had been no debate at all. Speeches are made not to influence opinion but

1. Influenced by American sociologists David Reisman (*The Lonely Crowd*), William H. Whyte (*The Organization Man*), and Vance Packard (*The Hidden Persuaders*).

to secure publicity, and are primarily aimed at the press table.

Meanwhile the electorate, whether national or local, becomes less effective in proportion to its growth in numbers, the difficulty of understanding public affairs, and the over-development of the party system.

Not long ago *Time and Tide*[1] made the following editorial comments on the decline of Parliament. Since the constitutional revolution of the seventeenth century, the theory of government has been that of 'a sovereign people making known their will through their representatives in Parliament and expressing that will in the name of a constitutional Head of State. Until the early years of this century the idea worked increasingly well, since it was generally agreed that the responsibilities of government were limited to certain restricted and well-specified functions which the citizens could not perform for themselves. These included the defence of the Realm, the protection of life and property at home and of British subjects abroad, and, in some degree, the support and regulation of the nation's commerce. It was the duty of Parliament to raise the revenue which was required for these purposes and to spend it wisely. The system assumed that under God's providence individual human beings had the wit to organize their own private affairs and the charity to relieve the distress of those who could not do so.

'These assumptions are now assumed to be false. In consequence Parliament in one sense plays too large a part in the life of every British subject and in another too small a part. Each Member of Parliament is today submerged beneath a flood of correspondence from his constituents, much of it concerned with matters so trivial that they should be handled at best by a Parish Council, and in many cases by the exercise of a little common sense around the family dining table.

'When the poor wretch, underpaid and overworked, has time to enter the House, or rather when he is driven into it by the Party Whips, he votes to order and accounts his duty well done if his record of attendances in the House and of letters dispatched to constituents satisfies his local Party Association. The

1. 30 May 1959.

country is largely governed through Orders in Council with which he is not concerned.

'In abolishing the University seats, the Labour Administration insured a few years ago that the last independent voices which could speak in the House of Commons according to their convictions were silenced for ever. Parliament today is made up for the most part of harassed men whose livelihood would be in jeopardy were they to defy the Party machine upon which they depend for their seats. They no longer depend upon the good sense of the voter. Many of the electorate realize this and, although they are unwilling or unable to give their Members more freedom, they are coming to despise them because they are not free men.'

In order to see how far from its true nature the machinery of democratic election can move we must cross the Atlantic. During the last twenty-five years in California, there has been a remarkable development in the employment, by political candidates, of professional campaign managers. Some of these agents operate as advertising agencies, some are lawyers, and some are 'public relations counsellors'. They are highly paid; for a state-wide campaign, a manager's gross takings may be 200,000 dollars. These managed campaigns are used for the election of congressmen and governors, and for other purposes such as the organized opposition of the American Medical Association to plans for national health insurance. Under the law of the State various matters can be referred to a direct vote. Certain questions have to be submitted to direct vote; but voters may force a direct vote on any action of the legislature by securing the signatures of five per cent of registered voters. Eight per cent of registered voters, by signing an initiative petition, can put almost any proposal to the vote. This means that anyone can get any proposal before the voters provided he can afford to spend up to 200,000 dollars on a professional agent to organize the campaign. Agents are employed to beat drums for railroads, school boards, lodges of churches, shipping companies. Whether the professional management of campaigns really sways the results is perhaps of less importance than the belief that it does.

Modern thinking about democracy has been bedevilled by
two heresies. One is the doctrine of the absolute right of the
majority. Democracy consists of counting heads. Anything that
you can get a majority to support must be right. Ironically, this
heresy owes something to De Tocqueville.[1] He was very much
alive to the dangers of an all-powerful majority, and went as far
as to say that 'the natural defects of democratic institutions
... increase ... in the exact ratio of the power of the majority'
He adds, with evident disapproval : 'The moral authority of the
majority is partly based upon the notion that there is more intelligence and more wisdom in a great number of men collected
together than in a single individual, and that the number of
legislators is more important than their quality. The theory of
equality is, in fact, applied to the intellect of man.' Nevertheless, De Tocqueville was convinced that the absolute sovereignty
of the majority was irresistible and inevitable; and this conviction did something to push history in the direction of his
opinion.

   Although no one has found a more workable practical device
than majority-rule, we must recognize that majority-rule is at
best a very crude way of trying to find out what is for the
common good. It is immensely inferior to the Quakers' technique of 'the sense of the meeting'. The trouble is that you
cannot govern a country, or even a town, by 'the sense of the
meeting'.

   The other democratic heresy is the doctrine of the absolute
right of a specially illuminated group. The doctrine had its effective origin in the teaching of Rousseau and its practical application by Robespierre in the Reign of Terror.

   Rousseau, in stating his fundamental principle that the
'general will' is sovereign, had the insight to observe that the
general will (that is, the will towards the common good) is not
the same as the will of all. That is to say, the majority does not
necessarily express the general will; the majority may be wrong.
How, then, are we to identify the general will? Where are we
to locate it? Into the gap left by this question-mark Robespierre, the first modern doctrinaire dictator, was quick to jump.

   1. *De la démocratie en Amérique*, 1835.

The general will was to be identified with Robespierre's party. Robespierre thus supplied the formula on which every modern dictatorship has been based.

The identification of democracy with the supremacy of a Party obviously avoids the error of sanctifying the majority, but equally obviously does so at the cost of destroying such protection as majority rule affords against the tyranny of a political group which imposes its authority by force. The one thing such a tyranny cannot afford to risk is a free election.

These two heretical doctrines, of the absolute right of the majority and the absolute right of the Party, are in one sense extreme opposites. But, with modern means of mass communication and pressure, the extremes can be made to meet. A powerful group can impose its will on the majority by mass persuasion, so that the rule of the Party seems to be the will of the majority. The more possible it becomes to 'process' human beings, the more difficult it becomes to distinguish the heresy of head-counting from the heresy of Party dictatorship. The more effective the means of influencing people's minds, the less need is there for crudely external methods of compulsion.

The best government is clearly that which combines the good elements which are perverted in the two heresies – that is, in which the leaders expect, and are expected, to explain themselves to the led, and in which no group will press too far its advantage of numbers, or power. Good government must be based on a proper mutual respect of persons and of groups. Such mutual respect cannot be ensured by any governmental machinery, though machinery can create, or destroy, opportunity. Which is another way of saying that the only true democracy is an educated democracy – educated in the appreciation of right values and in understanding of the ways in which attitudes are formed and changed. If power, whether of a majority or of a party, is to be exercised in a responsible way, those who possess power must acknowledge the proper limitation of power by the principle that human beings as such are sacred in an individual and ultimate sense. It is this principle which bids us respect the rights of minorities that are unable to make their will prevail. In other words, good government recognizes an ultimate authority to which *both* governors and governed are answerable. Whether we call this ultimate authority Reason and Justice, the Will of God, or the Law of Nature, its sacramental expression is that reverence of human beings for one another which is the essence of the democratic ideal in its purest form. It was implicit in the thought of Plato and Aristotle, but did not find full expression until the Christian Gospel broke down the barriers between bond and free. The Greeks could not think beyond the rights and duties of free citizens. The Christian revolution made it possible to think in terms of the worth that belongs to a human being because he is one – though after two thousand years we still find it hard to carry our faith in the value of human personality across the divisions of class and colour.

Human values are threatened not only in the political world but in economic relations. Large industrial organizations tend to be impersonal. In the small firm employers and employed know one another as people, even if they do not like one another. In the large organization the bosses become anonymous.[1] Most factory workers are still doing jobs that need little or no training. And unskilled work is often paid better than skilled work,[2] with the result that workers tend to forsake skilled for unskilled jobs which, owing to the extreme division of labour, offer little opportunity for the satisfaction of craftsman-

1. It must be remembered, however, that many employees are still employed in small firms. About 74 per cent of manufacturing establishments employ under 100 people, and about 95 per cent less than 500. Of employees about 52 per cent are employed in firms employing less than 500 people. (These percentages are based on figures given in the Annual Abstract of Statistics, No. 97, 1960, H.M.S.O.) As many schools have about 500 pupils 500 may perhaps be taken as a rough measure of the size of group beyond which relations become anonymous.

2. A skilled carpenter of my acquaintance, who works for a building contractor, earns about £12 a week. He could earn £20–25 a week by doing unskilled work in a factory. Up to now he has resisted the temptation.

ship.[1] No doubt we are in a transitional stage of development; and the indications are that we shall move into an age when we shall no longer use human beings as mere extensions of the machine, and the merely mechanical operations will all be done by machines. If and when that time comes, it will be all the more important that the people who make and use the machines should be intelligent and responsible. We are still, however, in the stage when we use large numbers of human beings as bits of machinery. Young people going from school into industry are paid too highly for jobs that have too little meaning and need too little skill. The discontent among the engineering apprentices is evidence of the overpayment of young unskilled workers.[2]

Industrial workers of any age find it difficult to understand the system of which they are part, let alone the world-wide pattern of relations on which their livelihood ultimately depends. With very incomplete understanding, they are at the mercy of any pressure group that can get hold of them. Their bewilderment is aggravated by the present anarchy in the trade union world. The rank-and-file worker does not know to whom he should listen, even within the ranks of Labour. It is not surprising if he contents himself with doing his job at the bench, collecting his pay-packet, watching TV, and doing his pools.

There is great need in our world for responsible individuals.

1. It is a mistake to regard craftsmanship as incompatible with machinery; from the flint axe to the electronic computer is only a difference of degree. But craftsmanship is incompatible with such division of labour as deprives a task of meaning.

2. In February 1961 Mr Selwyn Lloyd, Chancellor of the Exchequer, addressing the National Production Advisory Council on Industry, stressed the scarcity of skilled men. Mr Peter Thomas, Parliamentary Secretary to the Ministry of Labour, said that, in December 1960, there were four vacancies for every unemployed skilled man in the engineering industries, and that this situation would return. There was need for better apprenticeship training. It had been suggested that there should be more group apprenticeship schemes, operated by groups of companies, which would help small firms by sharing the burden of training. *Daily Telegraph*, 4 February 1961.

Quality of manpower will become increasingly important. Yet there is a great danger that human beings will find themselves 'processed' and will accept the situation. In these days not only the social order is provided ready-made, but so are attitudes. Outside the job (which in most cases requires only limited skill and little or no responsible judgement), the worker in industry need not think at all. This mental passivity is both sedative and frustrating; it accounts both for general conformity and occasional outbreaks of violence. It has been suggested that the greatest revolution of the past 100 years took place in 1914, when Henry Ford introduced an eight-hour day and at the same time doubled wages, thus lifting the modern factory worker from the subsistence-wage level, giving him leisure and a new power of consumer-choice. But this revolution can be for the benefit of mankind only if people know how to use their money and their leisure, and have some intelligent understanding of the world in which they live. Otherwise, whether they have motor-cars and washing-machines or not, they are mentally and spiritually as enslaved as ever.

The whole problem of industrial relations and 'job-satisfaction' is very difficult under the impersonal conditions of large-scale industry. Writing in *The Times*,[1] an ex-foreman and assistant works manager developed the thesis that the only nexus between employer and employed is the equivalence of the agreed reward and the agreed job of work – 'an appeal barefaced, simple, and at least honest, to the worker's self-interest' – which requires efficient completion of the job on one side and efficient 'workflow' on the other side. Given competence and reliability on both sides, there is a basis for loyalty, so long as conditions remain satisfactory. But we must not expect any other kind of loyalty. The job, in nearly all cases, is meaningless in itself. 'There are astonishingly few jobs in industry today of which you could imagine a small boy saying: "I should like to do so-and-so when I grow up." ' This article provoked some correspondence, in which it was argued that 'job-satisfaction' involves many things besides money – opportunity for promotion, acquirement of new skills, status, and so on. But it

1. 30 October 1959.

seems clear that we do not know nearly enough about the conditions on which job-satisfaction depends, and how to create them.

The whole picture of industrial relations is complicated by changes which make traditional attitudes and machinery out of date. One new factor is the much greater activity of the State as such in the last thirty years. Before 1930 the government's approach to industry was mainly negative and consisted of removing abuses. Since 1930 the government has positively accepted responsibility for providing employment (by the establishment of Special Areas, for example). Greater dependence on international trade and finance makes increased government intervention inevitable. In the next twenty-five years the population of this country will increase by four millions, but the working population by only one million. We have to face growing competition from other countries, especially from the U.S.S.R. We import fifty per cent of our food and eighty per cent of our raw materials; and all we have to offer in exchange is skill. The key problem for this country will be economic survival. As Sir Harold Emmerson, Permanent Secretary to the Ministry of Labour, pointed out not long ago, decisions have now to be made on political and social grounds rather than on purely industrial grounds, and at the highest level rather than by a few directors concerned with their own affairs. These changes require a new attitude on the part of industrial management and a broader view of national welfare and prosperity. A new attitude is also needed on the part of organized labour, which can no longer realistically think in terms of labour *versus* capital.

Our need is above all for quality in man-power, and for a new attitude towards industrial change, with the accent on intelligent understanding, responsibility, and self-discipline. It is not surprising that a good deal of thought is being given to the question whether the strike is not out of date as a means of settling industrial disputes. In *Trade Unions in a Free Society* Mr B. C. Roberts points out that strikes are increasingly self-damaging because they reduce the economic product from which wages have to be paid and make it impossible to raise wages without inflation, which injures everybody. He asks whether it is not time that the strike was recognized as an obsolete method, and some other means found for settling disputes by politically independent arbitration, though without reducing the trade unions to the position of totally controlled agencies of the State.

It can be reasonably maintained that technological development has outrun industrial organization so as to make the strike an impossible means of settling disputes. We can no longer afford strikes. But, if the strike is to be discarded as a means of settling disputes, there must be an efficient system of arbitration to take its place. This we have not got. Although the historical trend in British industrial relations has been towards the acceptance of arbitration awards, the system of arbitration is still largely voluntary, and could be quite easily dismantled if either side were prepared to terminate unilaterally the agreements they have entered into. The coal miners are the only major body of workers in the public sector with a water-tight compulsory arbitration system whose findings are binding on both parties. On the railways, for example, either side can take the other to arbitration but is not bound by the result.

Mr Leslie Stephens, Director of the Institute of Personnel Management, in a letter to the press,[1] emphasized the far-reaching effects of a minor strike when many other firms are dependent (as in the motor-car industry) on the product of the factory which is directly involved in the dispute.[2] He referred to the Minister of Labour's proposed working-party on industrial relations, and also to a conference on management responsibility and unofficial strikes which his Institute is planning.

Professor E. H. Phelps-Brown (one of the Cohen Committee), in *The Growth of Industrial Relations*, suggests a new code of laws (a) to define the rights of employers and employed, (b) to protect individual trade unionists against their trade unions and individual employers against their employers' associations, and (c) to protect the interests of the general public during strikes.

1. *Daily Telegraph*, 2 June 1960.
2. An example is the strike of workers at Smiths' Motor Accessories, Cricklewood, in June 1961.

A frequent cause of labour disputes in this country is the right to dismiss employees, one of the most cherished prerogatives of the British employer. So long as due notice is given, the employer's right to dismiss is not limited by law (indeed there is nothing to prevent him from dismissing a man for trade union activities), but only by the strength of the unions.

In other countries the employer's right to dismiss is limited in some way. There may be an obligation to consult, or to compensate. In some countries the employer must obtain authorization from a public authority before dismissing an employee. In the U.S.A. collective bargaining practice has virtually established the principle that dismissals can take place only for just cause. Britain is in fact almost the only industrial country in the world where the sole means of challenging dismissals alleged to be unjust is to turn them into industrial disputes.[1]

Apart from the difficult problem of strikes as such, there is the more obvious problem of the unofficial strike. This country has a worse record than any other for unofficial strikes. In November 1959 five strikes were in progress, all unofficial. In each case the official and elected leadership had urged the men to go back to work and use the arbitration machinery which was available; in each case the men refused to go back. In April 1962, an unofficial strike of 3000 men in the Austin works at Longbridge, Birmingham, resulted in 20,000 men being laid off by the B.M.C., and cost the Corporation £1,000,000 a day while it lasted (a week or so).

In April 1960, Mr W. J. Carron, President of the Amalgamated Engineering Union, in his presidential address at Blackpool, spoke very strongly against 'wildcat' strikes, which, by damaging exports, would jeopardize the future of the strikers' own children. He also attacked unofficial workers' organizations. The Communist Party, he said, had at one time tried to gain control of the union movement through the capture of executive authority. This attempt had for the most part failed. In more recent years the Communist emphasis had been more on gain-

1. *The Times*, 20 June 1960. An article summarizing a comparative study of dismissal procedures published in the *International Labour Review*, May 1960.

ing control among the shop stewards on the floor of the work-shop, and also on seeking, mainly by means of unofficial stop-pages, to undermine the authority of the executives which they had failed to capture.[1] Early in April 1960, the Executive Council of the A.E.U. warned the 10,000 shop stewards in the Union not to take part in unofficial strikes, and reminded them of the disciplinary measures that could be taken on breach of rules. These measures include withdrawal of a shop steward's credentials, a fine, or even expulsion from the Union. Breach of rules includes strikes or bans on overtime undertaken without instructions from district committees and the approval of the national executive.

A good deal of publicity has been given to the film *The Angry Silence*, which shows the persecution of a worker who dared to defy the call to strike engineered by a professional agitator. The National Union of Mineworkers banned the showing of the film in miners' halls in forty-seven South Wales villages.

It is impossible to resist the conclusion that the trade unions are in an almost chaotic condition. Two features seem to stand out. One is the near-impossibility for the rank-and-file member of a union to have a clear grasp of the issues in which he finds himself involved, and hence his susceptibility to all kinds of dubious pressures. The other is the fact that the trade unions, notwithstanding their considerable powers on paper over their

1. *Birmingham Mail*, 25 April 1960. The outstanding example is the long battle over the affairs of the E.T.U. The T.U.C. challenged the E.T.U. either to go to law over repeated allegations of ballot-rigging or submit to a judicial inquiry. The case came into court and, at the end of June 1961, five defendants (including the general president of the E.T.U., the general secretary, and assistant general secretary) were found guilty of preventing 'by fraudulent and unlawful devices' the election of Mr John Thomas Byrne as general secretary of the union in December 1959. The action was brought by Mr Byrne and others. The defendants admitted that the election of Mr Haxell as general secretary had been invalid, but denied the use of fraudulent practices. The false election in 1959 was the culmination of a struggle that had gone on for the leadership of the E.T.U. since 1946 or 1947. Important as the judgement in this case is, it has not put an end to the long struggle for leadership.

members, are by no means masters in their own house.[1] At the end of 1959 the Central Council of the T.U.C. appointed a Committee of Inquiry to study unofficial strikes and the general breakdown of normal trade union discipline.

In the words of a recent article in *The Times*, 'All three parties at Westminster know that the image of the trade union leadership has suffered ominous damage in the last few years. In consequence the Conservatives have at last lost their fear of the unions; some Labour thinkers are openly rebuking them, or challenging their constitutional entrenchments within the party; and the Liberals are campaigning for trade unions to be registered with the Registrar of Friendly Societies "in such a way as to ensure fair elections and prevent victimization".' [2] Labour thinkers point out that the jealousy with which individual unions guard their sovereignty is bound to weaken national leadership. And Mr R. B. McCallum, Master of Pembroke College, Oxford, remarks: 'It may be that one of the most important symptoms of the year 1959 was the appearance without causing undue commotion of two films satirizing trade union practices' (*I'm All Right, Jack* and *The Angry Silence*).[3]

The Labour Party Conference at Scarborough in October 1960 did not enhance the reputation of the trade unions in public opinion. For one thing, there was the disingenuous mental gymnastics and double-talk on the question of unilateral disarmament. For another, there was a fresh exposure of the unreality of the block vote. In the words of a leading article in the *Daily Telegraph*: 'As Mr Gaitskell himself confessed, his defeat is

1. The legal powers of the trade unions were much increased – some would say too much increased – by the Act of 1945 which repealed the Act of 1927. The Act of 1927 (passed after the General Strike) established contracting in – i.e., a union member did not subscribe to the political funds of the union unless he said that he wanted to do so. The Act also made it an offence for public bodies to compel their employees to belong to trade unions. The Act of 1945 substituted contracting out (i.e., it is now assumed that members will contribute to political funds unless they say they will not), and also laid the foundations of the closed shop.

2. *The Times*, 20 June 1960.   3. ibid.

partly the result of the constitutional fraud on which it is founded. Policy is supposed to be determined democratically by its members; it is in fact controlled by the block votes of trade unions, collected and wielded in a manner far from representative. How many of Mr Cousins's "million votes" really support Mr Cousins?' [1] Again, the conference underlined the question whether trade union leaders ought to use their block votes to exert influence in matters of national policy which, however important, are not the proper concern of a trade union as such.

An interesting study of mass culture was published some years ago by Dwight Macdonald in the international periodical *Diogenes*.[2] The author regards mass culture (German, *Kitsch*) as solely and directly an article for mass consumption, 'like chewing-gum'. He points out that it is not new, but goes back in the older art forms (the novel and music) to 1800. It has, however, been much developed along with political democracy and popular education, and the technological advances which made cheap books, periodicals, and furniture possible. The new media of the film, radio, and TV, which are adapted to mass manufacture and distribution, have given mass culture an enormous impetus in our own time.

Mass culture is distinguished by Dwight Macdonald from High Culture, and also from Folk Culture. High Culture is the traditional culture of an educated *élite*, and was formerly the monopoly of an upper class. Likened to 'a great formal park', it ignored the mob and sought to please only the *cognoscenti*. Folk Culture was, until the Industrial Revolution, the culture of the common people. It grew genuinely out of the life and work of the people, 'a spontaneous, autochthonous expression of the people, shaped by themselves, pretty much without the benefit of High Culture'. Mass culture, on the other hand, is fabricated, by technicians employed by the ruling social groups, and imposed from above. It consists largely of debased High Culture. Its audiences are passive consumers, and their exercise of choice is more or less limited to buying or not buying.

1. *Daily Telegraph*, 5 October 1960.
2. 'A Theory of Mass Culture', *Diogenes*, Summer 1953.

Mass culture is used as an instrument by power-groups in East and West. While the U.S.S.R. spoonfeeds with written-down Marxism, the U.S.A. debauches with coca-cola and comics. Ease of production and ease of consumption make *Kitsch* a serious rival to High Culture. For example, *Reader's Digest* maintains a circulation of fifteen million 'simply by reducing to even lower terms the already superficial formula of other periodicals. By treating a theme in two pages which they treat in six, the *Digest* becomes three times as "readable" and three times as superficial'.

The old fairly clear distinction between High Culture and Folk Culture has broken down. Mass culture vulgarizes High Culture, and the edges become blurred so that High Culture and mass culture melt into one another. 'A statistically significant part of the population, I venture to guess, is chronically confronted with a choice between going to the movies or to a concert, between reading Tolstoy or a detective story, between looking at old masters or at a TV show; that is, the pattern of their cultural lives is "open" to the point of being porous. Good art competes with *Kitsch*, serious ideas compete with commercialized formulae – and the advantage lies all on one side. There seems to be a Gresham's Law in cultural as well as in monetary circulation; bad stuff drives out the good, since it is more easily understood and enjoyed.'[1]

To describe this common, commercialized culture, in which differences of quality are blurred, the author uses the term Homogenized Culture. In it all barriers of class, tradition, taste, and even age are broken down. Everything is mixed and scram-

1. Dwight Macdonald is perhaps over-puritanical in his disapproval of trivial alternative entertainments. Even the best educated people cannot live all the time on the heights; and, if they could, they would become intolerable bores. There is a place for detective stories as well as for Tolstoy. Nevertheless, the general thesis is true, (a) that material of good and bad quality is jumbled together in modern periodicals and entertainments to a far greater extent than used to be the case, and (b) that, unless a person has a fairly strong drive towards material of good quality, he will easily forsake it for effortless indulgence in trivialities.

bled. Adults read comics, and children have access to adult films and TV programmes; adults are infantile and children are over-stimulated. Max Horkheimer is quoted: 'Development has ceased to exist. The child is grown-up as soon as he can walk, and the grown-up in principle always remains the same.' Reference is made to the cult of youth, which makes eighteen to twenty-two the most admired and desired period of life, and the sentimental worship of Mother ('Momism'), which suggests that we cannot bear to grow up. Values are destroyed in a culture which is 'democratic' by refusing to discriminate between anything and anything else.

The magazine *Life* is taken as an example of a homogenized mass-circulation periodical. It is read by rich and poor, and its contents are as mixed as its readers. The same issue may contain an exposition of atomic theory, the story of Rita Hayworth's love-life, photos of starving Korean children, the celebration of Bertrand Russell's eightieth birthday, and a full-page picture of a roller-skating horse.

With the development of mass culture has come greater and greater division of labour in its production, and the loss of the older individual touch. Every technical advance has brought further division of labour. In Hollywood today a composer for the movies is not *allowed* to make his own orchestrations, nor a director to do his own cutting. The older film directors of thirty years ago did everything. Mass art is increasingly syndicated. It is worth observing that, historically, *successful* collective creation has been possible only when the creators were part of a tradition, as in the building of a Gothic cathedral.

Dwight Macdonald is not very hopeful about the future. He considers the view of conservatives, like Ortega y Gasset and T. S. Eliot, who urge the rebuilding of the old class values in the hope of bringing the masses once again under aristocratic control, and also the view of Marxists and others of the Left, who regard the masses as intrinsically healthy, though the victims of exploitation, and believe that, given good material, mass culture would improve. He rejects both points of view because they both assume a mass culture which is a genuine expression of *people*, like Folk Art, whereas it is a manufactured article.

True culture can be produced only by and for human beings. But, in so far as people are organized (or disorganized) in masses, they lose their human identity and quality. 'The masses are in historical time what a crowd is in space: a large quantity of people unable to express themselves as human beings because they are related to one another neither as individuals nor as members of communities – indeed they are not related *to each other* at all but only to something distant, abstract, non-human: a football game or bargain sale in the case of a crowd, a system of industrial production, a party, or a State in the case of the masses. The mass man is a solitary atom, uniform with and undifferentiated from thousands and millions of other atoms who go to make up "the lonely crowd".'

In the mass the lowest standards dominate – it coheres along the line of the least common denominator. The technicians of mass culture degrade the public by treating it with the lack of ceremony and the objectivity of medical students dissecting a corpse, and at the same time flatter it by pandering to its level of taste.

In the last resort the mass has its revenge. 'Complete indifference to their human quality means complete prostration before their statistical *quantity*, so that a movie magnate who cynically "gives the public what it wants" ... sweats with terror if box-office returns drop ten per cent.'

A fairly full summary of Dwight Macdonald's article has been given because it is vigorous, shrewd, and, I believe, substantially true. It is questionable, however, whether we need accept his negative conclusion. Great as are the dangers confronting our civilization, we need not give up our future as hopeless. There would seem to be at least two positive suggestions worth making.

In the first place, it is not beyond the bounds of possibility that we could build up a cultural *élite* that held authority. All the great cultures of the past, with the possible exception of Periclean Athens, were *élite* cultures, fairly closely linked with an aristocracy, from which they drew their social authority. It is true that the *élite* of birth has gone and that the new *élite* of brains has no recognized authority in the general field of

social values, though it has increasing authority in the technological field. The *élite* today is anyone who can pass the eleven-
plus. Our present intelligentsia, in Dwight Macdonald's phrase,
is 'small, weak, and disintegrated'.

Yet, slender as the prospects may seem, the re-creation of an
authoritative cultural tradition, through good general education which lays emphasis on those abiding values which stand
fast in a world of rapid technical change, is surely worth
attempting, if only because without it we can expect nothing
but disaster. The vehicle and repository of such a culture would
be an acknowledged tradition rather than an insulated social
class, and there would be a good deal of social fluidity in the
élite which, generation by generation, found themselves guardians of the tradition. It would be important for the *élite* not
to be emotionally out of touch with the wider public; if out
of touch they would have no influence. This idea of a cultural
élite will be discussed further in later chapters.

In the second place – and this suggestion will also be discussed later – we ought to do everything possible to encourage
neighbourhood activities of all kinds (ranging from formal adult
education to informal dramatic, musical, or gardening clubs)
which create opportunities for cooperation and for the exercise
of responsibility, and which are on a sufficiently intimate scale
for personal relations to count. The voluntary neighbourhood
group is the basic unit of democracy, and from it people can
graduate to larger responsibilities. Not only is neighbourhood
activity of this kind a positive retort to the passivity invited
by mass entertainment, but it possesses, in its own contemporary context, the essential qualities of a genuine Folk Culture,
a culture made by people for themselves which enriches their
lives because they are doing things which they honestly believe
are worth doing.

Meanwhile it is salutary to recognize how hard it is for the
free, responsible human being to escape being crushed between
a competitive economic system and a socialized political system – between the advertising salesman on the one side and the
organizing bureaucrat on the other.

Part II

CONDITIONS OF PERSONAL VALUES

CHAPTER 5

The Need for a Coherent View of Life

IT has been assumed that personal values – the sacredness of human personality and the proper reverence of human beings for one another in their dealings – are necessary to the good life. And it has been suggested that, in the world as it is, there are many influences operating to undermine personal values.

It is the purpose of this and the following two chapters to consider some of the conditions upon which the promotion and maintenance of personal values would seem to depend. This chapter is concerned with the need to rediscover a coherent culture or view of life.

'Fragmentation' is a vogue word nowadays. We are well aware of the disintegration of thought and knowledge into an increasing number of separate systems, each more or less self-contained, with its own language, and recognizing no responsibility for knowing or caring about what is going on across its frontiers. The polymath is an extinct species. He cannot exist in the modern world; and attempts to follow in his footsteps are suspect in respectable academic circles. The story of the Tower of Babel might have been a prophetic vision of the modern university; and the fragmentation which is spotlighted there affects the whole of society.

The most striking instance of cultural disintegration is the cleavage between the sciences and the humanities, of which Sir Charles Snow has written in *The Two Cultures*.[1] Up to the seventeenth century the emphasis in Western culture was upon

1. It makes little difference whether we accept Sir Charles Snow's view or prefer that of Mr Kingsley Amis, who says that we have one culture which has been disintegrating.

the humanities. From the seventeenth to the nineteenth century the emphasis swung over increasingly to science, and the growing body of scientific knowledge was less and less related to the traditional values of the humanities. In the present century we have become uncomfortably aware of the cleavage between the two main cultural traditions and of the need to bridge the gap. With the growth of human sciences – anthropology, sociology, psychology – science has come near to claiming that the whole of human life can be brought under the dominion of scientific method. No doubt there is much to be gained by scientific study of human behaviour. But the human sciences carry with them the danger that those aspects of human behaviour which are not susceptible to scientific treatment will be ignored, and the truth be obscured that the really important thing in human life is the quality of relations between persons, which in the ultimate analysis eludes scientific assessment.

Although the sciences have extended their frontiers to include great areas of human behaviour, it cannot be said that any very systematic effort has been made, from the other side of the gap, to bring the findings of science within the interpretation of human values. In these days of tremendous technological development it is of the utmost importance that scientific discovery should be evaluated and used in relation to the highest human good, and that human values should not become subservient to technological discovery. In homely terms, labour-saving devices can be a blessing if they liberate the human spirit for worthwhile creative activity; but they become a curse if they are identified with the good life. Spin-dryers and the rest are not a recipe for happiness. The technological age will end in disaster unless the use of scientific knowledge is governed by the broadest and deepest consideration of human welfare.

It is one thing to pay lip-service to spiritual values. But in a generation which is breathless with admiration for its own technological achievements, in a world where science commands so much popular prestige that for many people scientific truth is the only truth, it is another thing to resist the inducements to bow down in spite of ourselves to the Baal of material values.[1] In the West we accept too easily material standards as the criteria of civilization, and then apply them to our thinking about the rest of the world. Not long ago Mr Aidan Crawley observed that the 'gap' between the industrial and under-developed countries can be very misleading if expressed only in terms of the standards of Western civilization. 'Statistically the inhabitants of Burma must be among the most miserable in the world. They have an average annual income of only £20 a head. In fact, the Burmese are a gay and carefree people and probably extract as much fun out of life as we do. They enjoy something which statisticians have not yet learned to measure, the sun.'[2] Income per head is a very misleading measure and takes no account of things which Eastern people can do without or do much more cheaply – they can, for example, carry on their business out of doors. 'When, as Professor Galbraith suggests, statisticians tell us the number of laughs emitted at different levels of income, when they let us know which income-groups derive most pleasure from the company of other human beings and which are most consistently bored; when they tell us what occupations develop ulcers and in what income-groups family life is at its best, then we shall be getting somewhere. For in a society in which leisure begins to play an increasingly important part these things may have greater importance than most of the items in the cost-of-living index.'[3]

Our concern is not so much with the undisputed fact of the fragmentation of thought and knowledge as with its consequences – and in particular the consequences of the falling apart of the scientific and humanistic traditions which has been such

1. In the second of his Reith Lectures on *Artistic Participation* (November 1960), Professor Edgar Wind said that, although artists today understood much less of science than they did in the sixteenth or seventeenth centuries, their imaginations were haunted by a desire to mimic scientific procedures. Many of them seemed to act in their studios as if they were in a laboratory. He shared André Gide's opinion that wide stretches of art had been dehumanized.

2. *Sunday Times*, 23 October 1960. The last of four articles on 'Our Affluent Society'.

3. Aidan Crawley, ibid.

a marked feature of the past hundred years. The divorce between the sciences and the humanities exposes our civilization
to two main dangers.

(a) One danger is that our civilization may become wholly
materialistic, given over to material convenience and luxuries.
It would be quite unjust to accuse the professional scientist of
being a materialist or fostering materialistic values. The true
scientist is probably much less materialistic – certainly much
less mechanistic – than his predecessor of fifty or a hundred
years ago. If physical science has penetrated increasingly into
regions which used to be regarded as non-physical (as in the
medical and even surgical treatments now used in psychiatry),
the modern scientist knows that there is no clear and convenient partition between the material and the non-material;
and physical science has to reckon with phenomena the very
acknowledgement of which would have embarrassed the Victorian physicist (for example, the manifestations of extra-
sensory perception and psycho-kinesis or action-at-a-distance).
There are, indeed, no reputable materialists today in the sense
in which that word was used two generations ago.

If we speak today of the danger of materialism we are thinking rather of the effects of popularized science on the attitudes
of ordinary people. Never has science enjoyed such high popular prestige, especially among people who do not understand it.
Science is the new magic; and it has placed so many wonders
within our grasp that we are tempted to think it can solve all
human problems. If we are told that something is 'scientifically
proved', the word 'scientific' is simply a prestige-intensive,
meaning 'proved beyond all doubt or contradiction'. We too
easily identify the achievements of applied science with the
conditions of human happiness and regard technology as the
gateway to the millennium.

In this sense nothing could be more unscientific than the
popular attitude to science. Given that attitude, however (and
the mass media offer plenty of inducement to adopt it), there is
a real danger that an attitude to life may prevail which puts the
gifts of applied science, glowing with prestige, at the top of the
list, but is shallow in its appreciation of those non-material

values which give deeper meaning to human life. For, while our minds are perpetually bombarded by achievement, the prophetic message of the humanistic tradition (whether Plato's cardinal virtues or the Christian gifts of the spirit) is muted if not silent. It is worth reminding ourselves that the classical Greeks, whose values were healthy and discerning, were not exposed to the irresistible temptations of a world in which enormous wealth can be amassed by doing things of doubtful worth. Too many teenagers in these days have a dream-world of luxuriant affluence, achieved quickly and without too much effort by a combination of luck and the right gimmick.

Mr Adlai Stevenson, early in 1959, said: 'The dreary failure in history of all classes committed to pleasure and profit alone, the vacuity and misery accompanying the sole pursuit of ease, the collapse of the French aristocracy, the corruption of Imperial Rome; all these facts of history do not lose their point because the pleasures of today are no longer the enjoyments of an *élite*. If we become a nation of Bourbons, numbers won't save us. Vacuity and indifference are not redeemed by the fact that everyone can share them. They merely restrict the circle from which regeneration can come.'

(b) The other danger is that power (and largely destructive power at that) may be developed without proper understanding of the uses to which it may be put – the danger, in fact, that human problems may be thought about and handled as if they were purely technical problems; and the related danger that the technologist, preoccupied with means rather than ends, may be used as a tool by political or other power-groups.

Perhaps this danger that human problems may be treated as purely technical problems is the clearest illustration of the cultural disintegration of our time and of the need for a coherent pattern that could once more bring our thought and knowledge into an organized whole.

The difficulties of a coherent, or total, handling of human problems can be illustrated from the medical field. Not long ago Professor Fraser Brockington, speaking on the work of the World Health Organization, emphasized the fact that no important problem is a purely technical one and suggested that people who cannot see beyond the technical aspects of our problems are not likely to be of much help in coping with the state of the world.

In the Western ('developed') countries, at least sixty per cent of deaths are due to old age or to the degenerative diseases of age. In the Eastern ('underdeveloped') countries, at least sixty per cent of deaths are due to infectious diseases, largely water-borne. As to the age distribution of mortality, in the West there is a comparatively small, but still significant, rate of mortality below the age of five, and then comparatively little until middle age and old age. In the East, the largest mortality age-group is under five, and then there is comparatively little variation from age-group to age-group.

We already possess the technical knowledge to prevent or cure most of the worst Eastern diseases. If the problem were a purely technical one, it could be solved tomorrow. But it is a social, political, ethical, and religious problem. To solve it we need to awaken the social conscience of the West to do some-thing about it, especially in the matter of money and personnel. We need also to educate the East to accept Western ideas and practice in medicine and hygiene. Religious and other taboos, together with sheer inertia, are strong and resistant. For ex-ample, in Bangkok (a kind of far-eastern Venice), the banks of the *klongs* (canals) are crowded with colourful but squalid tene-ments. The people take their water from the *klongs* and are not in the habit of boiling it. The *klongs* receive all the sewerage. Three-quarters of the children die under the age of five.

Underlying the educational problems implicit in this situa-tion there is the great difficulty created by the slowness and apparent ineffectiveness of democracy, working by persuasion. The fact is that the U.S.S.R. and China, in the countries under their control, have advanced considerably further than the countries under Western influence towards the establishment of health services. But they have done so by methods which democracy could not feel at liberty to use.

Technical knowledge of itself does not take us very far to-wards the solution of problems of this kind. We also need will and purpose, which are born of faith. If world problems of health need an approach which is broadly human and not purely technical, so do all the important problems of our time – most of all, perhaps, the use of atomic power and its place in international relations. We cannot hope to see and deal with these great human problems unless we can give new meaning to our fragmented culture by means of unifying beliefs.

The trouble is that technical development is taking place on such a scale and at such a rate that we find it hard to believe that anything else matters. Technology tends to steal the show and blinds us to the fact that the drama of human life is essentially the same as it ever was. The central theme of the drama is that the quality of life in any society depends on the amount of courage and sense of purpose, truthfulness, compassion, and unselfishness in that society, rather than on the amount of technical achievement. That is not to say that technical achievement does not matter. Rightly used, technical achievement can enhance the spiritual quality of life. But no technical achievement is a substitute for spiritual quality; and in the final reckoning, when the account of human history is made up and closed, technical achievement alone will not count for very much. The play is the same play, and it is a classic. A revolution in the techniques of production ought not to delude us into thinking that it is a new play, or – worse – losing the play itself in an orgy of producer's gimmicks.

Our age is one of cultural ferment. A plea for a new cultural synthesis might be taken to imply that cultural ferment is a bad thing. That was certainly not the purpose of this chapter. Times of cultural ferment are inevitable in human history. Our own time is one of them; and to that extent it is beside the point to ask whether cultural ferment is good or bad. But we can say that cultural ferment is a good thing in so far as it is healthy to recognize a disturbance of traditional attitudes and values and unhealthy to shut our minds against changes with which we do not know how to deal.

What has been condemned by implication in this chapter is not cultural ferment but an indifferent, enervated or imperceiving acceptance of cultural disintegration, such as marked the long sunset of the Roman Empire. What has been affirmed is our responsibility for striving towards cultural coherence – towards meaning and purpose.

If we say that a healthy society has a coherent culture, we are not saying that a coherent culture is a static culture. Culture can be at the same time coherent and growing. It is important to distinguish between a unifying belief which inspires effort and a complacent or apathetic acceptance of a situation. There is all the difference between the medieval belief in Augustine's vision of the Commonwealth of God and the mid-eighteenth-century acceptance of Gibbon's description of 'our general state of happiness, the system of arts, and laws and manners, which so advantageously distinguish, above the rest of mankind, the Europeans and their colonies'. The deep spiritual insight and sense of national unity which the Jewish people reached after the Exile could not have been attained without bitter experience; nor could Athens have touched the heights of Pericles' Funeral Speech without the Persian and Peloponnesian Wars. An age of faith is no more static than an age of disillusionment or of bland complacence. But an age of faith has a cohesion which disillusionment and complacence both lack. Faith makes for coherence of thought and effort; it is the positive element in human history, without which the human mind and human society fall to pieces. Lionel Curtis ends his book, *Civitas Dei*, with some words of Goethe's : 'The deepest, nay the unique, theme of the history of the world, to which all other themes are subordinate, is the conflict of faith and unbelief. All epochs in which faith prevails – whatever its form may be – are noble, soul-elevating, and fruitful for the present and for after times. All epochs in which unbelief, be it under what form it may, wins an unhappy victory ... vanish and are forgotten by posterity; because no one willingly wastes his pains on what is barren and unfruitful.'

A culture inspired by a faith is no more static than a healthy body is static. The healthy body is growing and changing; but it is coordinated and functions, so to speak, in one piece. What is to be deplored at the cultural, as well as the physical, level, is locomotor ataxy.

It has been maintained in this chapter that cultural coherence depends not only upon the intellectual operation of relating the various fields of thought and bodies of knowledge, but also upon the will and purpose which come from a unifying faith. From this point of view the example of the Communist countries deserves attention, though it may be doubted whether creeds can be imposed, and whether truth in scientific inquiry ought to be subordinated to doctrinal orthodoxy.

It is not suggested that a coherent culture, or the faith in which it is rooted and which gives it power, can be manufactured to order. It must be a natural growth. We are historically conditioned; and, if we live in an age of cultural ferment, we must accept its opportunities, and not deny the fact of it. What we can do, however, is to use those opportunities for striving towards a coherent and purposeful view of life. Confused as our predicament may be, it has its growing points.

If we ask what are the growing points for a faith that could give impulsion and direction to our thought and action, the outlook might at first sight look unpromising. Ours has not the excitement of upsurging national greatness of the first Elizabethan age. Nor does our age offer the individual opportunities for making fortunes which Victorian industrial expansion created. Certainly there are ways of getting rich today, but they tend to be somewhat bogus compared with the solid worth of the countless Victorian success stories by which people of obscure origin built up and established family businesses. For most young men and women in these days a career in industry means entering a huge organization and expecting promotion much as in the armed forces. The affluent society is not, for most people, a very romantic or adventurous affair; whether you earn £10 or £50 a week there is not much to aspire to except a washing-machine, a better car, or colour television.

Ours is not an age of faith. The beat mentality may accompany success as well as failure. The sense of deep insecurity is no monopoly of the materially unsuccessful. Federico Fellini, director of the film *La Dolce Vita*, speaks for numbers of our generation when he says: 'Like many people, I have no religion and I am just sitting in a small boat drifting with the tide. I live in the doubts of my duty, which is to make the best possible films. I think there is dignity in this, just to go on working, shooting, cutting, editing, looking at life, then looking again and trying to make others see. This is the way things are, you say, now what are we to do? Today we stand naked, defenceless, and more alone than at any time in history. We are waiting for something, perhaps another miracle, perhaps the Martians. Who knows?'[1]

Nevertheless there are growing points in our contemporary situation from which hope and faith and courage may stem. To begin with, we are aware of our predicament; and self-criticism is the advance guard of reconstruction. Through history the prophet's first word has been: 'Repent!' and his second: 'The Reign of God is at hand!'

If we look more particularly at our industrial situation, we must recognize the obvious need for industry to be run as a national service (with the ethics that govern the running of education or the medical service) and not as a private dog-fight. Again, we cannot in these days shut our minds to the knowledge (brought home by vivid means of communication) of the needs of the underdeveloped countries, seeking independence but handicapped by ignorance, inexperience, and want. There are plain challenges to clear thinking and unselfish action both at home and across the world.

Another hopeful sign of the times is the great drive for more and better education. Never has there been so much public interest in education as there has been since the Second World War; never has the general public been better informed about education; and never have we as a people been more self-critical about our educational system. There is clearly a greater belief in education than ever before, and a greater resolution to give our people the best opportunities to fit them to meet the challenges of our time.

It is impossible to discuss the part that education can play in the achievement of a coherent view of life without recognizing the special responsibility of the universities and other places of higher learning. If a coherent cultural tradition, holding

1. *Sunday Times*, 4 December 1960.

authority, can be created, who should be the guardians and trustees of such a tradition? In the world of today and tomorrow a cultural tradition can no longer derive its authority from its association with a social class. Rather the guardians of a cultural tradition will have to be the universities and other places of higher education. But if they are to perform this function they will have to do two things which at present (with notable exceptions) they are failing to do. The people working in higher education will have to be more ready to look beyond the hedges that separate their narrow academic specialisms; if a view of life is to be presented which commands authority, it must be a whole view. Again, the places of higher education must make more effort to reach the general public effectively. The universities have a mission to the general public, and there are welcome signs that they are beginning to recognize the fact, not only in the scientific field.[1]

Implicit in all these challenges is the problem of the value of human personality as such. Our attitude towards economic conflict in our midst, or towards undernourishment on the other side of the world, turns upon whether or not we believe that human beings are of ultimate worth because they are human beings. This belief is the common and precious possession of our Western culture, and historically has inspired our best thoughts and actions. As Mr Victor Gollancz wrote in 1946: 'Our central value – or, to put it in another way, the value that includes all other values – is respect for personality.'[2] Discussing the possibility of another world war, he sees an even greater danger. 'The more pressing danger is of a different kind: it is nothing less than that the typical values of Western civilization may so nearly vanish – they can never, from their nature, vanish entirely – as no longer to contribute to what Mr Churchill has called "the forward march" of mankind. And if war does come, it will not come, essentially, because the machinery for preventing it is imperfect: it will come because day by day those impulses in our hearts which make for har-

1. The problem of the responsibility of the intellectuals to the general public is discussed further in Chapter 6.

2. *Our Threatened Values*, p. 9.

mony are growing weaker. At the crucial moment it will not be paper constitutions that men and women will obey: they will obey their own nature, and their own nature such as it has become.'[1]

The argument of this chapter is that the quest for an effectively coherent view of life involves two things. One is an understanding of the relations between the different departments of thought and knowledge. This does not mean that we must be versed in all the arts and sciences. That is neither possible nor necessary. But it does mean that we should have some grasp of the kind of contribution which they severally make to the whole human outlook – what questions they ask and answer. We must be clear about the limitations, as well as the value, of the various branches of knowledge; there is no more fruitful source of confusion than the assumption that what lies outside the terms of reference of a particular branch of knowledge does not exist.

The second thing needed is a governing principle, or master-idea, about which our thought and knowledge can cohere, and which gives them meaning and purpose. In the present world, belief in the sacredness of human personality has the best chance of acceptance as a common, uniting principle. People of different political and religious creeds are prepared to affirm that the quality of human society is the quality of human relationships; and this depends on the respect – reverence is not too strong a word – which one human being feels for another. The sacredness of human personality is the ultimate foundation of good government, decent society, and enlightened culture. The question *why* human personality is sacred goes beyond the scope of this chapter.

1. ibid.

CHAPTER 6

Communication

THE problem of unifying our culture brings with it another problem – that of communication. A society cannot have a coherent culture – it cannot even have a coherent existence – unless there is effective communication among its members.

There are two main reasons for the contemporary interest in communication. One is the enormous development of the technical means of communication. The other is the fact that our national and international problems increasingly depend for their solution on effective communication, and our failure to solve them is largely due to failure of communication.

In these days no important problem is a local, self-contained problem. Our problems cannot be insulated, but involve increasingly complex interrelations. Food, clothes, and fuel, which in the pre-industrial society could be purely local problems, are world problems. Social groups, industrial organizations, nations and groups of nations, cannot ignore one another; if they cannot come to terms with one another, something is likely to go wrong on a large scale.

The outstanding example of failure of communication is the great international barrier of the Iron Curtain. The deep distrust between East and West is the result of two fundamentally irreconcilable views of life. It is not a mere matter of disagreement; for disagreement presupposes that the parties have something in common to disagree about. It is rather a matter of two sets of assumptions which are so alien to one another as to preclude discussion. You cannot argue with people who, starting from different assumptions, do not know what you mean.

If we look within our own national borders, we must recognize that communication is hindered not only by the fragmentation of thought and knowledge which was described earlier, but also by the breaking-up of society itself into homogeneous groups out of touch with one another. One of the most important results of the Industrial Revolution has been the virtual disappearance of the old mixed community of the village or market town, in which all ranks of society shared traditions and customs and, to a large extent, a common life. The industrial town is an unpleasant place to live in, and improved transport enables those who can afford to live elsewhere to do so. Our social distribution has thus developed away from the old mixed community towards the one-class communities of slum, suburb, and (more recently) housing estate. Town planners have tried to re-create the mixed community; but their efforts are perhaps rather artificial. Meanwhile the impersonal character of large organizations (large industries, large public services) does not help to establish understanding between people. There is nothing more frustrating than trying to deal with an organization (local education authority, hospital, or telephone service) where one cannot get hold of anyone who will talk to one on a man-to-man basis. It is small wonder that the general public tend to accept, with passive docility, the treatment they receive from the organized social services. Impersonal treatment is in the long run more undermining to morale than hostility.

The problem of communication can be seen from two standpoints – from the sending end and from the receiving end.

On the one hand are those who, by ability and training, should be equipped to lead thought and set standards. Professor C. Wright Mills of Columbia University, in *The Causes of World War Three*, says that the intellectuals are cut off from the control of communication, encapsuled in their specialisms, out of touch with the world at large, and at the mercy of power groups who can use them as instruments of policy which the intellectuals have not determined. He urges that the intellectuals should try to repossess themselves of the cultural apparatus, including the mass media. In effect he is asking for a revival, in a modern context, of Plato's idea of the philosopher-king.[1] The *Universities Quarterly* for Autumn 1959 was given up to a symposium on the place of the creative writer in the university. No very startling conclusions were reached. There was in fact little more than what *The Times* described as a 'guarded admission that for those who like teaching a university job is not incompatible with creation'.[2] *The Times* suggested that we ought to go much further in the direction already opened up by the American universities; that is to say, we should 'support creative writers without exacting from them too precisely measured a pound of flesh'. After referring to the fact that for the past thirteen years Mr E. M. Forster had been an honorary fellow of King's, Cambridge, and that Mr W. H. Auden's duties as Professor of Poetry at Oxford are not very arduous, *The Times* went on : 'May not the moral be that writers ought to be employed more extensively in universities for the sake of their indirect rather than their academic influence?' It might be added that the same principle could apply to people who work for the films and radio as well as to writers of books. The important thing is that artists in language and other media whose work reaches and influences the general public should be recognized by and associated with universities.[3] In that way it might be possible to establish some con-

1. In this connexion it is worth noting a suggestion by Professor Lowenstein of Birmingham University that the British Association might take on the job of processing scientific knowledge for public consumption.

2. *The Times*, 17 October 1959.

3. In February 1961 the Universities Council for Adult Education submitted a memorandum to the Pilkington Committee on Broadcasting. In it the Council proposed the establishment by the Government of an Educational Broadcasting Council, widely representative of educational interests, to advise the Broadcasting Authorities on the enlargement and improvement of the educational aspects of broadcasting. In the Council's opinion, all broadcasting is in some respects educational and there is no dichotomy in broadcasting between education and entertainment. There should be no separate, specifically educational, broadcasting, but the educational potentialities of all programmes should be developed in a balanced service by both the BBC and the Independent Companies.

nexion in the public mind between the world of entertainment and the world of scholarship. In 1962, in addition to the examples mentioned above, four universities in Great Britain have established fellowships in literature, music, and fine arts, the purpose of which is to encourage creative work that will reach the general public. In one of these universities, fourteen people have held such fellowships since 1950. At least one other university plans to establish fellowships of this kind. Two universities have departments of drama, and two plan to have them. A few universities are engaged in research into the techniques and effects of television.

On the face of it there is a good deal to be said for Professor Wright Mills's view about the role of the intellectual. The trouble about the intellectuals, however, is that too few of them have any message for the general public. With ever-increasing specialization, fewer highly-educated people have a whole view of life, or observations on life as a whole, to communicate. Nor does the intellectual find it easy to communicate to the general public anything from his special field of study. The restricted range and esoteric idiom of modern scholarship are a barrier to communication which – as some laudable examples show – needs determined effort to break through. Moreover the scholar who tries to 'popularize' his subject is unlikely to arouse the enthusiasm of his academic colleagues.

The modern intellectual, who might be expected to play the role of Plato's philosopher-king in modern dress, is thus doubly handicapped. On the one hand he seldom has a whole view of life to communicate to the general public. On the other hand, even if he has a message for the general public, he is unlikely to be able to utter it in a way that ordinary people can understand. Here is the other side of the problem of communication. The kind of education which qualifies a 'leader of thought' tends to make him unintelligible to the man in the street. 'He doesn't talk our language.' Worse still, he is liable to be distrusted, even if his social origin was among the very people with whom he wants to communicate. He has been separated from them by his education, by the manners he has acquired, by the company he keeps. 'He's no longer one of us.'

It is one of the hazards of educational opportunity that an intelligent working-class boy may be estranged from his original social background, and yet not fully assimilated into his new milieu. With the increase of educational opportunity there has been coming into existence a new intelligentsia, sprung from comparatively humble origins and without much background of social confidence and security. They are highly intelligent but for the most part do not earn very much money or gain very much power. They are a main source of teachers for schools and for the newer universities. Their quality is high, but their influence does not compare with that of organized labour or of the 'establishment'. Indeed they may be made use of by power-groups.

Those whose education ought to equip them to be leaders of thought have a double obligation to fulfil if they are to exert effective influence. In the first place they must think out a coherent view of life which can give meaning and purpose to the various forms of work and leisure. Secondly they must study ways of sharing their thoughts with the general public – an activity which involves a sensitive awareness of what is going on (confusedly no doubt) in the minds of people at large.

This double task is not easy. We shall not begin to cope with it unless we can move a long way beyond the assumption, common in academic circles, that communication consists primarily of exposition. As a means of communication exposition has a limited range and function. The existentialists know very well that drama, fiction, and other forms of art are not only more potent than exposition but have a much more general appeal. We are scarcely beginning to realize the possibilities of the mass media as means of serious communication. One of the difficulties of our age is that, being an age of doubt and not an age of faith, it produces fiction and drama which are analytic rather than constructive. Much contemporary drama, both high-brow and middle-brow, is negative rather than positive, depressive rather than inspiring.

If communication is not primarily a matter of exposition, neither is it primarily a matter of words. Words can obstruct communication, as everyone knows who has argued for an hour and a half only to discover at the end of it that the two parties were meaning different things by the same terms. Communication, indeed, is not primarily an intellectual activity; though intellectual activity, properly conducted, can greatly aid communication.

The basis of communication is shared feeling. And failure of communication is ultimately due to there being no common feeling or experience to share. Language barriers can usually be overcome between people who have a strong interest in common, whether it be bargaining, escaping, or making love. But where the lives of people or groups of people do not touch at any point, there can be no communication. In this connexion it may be worthwhile to recall what was said earlier about the virtual disappearance of the pre-industrial mixed community, and the appearance in its place of the various one-class, one-type communities.

If, however, a common interest – such as gardening – can be found among a miscellaneous group of people (say a factory worker, a business executive, a smallholder, and a professor) communication will begin. Not only that, but communication, once begun, will spread to other topics as mutual confidence is established. Once people begin to trust one another, they will want to explore each other's minds and share their experience. To this end there is great value in voluntary social activities, such as dramatic societies, rambling clubs, Women's Institutes, and the like, which bring a varied assortment of people together for a clear and limited purpose, in the pursuit of which they can lose their self-consciousness. As they get to know one another better, they will make friends, widen their general experience of life, and find more things in common than the original object of association.

Experience is wider and more common than language. A professor of philosophy and a factory bench-worker may be quite unable to *discuss*, say, the problems of moral behaviour. But, provided neither party has had the edge taken off his natural perceptions by the attrition of civilized life, both will know in terms of living experience what the problems of moral behaviour are, and both will be able to respond to situations where courage and compassion are matched against oppression and greed.

The parables of Jesus of Nazareth were understood equally by his humblest listeners and by the scribes. The understanding of goodness and beauty is not restricted to an intellectual *élite*, nor has it to be 'intellectualized'. Moral and aesthetic judgement springs out of experience approached sensitively and is essentially an active response to an actual situation. The formation of principles is not a precondition, but a convenient sequel, of moral and aesthetic experience. The best moral or aesthetic education is that which, through suitable experience, stimulates sensitiveness and sympathy with others.

Natural man, however naïve and untaught, wants to ask the important questions about life – What are we for? What are the things that matter most? What is the highest good? Comfort without effort, achievement irrespective of comfort, getting as much as possible, giving as much as possible, looking after Number One, losing ourselves in something more than self? The real problem of education at all levels is not to provide answers to questions but to get people to ask the important questions, and especially to reawaken those who have become incapable of asking any questions at all. To stimulate honest and resolute inquiry, at whatever cost to comfort and convenience, has always been the aim of the greatest teachers, from Socrates onwards.

A further truth about communication is that true communication is personal – and in two senses. In the first place communication is between persons conscious of themselves and of one another as persons. There is a mutuality in true 'communication, with an active, questioning attitude on each side. The word itself has the implication of shared discourse. Mass communication, in which people are passively receptive to impressions, is an impersonal affair, sedative rather than stimulating, and tends to break down rather than build up the individuality of those who are habitually exposed to it. If we stop to think, that is not what we really mean by communication.

Secondly, communication is personal in the sense that the

deepest truths are manifested in persons and not in propositions. As Lord Lindsay put it: 'The question as to the nature of justice was one which it was natural for Socrates to ask, and impossible for him to answer.... And so Plato has given the Republic this curious form, because he believed that *Socrates in his person and his life offered the real answer to the questions he propounded,* and which his teaching never solved.'[1] A great teacher does not merely preach his gospel; he *is* his gospel.

These reflections may remind us of the supreme importance of maintaining and promoting relations between people at a truly personal level. Whenever the person-to-person relation is lost within a community, that community loses value and significance as an electric battery runs down.

1. *The Republic,* translated by A. D. Lindsay, 'Introduction', pp. xv, xvi. Italics mine.

CHAPTER 7

Voluntary Activity

PERSONAL values are endangered by inducements to passivity at the receiving end of a laid-on system of services and entertainments. The thesis of this chapter is that the more collectively organized life becomes and the more aspects of life are brought into the scope of public administration, so much the more important is it to maintain and promote voluntary initiative both alongside and within the public services. The growth of the social service State has diminished the need for some forms of voluntary action. But it has created new opportunities for voluntary action and enhanced the importance of the *principle* of voluntary action.

In this chapter a good deal of use will be made of Lord Beveridge's book, *Voluntary Action.*[1] 'It is clear', he says, 'that the State must in future do more things than it has attempted in the past. But it is equally clear, or should be equally clear, that room, opportunity, and encouragement must be kept for Voluntary Action in seeking new ways of social advance. There is need for political invention to find new ways of fruitful cooperation between public authorities and voluntary agencies.'[2] 'Voluntary Action is needed to do things which the State should not do, in the giving of advice, or in organizing the use of leisure. It is needed to do things which the State is most unlikely to do. It is needed to pioneer ahead of the State and make experiments. It is needed to get services rendered which cannot be got by paying for them.'[3]

Voluntary action would appear to have four main values. It is good in the first place because it represents the spon-

1. Allen and Unwin, 1948.   2. *Voluntary Action*, p. 10.
3. ibid., pp. 301–2.

taneous initiative of individuals and groups and thus actively counteracts the tendency to passive acceptance. Secondly, in most of its forms it creates opportunity for cooperation between people and thus aids communication and mutual understanding. Thirdly, it provides experience in administration and management and can be a valuable school of public responsibility; people can graduate from small and informal neighbourhood groups to larger spheres of activity. Fourthly, when voluntary action takes place within the framework of public administration, it helps to humanize public affairs. An example is the governing body of a publicly maintained school – a group of people including some members of the city or county council, probably a representative of the nearest university, and others, giving their services and, through their personal interest in the school, forming a valuable link between the school and the officers of the local education authority. Another and very different example is the work done in hospitals by members of the Women's Voluntary Service. English public life abounds with examples of the combination of voluntary service and official administration, so that it is sometimes difficult to say where one ends and the other begins.

For the purpose of the present discussion, voluntary action is taken to mean action arising from private initiative, but not necessarily unpaid. In Lord Beveridge's words, voluntary action means 'private action, that is to say action not under the directions of any authority wielding the power of the State'.[1] In his book the term is limited to voluntary action for a public purpose, namely social advance. 'Its theme is Voluntary Action outside each citizen's home for improving the conditions of life for him and for his fellows.'[2] That description will serve for the purpose of this chapter if it is interpreted to include such cultural amenities as a free press and associations for the promotion and practice of science and the arts.

There is a long and rich tradition of voluntary action in this country. Our public services had their historical origin in voluntary action. The great movement towards universal education began before the end of the eighteenth century; but

1. *Voluntary Action*, p. 8.   2. ibid., p. 8.

almost another century had passed before there were any publicly provided schools. The State did not establish a training college for teachers until voluntary training colleges had existed for over sixty years. The development of the medical service follows the same pattern of the State coming in late in the day to coordinate and supplement voluntary effort.

As the public services have grown, voluntary action has not ceased, but (as in the medical service) has continued alongside. Certainly the nature and objectives of voluntary action have changed with the growth of the public services. Broadly speaking, the emphasis of voluntary action has shifted from the relief of dire necessity to the provision of additional benefits and cultural amenities. But there is still an immense range of opportunity for voluntary agencies.

The Friendly Societies, for example, still have some eight million members. Their original function of enabling their members to escape from pauperism has been taken over by the State. They are no longer societies whose members meet in person; they no longer represent good fellowship but rather a means of insurance by contract. Yet there is still plenty of scope for insurance above the state minimum and of opportunity for the discipline of not spending week by week up to the limit. There is valuable education in learning not to live from hand to mouth, especially in a country where the State provision for sickness, unemployment, and old age is on a flat rate. Friendly Societies can also develop their usefulness in the direction of homes for old people, convalescent homes, clubs, and provision for holidays.[1]

Not only has voluntary action continued and developed alongside the public services, but it has been integrated into the very structure of those public services. This combination of voluntary action with public administration is peculiar to this

1. Another type of voluntary association which has changed its function – and much less happily – is the trade union. As was observed in another chapter, the trade unions' original function of securing fair wages and conditions of work has been overshadowed by the problems of individual freedom within the union and of the unions' political relations with parliamentary government.

country. 'The practice of public bodies, whether they are central government departments or local authorities, using voluntary institutions and individual volunteers as responsible agents is well-established. Some observers rank this practice as a contribution of British political sense to world affairs comparable to the inventions of representative government and of the British Commonwealth of free and independent nations.' [1]

The education service affords many examples of this use of voluntary effort by public bodies – in the constitution of Local Education Committees, governing bodies of schools and colleges, and advisory committees. Our judicial system also exemplifies the cooperation of volunteers and professionals.

The use of voluntary service by public authorities is one side of a coin, the other side of which is the granting of public money to voluntary associations, usually with very few 'strings' attached. Obvious examples are the grants made by local education authorities to youth organizations, and the seventy-five per cent capital grants made by the Ministry of Education to voluntary training colleges. It must be acknowledged, however, that there is a certain tendency for public control to increase as the grants increase. For example, the universities have lost a good deal of the independence which they enjoyed before the Second World War. The University Grants Committee, which channels the money from the Treasury to the universities, began as a means of explaining to the government the needs of the universities; it is increasingly becoming a means of conveying to the universities the requirements of the government. The Treasury's dictation to the universities has now become so direct (an example is the severe cut back in grants in March 1962) that the question is being asked whether there is any point in the continued existence of the U.G.C. in its present form.

In general, however, it is true that the granting of public money to voluntary bodies is a well-established tradition in this country, and that on the whole there is little tendency to hamper the use of these grants by attaching restrictive con-

1. *Voluntary Action*, p. 308. Lord Beveridge thought this opinion extravagant.

ditions. Lord Beveridge gives a list of nearly seventy voluntary organizations, excluding educational institutions, which receive grants from the Exchequer. Many of these, such as the Women's Institutes, have numerous local branches. And many more organizations, such as the Citizens' Advice Bureaux, receive grants from local authorities.[1]

It is not always realized what a variety of voluntary associations exists. Excluding trade unions, Friendly Societies, Co-operative Societies, and also excluding the thousands of purely local groups such as dramatic societies and gardening clubs, *Whitaker's Almanack* for 1961 lists well over a thousand societies and institutions. In very round numbers these are distributed in different fields as follows: the arts (5 per cent); learned and scientific (23 per cent); social and recreational (3 per cent); philanthropic, humane, and mutual aid (excluding Friendly Societies and others excepted above) (23 per cent); professional and industrial (30 per cent); religious (10 per cent); preservation of buildings and countryside (2 per cent); youth (2 per cent); trusts and foundations (2 per cent).

Lord Beveridge distinguishes two main motives for voluntary action. The first is mutual aid, which has given rise to many associations, of which the largest numerically are the Cooperative Societies, the most powerful are the trade unions, and the most typically British are the Friendly Societies. The earliest of the Friendly Societies was founded in 1555, and many existed before 1800. In 1945 there were about 20,000 societies registered under the Friendly Societies Act, with a membership of about ten million and funds of over £165 million.[2] The motive of mutual aid is often combined with the secondary motive of personal thrift (as in the Friendly Societies) and the business motive (as in insurance societies).

Mutual aid is clearly the motive behind the immense number of professional associations, from such obvious organizations as the Institute of Directors, the Incorporated Society of Auc-

1. ibid., Supplementary Volume, pp. 92 ff.
2. ibid., p. 88, Table 7. Individual examples are Manchester Unity (three-quarters of a million members, 1946), Foresters, Oddfellows, Hearts of Oak.

tioneers and Landed Property Agents (1924) to such unexpected
bodies as the Association of Circus Proprietors of Great Britain
or the Oyster Merchants' and Planters' Association. The same
motive is responsible for societies whose function is the ad-
vancement of knowledge – for example, the British Association
(1831), the Mathematical Association (1871), the British Glacio-
logical Society, the British Goat Society (1879); for the many
social and recreational associations – British Drama League
(1919), National Federation of Women's Institutes (1917), British
Gliding Association (1930), British Field Sports Society (1930),
etc.; and for some unclassifiable bodies such as the Income
Tax Payers' Society.

It must be pointed out, however, that this category of 'mutual
aid' blurs an important distinction between associations whose
genuine function is to benefit people in general and those
which exist to defend the interests of a particular group and
therefore lend themselves to use as weapons of pressure against
the rest of the community. There is no doubt of the value of
the former kind of association; the value of the latter kind is
much more doubtful. The essence of the distinction is one of
function, not of structure. On the one hand are those mutual
aid societies (like the British Drama League or Women's Institutes) which are open to any who choose to benefit from them.
On the other hand are those which exist to protect a group
interest. Within this latter type there is a further distinction
between the legitimate protection of certain group interests,
without harm to the rest of society, and the defence of those
interests by holding the rest of the community up to ransom.
This is not always a clear distinction, as a second glance at the
preceding list of societies will show.

The second main motive for voluntary action, according to
Lord Beveridge, is philanthropy, springing from social conscience. 'To have social conscience is to be unwilling to make
a separate peace with the giant social evils of Want, Disease,
Squalor, Ignorance, Idleness, escaping into personal prosperity
oneself, while leaving one's fellows in their clutches.' [1]

Beveridge's 'philanthropic' category can be extended to in-

1. *Voluntary Action*, p. 9.

clude a great variety of institutions and societies for cultural amenities. Some examples may help to show the range of activities covered. Strictly philanthropic enterprises include Dr Barnardo's Homes (1866), the Aged Poor Society (1708), the R.S.P.C.A. (1824), the N.S.P.C.C. (1884), the Guide Dogs for the Blind Association, the Pit Ponies Protection Society (1927). But they extend to societies in the field of the arts – Royal Academy (1768), English Folk Dance and Song Society (1931); religion – S.P.C.K. (1698), C.M.S. (1799), Catholic Truth Society (1868), the Open Air Mission (1853); preservation of buildings and countryside – National Trust (1895), Commons, Open Spaces, and Footpaths Preservation Society (1865), Society for Protection of Ancient Buildings (1877); and social science – National Marriage Guidance Council, Citizens' Advice Bureaux, National Council of Social Services.

Not only do many voluntary associations receive grants of public money, but the State has facilitated private gifts of money for charitable purposes by exempting such gifts from income tax. There is plenty of evidence that, despite heavy taxation, the public are still willing to give money (the response to the Week's Good Cause is an example). 'The democracy can and should learn to do what used to be done for public good by the wealthy.'[1] But a good deal of education is needed to channel the public's generous impulses in the best directions. It is difficult to persuade the public to give money for new and unfamiliar things. There is evidence that, while people will give freely for sailors, animals, and children (in that order), they do not readily contribute to such objects as the National Trust or the Marriage Guidance Council.

It is worth observing that voluntary action needs service as well as money. Money is useless unless there are people willing to give their time and energy to its administration. Lord Beveridge suggests that there should be, in every locality, an organization which people offering voluntary service can join, so that voluntary manpower can be deployed to the best effect.

Professor Galbraith has recently drawn attention to the contrast, in Western industrial societies, between private affluence

1. ibid., p. 302.

and public squalor. In this country education, including the universities, costs only 4·7 per cent of the national income; 5·6 per cent of the national income is spent on tobacco. The last chapter of Lord Beveridge's *Voluntary Action* is entitled 'First Things First'. There should, he says, be bread and health for all before cake and circuses for any. It is clear that, in Britain today, first things are not being put first, whether economic or cultural. People are being exploited who have money which they do not know how to spend wisely. Dog tracks and football pools flourish alongside bad housing and conditions of living barely at subsistence level. In the world as a whole, plenty in the West contrasts with want in the East.[1]

If we ask why, with social security established by law and virtually full employment, life in Britain is not better, there are two answers. In the first place the State, though master of money, in a free society is master of little else. The making of a good society depends not on the State but on the citizens, acting individually or together. Secondly, we in this country have been slow to recognize how the world has changed after two world wars. We have not yet realized how much of the early prosperity of the nineteenth century was due to our being the first country to be industrialized. 'If we want to live as well as our fathers, we must either work harder or work more effectively, not rejecting or limiting any machine that will make work easier.'[2]

The building of a just and good free society has to overcome two difficulties. Something other than the pursuit of gain must be kept alive as the dominant force in society. And, with the passage from class rule to representative democracy, the mass of the people must be influenced by education; otherwise they will be economically and culturally exploited by power-groups animated only by greed.

When the whole problem of making a good free society is seen in this light, two indications clearly emerge. One is that

1. It is, however, important to avoid sentimentality about these problems. The U.S.A. has enough corn stored to feed India for three years; but India's problem would not be solved by giving her this corn.   2. *Voluntary Action*, p. 321.

the problem is essentially educational; the operations of government are a means, not an end, and the character of the national life is determined, not by systems, but by the quality of men and women. The other is that voluntary action is a most potent means both of educating those who share in it, and also of lifting the quality of national life to levels which governmental administration alone can never reach.

'Time in his course will bring to us endless successors in spirit of the Victorian pioneers of social advance – men and women with the conscience and industry of Shaftesbury, the strength of purpose of Elizabeth Fry, the courage and inventiveness of the Barnetts, the untutored fervour of William Booth, the passion to understand of Charles Booth, the exuberant humanity of Quintin Hogg, the pity and the anger of Benjamin Waugh. But who will restore the conditions in which these men and women did their work? When and how shall we replace the lost power of widespread religious belief, the material resources which must support the Philanthropic Motive as the body clothes the soul, and the sense of brotherhood in the human race? None of the Victorian pioneers dreamed of a world with dangers such as ours. None of them doubted that man could and would be master of his fate.

'To restore the conditions in which these pioneers did their work will not be the work of any one man. But restoration may come through one spirit breathing again through many men, as it did in the special field from which this study began. So at last human society may become a friendly society – an Affiliated Order of branches, some large and many small, each with its own life in freedom, each linked to all the rest by common purpose and by bonds to serve that purpose. So the night's insane dream of power over other men, without limit and without mercy, shall fade. So mankind in brotherhood shall bring back the day.' [1]

1. ibid., p. 323. Although this passage was written just after the Second World War, it has no less, though a different, relevance today.

In his recent book, *Heavens Below: Utopian Experiments in England, 1560–1960*, Professor W. H. G. Armytage argues the historical value of voluntary utopian communities which have 'tried to save the English behind their back', but have had a raw deal at the hands of the historians. These social experiments, from the Levellers to the Garden City, are almost bound to fall short of their ideal aims. But, Professor Armytage claims, they should be seen as a normal part of social development rather than as pathological symptoms. They work like leaven to regenerate society by affirming the basic human values of respect for honest work and the respect of one human being for another and for the fellowship of men. They offer, in the freely cooperative community, a viable alternative to economic competition on one side and the collectivist State on the other.

Part III

EDUCATION

CHAPTER 8

The Education of the Adolescent

IN Part I an attempt was made to describe our contemporary culture. Part II was a discussion of personal values, which are the foundation of all else that is worth while in human life. The next question is: What means have we for maintaining and reinforcing those personal values which are so gravely threatened in the modern world?

It has been suggested many times in earlier chapters that the main problems with which this book is concerned are essentially educational questions. The purpose of Part III is to examine the thesis that the promotion of personal values is the business of education. Education is the nurture of personal growth. Education, as an organized process, is concerned not only (or even chiefly) with the communication of knowledge and the acquisition of skill, but also with the formation of right attitudes — attitudes towards learning, towards work, towards truth and goodness, towards other people, towards life in general. Education, morever, is a person-to-person activity; it can function only when there is personal communication under conditions of mutual respect. Mass communication is not education in any true sense of the word. And whenever education has to be carried on under conditions where relations are less than personal (where, for example, classes are too large and mass-production methods have to be used) something less than true education is bound to result. By its very nature, then, education testifies to, and vindicates, our central values. By undertaking education we proclaim our belief in those values.

Since the scope of education is as wide as life itself, some limits must be set for the purpose of manageable discussion.

The three chapters that follow are concerned for the most part with aspects of work in schools. It must not be forgotten, however, that adult education is becoming increasingly important in modern society, that formal education shades into all kinds of informal education carried on in voluntary associations, and that, wherever two or three are gathered together for any activity, some kind of education, good or bad, is bound to happen. If, however, we are thinking of education as a social instrument deliberately created by a community to help its members to be the best that they have it in them to become and to make their fullest possible contribution to the community life, then we naturally think first of the schools.[1]

The education of young children is not discussed in this book, not because it is unimportant – far from it, but because the main issues under consideration become obviously and painfully acute in adolescence. This chapter is concerned with some of the problems of educating teenagers.

A century ago public education in this country was still concerned with the rescue of the young child from industrial exploitation. Today the emphasis has shifted. Our primary schools represent, on the whole, the most successful part of our educational system. Our most pressing modern problem is the education of the adolescent. And it is a very difficult problem. It is thirty-five years since the publication of the Hadow Report, entitled *The Education of the Adolescent*; and in the intervening time we cannot claim to have made more than modest progress in that field, though we are more acutely aware of the nature of the problems that we have not solved.

The present world is not an easy one for young people to grow up in, and young people are maturing earlier, and marrying earlier, than their predecessors. Economically the teenagers are the new rich of our time, and are fair game for advertisers of all kinds. Young people aged between fifteen and twenty are earning in total about £900,000,000 a year – an average of

1. Something has been said in other chapters about higher education, and universities in particular.

about £5 per head per week. The high wages obtainable on leaving school are a strong temptation; and it is much to the credit of the more sensible young people that the numbers voluntarily staying on at school beyond fifteen have more than trebled in the past ten years. Among those aged between eighteen and nineteen, gross weekly earnings are, generally speaking, *inversely* proportional to length of schooling, and directly proportional to the time that has elapsed since leaving school. That is to say, by the age of eighteen or nineteen, the earlier school-leavers are still earning the most money. It is only by the age of twenty-one to twenty-two that higher educational attainment begins to tell, and those who stayed longer at school catch up on those who left school earlier.[1]

The best teenagers with jobs hand over a good proportion of their earnings to their mothers, to help with their keep. But they usually retain a very ample sum as pocket money which, for the most part, they are free to spend without any sense of responsibility. A 'good' boy of seventeen, who worked in a slaughter-house and was paid £5 5s. od. a week, handed over his pay-packet, receiving back 25s. a week for 'boppin' an' fags an' pictures. An' I don't have to worry about savin' enough for clothes. No, I don't save nothin'.'[2]

The relatively high earnings of boys and girls in comparison with their parents' encourage a feeling of independence which does not always foster the best relations between parent and child. A girl remarked of her mother: 'She takes £4 a week off me, and I can't get a winter coat. *And* she smokes like a chimney.'[3]

The desire of young people to have money to spend accounts for the increased tendency of boys and girls still at school to take part-time jobs. About fifty-four per cent of boys and twenty per cent of girls earn money in this way,[4] and spend it on amusement, clothes, holidays, bicycles, gramophone records, guitars. The pursuit of entertainment takes boys and

1. *Crowther Report*, Vol. II.
2. *Sunday Times*, 14 December 1958.
3. ibid.
4. *Crowther Report*, Vol. II.

girls out of their homes in the evenings. Between the ages of fifteen and eighteen, boys on an average spend four or five evenings out a week and girls three or four.[1]

Teenage morality has been the subject of a good deal of lurid writing in the past few years. No doubt some of the more sensational secondary modern fiction and spine-chilling accounts of youth clubs are, if not exaggerated, at least not fairly representative. But the smoke does not arise without fire.[2] And there is no doubt that most teenagers are morally insecure and not a little confused. They have money. Advertisers press all kinds of invitations upon them. They get little guidance from their parents. Lack of sound parental guidance, and – consequently – failure to think out problems of conduct, seem to be the lot of ex-secondary modern boys and girls to a much greater extent than of grammar school pupils. This distinction between the two types (of individual and of home background) has been recently emphasized by Dr Donald Soper and the Bishop of Southwark (Dr Mervyn Stockwood). The ex-secondary moderns, industrialized from the age of fifteen, appear to be largely philistine and pagan. The Bishop of Southwark wrote: 'A few years ago I had the alarming privilege of addressing the physics students at the Cavendish Laboratory on the Christian Faith. It was interesting to contrast their thoughtful approach with the attitude of a group of young apprentices in an engineering firm, who automatically assumed that I was a "Magic" man.'

To these young people with little firm moral background – much bad entertainment material is offered. One has only to glance at a railway bookstall to see how much suggestive material is exposed, and how few magazines there are which can suitably be placed in the hands of teenagers. It is also worth observing that suggestive material (pictorial and other) is now finding its way into traditionally respectable periodicals. Magazines that used to be as safe as the Bank of England are

1. ibid.
2. In July 1961 attention was drawn, by the British Medical Association as well as by leading clergy, to the publicity given by some television programmes to sexual promiscuity among teenagers. There were, about this time, some shocking disclosures.

taking on a new look, and the new look is not always to their credit.[1]

Television makes easily available a wide variety of material, good, bad, and indifferent. The notorious *Living for Kicks* (A.T.V., March 1960) with its suggestion that 'eighty per cent of us have sex before marriage', was the kind of thing that encourages the comment: 'If it's O.K. for them, it's O.K. for us.' Granada's *The Shadow of Ignorance* was referred to in an earlier chapter. Although the programme was on the whole well done as a piece of public prophylaxis, it carried an under-current of suggestion that the moral law had been lifted and the abdication of personal responsibility invited.

The whole problem of sexual morality is bewildering to the teenager, who gets little enough wise guidance from parents and other grown-ups. For too many teenagers the problem appears as a question of 'where to draw the line', and they do not see that this view misses the whole point of the mean-ing of sex in civilized human relations – that sexual feelings and their expression are decent only when they form an integral part of a sincere and deep love between two people. What teenagers (and many grown-ups for that matter) need to learn is that personal values are central, and that the physi-cal expressions of love-making find their proper place only within a relation of sincere love and mutual respect. As Ken-neth C. Barnes puts it: 'Only when our sex experience is at this personal level can all our sexual thoughts be taken into a loving relationship and made good there.'[2] Mr Barnes is head-master of a co-educational school, and elsewhere in his book makes the salutary observation, re-emphasized by the Marriage Guidance Council (July 1961), that factual information about sex does *not* allay curiosity.

Behind these and other particular problems there is the un-reality and shallowness of urban life for millions of young people. Ignorant of the basic activities that go to produce food and clothing and generally sustain life, drawing their wage

1. There is of course another class of material, increasingly avail-able and thoroughly disreputable, of the kind represented by American 'comics'.   2. Kenneth C. Barnes, *He and She* (1958).

packet from a limited job the meaning of which in relation to other processes they know little of, and in their spare time absorbing mass-produced 'homogenized' entertainment, many of them (though certainly not all) are culturally rootless.

'Judging by the experience of one social worker in Birmingham, however, someone has to go down to bed-rock with some children. She has found boys unwilling to pay the very modest cost of a weekend's camping because they think it too much in relation to other things they want to spend their money on; and she is convinced that they do not realize the cost of food. The same trouble is not experienced with girls. She has also had boys out in the country ask whether the noise they heard was a sheep or a cow, and ask, in February, whether there would be fruit on the trees.

'Where there is ignorance of this sort it is not to be wondered at that we are breeding people in our cities with no firm scale of material, let alone moral, values. As human beings our basic needs for simple survival are food, clothing, and shelter. It is not difficult to see how an appreciation of this is overlaid by the bricks and mortar of our great urban agglomerations until the necessities are taken for granted and the substance of life dissolves in a fantasy of the "telly", the low-grade dance hall, the pub at the corner, and a he-man make-believe.' [1]

It is doubtful whether these young people, although they have money in their pockets and an unprecedented range of opportunities open to them, are in any deep sense happy.

In spite of the fact that boys and girls who leave school at fifteen and go to work gain more money than those who stay on at school, there is a prestige distinction between 'grammar' and 'secondary modern' which amounts to a class distinction, and of which the young people themselves are very conscious. A boy who left school at fifteen to work in a garage would not hope for the favours of a girl who is still in full-time education. Whether the comprehensive schools will break down these distinctions, and whether – if they do – it will be a good thing, there is not yet sufficient evidence to show. It is worth

1. From an anonymous article in the *Birmingham Post*, 30 June 1958.

observing however that Mrs Chetwynd, headmistress of the first comprehensive school opened by the L.C.C. (Woodberry Down), records in her book a comment by her head girl, who said that her friends at grammar schools did not seem to understand boys and girls at other kinds of schools and spoke a different language.

The comprehensive school is not the only alternative to the traditional 'tripartite' system of grammar, technical, and secondary modern schools. Leicestershire is experimenting with an arrangement by which all pupils stay in secondary modern schools (renamed High Schools) for three years; at 14-plus those who wish may go to grammar schools provided an undertaking is given to keep them there until 16-plus. For this system, it is claimed that it eliminates once-for-all selection at 11-plus and, since it will fit into existing buildings, it avoids the big rebuilding operations involved in a policy of comprehensive schools. Other local authorities (for example, Derbyshire and the West Riding) are experimenting with a two-tier system. There is a good deal of support for the view that the best age for transfer is not 11-plus, or 14-plus, but 13-plus. If 13-plus were established as the age of transfer to the grammar school, a consequential rearrangement of the earlier stages of education would seem to be necessary. The pattern that eventually emerges may be 5–9, 9–13-plus, 13-plus–18.

The grammar schools, and grammar streams of comprehensive schools, through which pass nearly all boys and girls destined for higher education, account for about twenty-five per cent of an age-group during the age of compulsory schooling. Only about fifteen per cent of the population have I.Q.s of 120 or over; it would appear, therefore, that the grammar schools are receiving at least the great majority of those who can profit by the kind of education offered in them. The grammar school population is increasing, partly because of the upward move of the birthrate 'bulge', and partly because more boys and girls are staying on into the sixth form. The numbers in sixth forms have doubled in the last ten years, and are likely to double again in the next five.

Generally speaking, the grammar schools do a very good job,

and the products of the sixth forms are well-informed, sensible, and intelligently critical. Anyone who has had first-hand experience of the sixth-form conferences arranged by the Student Christian Movement will agree that it would be difficult to find more interested and stimulating groups of people.

The great defect of grammar school education at present is the premature and too narrow specialization which sets in as soon as 'O' levels in the G.C.E. have been passed. For many pupils this narrowing of scope begins at fifteen. Three-quarters of a sixth-former's time is now spent on specialized studies very little wider in scope than the programme that the boy or girl would follow afterwards at the university. Very few pupils combine elements from both the arts and science sides. According to a recent report published by the University of Oxford Institute of Education, only 2·3 per cent of sixth-form boys and 9·8 per cent of sixth-form girls combine major arts and science subjects. Apart from specialized studies the rest of the sixth-former's time (which the Crowther Report calls 'minority time') is normally divided between a considerable number of subjects and activities, none of which receives much time or serious attention.

This premature, excessive, and usually lop-sided specialization has been forced upon the grammar schools by the increase of knowledge in all fields and by the pressure of the universities upon the schools. The universities, in order to bring their students in three years to the standard of knowledge now required for the first degree, require a good deal of the ground to have been already covered before leaving school. The effect of this pressure on the schools is not only to narrow the educational front on which the sixth forms advance, but also (in some ways more serious) to put a premium on the memorization of factual material at the expense of imagination and critical thought.

One of the most hopeful indications in the present situation is the grave concern felt in the universities themselves about the educational effects of the premature specialization for which the universities are themselves largely responsible. The universities, which control the various examining boards for the G.C.E., are giving a good deal of thought to the reform –

and broadening – of sixth-form courses (that is, 'A' level syllabuses for the G.C.E.). The problem, however, in school and
university alike, calls for a more radical solution. The only
long-term answer to the question would appear to be a much
greater development of courses of further study, available at
universities and other places of higher education for people
who have been earning their livings for at least several years
after taking their first degrees or equivalent qualifications. The
provision of such courses of further study, including sandwich
courses, has increased enormously since the Second World
War; and there is no reason in principle why it should not continue to increase, supported by appropriate provision for sec-
ondment on salary, until it becomes a normal thing for people
to return to universities and colleges for further study after
spending several years out in a job. The advantages of such an
arrangement are twofold. In the first place, young men and
women who have some years of experience in employment can
profit far more from an interlude of further study than inex-
perienced students can from the same courses. Secondly, the
provision of fuller opportunity for further study would relieve
the first degree course (or its equivalent) from the hopeless
attempt to produce a finished product. The first degree course
could once again become, as it once was, a personal education
rather than a high-pressure knowledge-stuffing process. If this
change took place, the sixth forms of the schools would in
turn be liberated from excessive pressure from above, and
could be devoted to education rather than intensive training.

This, however, is a long-term solution of the problem, though
there are clear indications that events are moving in that direction. Meanwhile it is worth observing that the Crowther Report
recommends certain changes in the organization of sixth-form
work. In the first place the curriculum should normally combine elements from both the science and arts sides. Secondly,
there should be three elements in a sound sixth-form curriculum : (i) The specialist work, occupying two-thirds of the total
time, and not three-quarters as at present. It is worth noting
that the Crowther Committee were fully alive to the educational value of specialized study – study in depth – provided

it did not occupy too large a proportion of the timetable. (ii) Common elements in which arts and science students can come together (religious education, art, music, physical education). (iii) Complementary elements to redress the balance of science and arts specialization respectively – to save the scientists from illiteracy and the arts specialists from 'innumeracy'.

Another answer to the problem of premature and excessive specialization is proposed by Mr A. D. C. Peterson in a Report (*Arts and Sciences in the Sixth Form*) sponsored by the Gulbenkian Foundation. He suggests that four 'A' level subjects should be taken, two in arts and two in science, and that the choice of university course should be postponed until the end of the sixth-form career. If four 'A' level subjects were taken they presumably could not be quite of the present 'A' level standard, unless a year were added to the school course and students went on to the university at nineteen rather than at eighteen. Other proposals have been made besides those of the Crowther and Peterson Reports; but none as yet generally acceptable.

The secondary modern school or its equivalent has the extremely difficult task of educating the 75 per cent of boys and girls who will leave school at fifteen or sixteen and go to work. The task is difficult for three main reasons. First, the range of intelligence in these schools is very wide, extending from, say, I.Q. 120 to I.Q. 80 or under. In the fourth year (chronological age 14–15) of a school large enough to have four streams the mental age of the A stream will be perhaps 16·0, of the C stream 13·1, and of the D stream only 11·6. In other words, the mental age of some school leavers will be no higher than that of many first-year children. Secondly, the average intelligence of these boys and girls is not high; for the most part they find great difficulty in thinking in terms of abstract ideas, and therefore in appreciating general principles underlying a number of particular situations. This difficulty of discerning the general behind the particular handicaps the moral as well as the intellectual education of these boys and girls. They tend to operate at a purely empirical level and are not interested in the reasons why a certain proposition is true or a course of action right. Thirdly, these young people are on the brink of adult life. Limited as many of them are mentally, they are mature physically (because of higher standards of living they mature earlier than the previous generation), they become impatient of school, they look towards the well-paid jobs that they can get, and they expect to marry young. The maturity of the fifth- or sixth-former at the grammar school is to a great extent masked by his remaining *in statu pupillari* until the age of eighteen. There is no such masking effect in the case of the products of the secondary modern school.

The truth is that we still know all too little about the best ways of educating boys and girls in the secondary modern schools. To say this is not to belittle the valuable and often heroic pioneer work done by countless teachers in these schools. It is only to acknowledge the difficulty of a problem that is still far from solved. One of the most interesting pieces of pioneer work is described by Mr A. W. Rowe (for the past seven years headmaster of a mixed school in Buckinghamshire) in his recent book *The Education of the Average Child*. The school works on an adapted Dalton plan, with programmes based on 'job-cards'. There is a good deal of practical and vocational work — technical drawing, typing, building, nursing, music, dancing, electrical work; but Mr Rowe lays great emphasis on the importance of literacy, and insists that every child must make his own notes on the work he has done, and not merely copy from books. The fundamental principle on which the school is run is that education means making choices and experiencing responsibility.

Perhaps the solution to the problem of how to educate the boys and girls in the secondary modern schools lies along two lines. In the first place, those who are capable of taking a public examination should have the opportunity of doing so. These boys and girls need a tangible objective. It is doubtful whether the G.C.E. is the right examination for any but a very small minority of secondary modern pupils, since few can pass in more than one or two subjects at 'O' level. A recent report of a Committee of the Secondary Schools Examinations Council (*Secondary School Examinations other than the G.C.E.*), known as the Beloe Report, recommends a new recognized secondary school certificate to be taken at the age of sixteen. This examination would replace the very varied assortment of examinations now taken. It would be on a subject basis, and would be so designed that forty per cent of the age-group could pass in four or more subjects, and the next twenty per cent below that might attempt individual subjects. An obvious danger in any programme for a standard examination is that employers may come to require more than many candidates are capable of, as we have seen in the demand for 'matric' by employers who often did not understand what 'matric' involved.

It has been suggested that those boys and girls who have not the ability to take the kind of examination proposed by the S.S.E.C. are perhaps better not kept in full-time schooling to sixteen, or even to fifteen, but apprenticed so as to spend part of their time in school and part in the workshop, as now happens in Russia. Many heads of secondary modern schools, however, urge that all boys and girls should continue in full-time education until at least sixteen.

Important as are the problems of the secondary modern school, it is perhaps of more interest to the present inquiry to consider what happens to the boys and girls when they leave school at fifteen (or, increasingly, at sixteen). Even at sixteen they are not, and cannot be, educated to the limits of their capacity. It is well known that those who have no further education after leaving school rapidly lose a great deal of what they had attained by the age of fifteen; in the following three or four years many relapse virtually into illiteracy.

At present about sixty per cent of boys and girls who leave school at fifteen-plus get no further education or training at all. Of the rest, half continue in full-time education and half have some continued part-time education.

Part-time education continued beyond school has been with us for many years in the form of evening classes; but in the form of day-time classes it is virtually a development since the Second World War. It is of the utmost importance that, as a community, we should learn to think of the young worker up to the age of eighteen as a ward of the community, whose education is continuing, and whose industrial employment is thought of and planned as part of a total educative programme. In this connexion it is worth noting the new Russian secondary education plan announced in September 1958, under which boys and girls do part-time work in State enterprises. The purpose of this combination of industrial work and continued study is not to create juvenile labour but 'solely in the interests of the children's upbringing' – that is to say, to demonstrate the connexion between school and life.[1] So long as the young worker is regarded primarily as machine-fodder, with perhaps an incidental bit of continued education on the side, neither his employment nor his education can be seen in the right perspective. The importance of developing a coherent system of further education is all the greater in view of the fact that by 1964 a million more teenagers will be looking for jobs.

The Crowther Report recognizes that release of young workers for one day a week for further education has not been a great success. It has emerged as a standard pattern in comparatively few industries and is almost entirely confined to boys. The rate of increase of day release is slowing down, which suggests that it is not an unqualified success. Where possible, concentrated periods of continuous study, on the lines of sandwich courses, would probably be more fruitful than one-day-a-week release. The Report however recommends that the provisions of the 1944 Act for the part-time education of all boys and girls from school-leaving to the age of eighteen should be implemented in three stages. The proposed programme would mean that county college education would be universal for those not in full-time education, by a date between 1977 and 1979; and the Report expects that, by 1980 or thereabouts, roughly half the boys and girls in the country will be continuing full-time education to eighteen and the other half receiving part-time education to eighteen. The fact that the Minister of Education has not felt able to announce a starting date for this programme leaves the whole matter somewhat in the air.

What kind of education should the county college provide?

1. *The Times*, 24 December 1958. Report of statement by Professor Ivan Kairov, president of the Russian Academy of Pedagogical Sciences.

While it should not be purely vocational, county college education should be realistic in the sense of recognizing that the students are young workers entering upon adult life, and already economically important. The Crowther Report recommends that the county college should try to do four things:

(i) Help young people to understand and appreciate the adult world in which, as young workers, they find themselves.

(ii) Give them guidance in working out human relations and moral standards.

(iii) Help them to develop physical and aesthetic skills.

(iv) Continue their basic education, with a vocational bias where appropriate.

Although the county college ought to offer a good deal more than vocational training (and in any case is probably not the best place for specialized vocational work), vocational training should not be despised as a form of education. If the young worker can be induced to make a real mental effort to improve his technical equipment and prospects, it is far better than no mental effort at all. Education must start from where people are, not from where we think they should be; and for most people the effective spur to effort is the ambition to get a better job.

Since the Second World War a great deal of valuable experience has been accumulated in the field of further education. A number of big industrial firms, such as Cadburys and Stewarts and Lloyds, have been pioneering for a good many years. The work of many colleges of further education is now being systematically and comparatively studied. A foundation is being laid on which could be built the developments of a generation to come.

Young people need not only formal education but opportunity for the worthwhile use of leisure. It is rather discouraging that in the development of the Youth Service we are virtually back where we were in 1945. But the Albemarle Report (1960), *The Youth Service in England and Wales*, at least indicates that the Ministry of Education are again taking the view that an efficient Youth Service is a necessary part of further education. The Report recommends that the number of full-time workers in the service should be about doubled (from the present 700 to 1,300) by 1966. 'This is the least that is needed to provide a better service for the larger number of young people to be expected in the early sixties,' when the 'bulge' together with the ending of national service are expected to add about a million more young people aged fifteen to twenty in civilian life to the present 3¼ millions. There are some 4,000–5,000 part-time youth workers.

The Youth Service can never be put on a proper footing as an integral part of the educational system until youth leaders and organizers are on a par with the teaching profession as regards salary and superannuation. The Albemarle Report recommends a revision of salary scales and superannuation arrangements. At present the Youth Service is a sadly underpaid profession; the club leader of a large club (who has a difficult and responsible job) may get £600 or £700 a year.

The development of the Youth Service is further hampered by the fact that the Local Education Authorities have adopted different attitudes towards the Youth Service. For example, of two large adjacent Local Authorities in 1958 one had a Youth Officer with eight district organizers to assist some 450 clubs, while the other had no full-time Youth Officer. The one Authority spent four or five times as much as the other on the Youth Service in 1958.

The problem of what kind of programmes should be offered in youth clubs is a very difficult one, to which much thought is being given, but which cannot be regarded as solved. It is well known that some of the older-established voluntary organizations are losing their hold on young people; for example, it is difficult to get scouts to stay on in the movement when they reach adolescence. On the other hand, the clubs that try to attract teenagers by offering rock 'n' roll often attract a certain amount of hooliganism as well; club leaders need to be both vigilant and tough. It is very much the old and familiar story : give them what is good for them and those who most need it do not come; give them what they like, and they take advantage. It is very difficult to steer a course between catering only for a nicely behaved *élite* and so defeating the real object of the operation, and on the other hand throwing open the doors to all and sundry and having the place broken up. One thing at least is clear as a matter of long-term policy – the Youth Service ought to provide something more than organized opportunity for amusement. It will fail in its main purpose unless it can help to produce a generation who are willing to put skill and effort into the intelligent use of spare time and who can work together in drama, camping, building, debating, or other cooperative activities.[1]

This chapter began with a reference to teenage morality. It may fairly be asked whether any constructive suggestions can be made towards dealing with this important side of education. There can be no magic formula. But some lines of approach suggest themselves. To begin with, every effort should be made to encourage boys and girls to continue their education, both full-time by staying longer at school, and part-time in the county colleges for which we are still waiting. The secondary modern curriculum, especially in its later stages, and the county college curriculum need more thought and experiment. The moral education (including sex education) of young people needs to be tackled in a planned and concerted way by teachers, clergy, doctors, and such organizations as the Marriage Guidance Council. We have not really begun to work systematically in this field. Together with better education in school, we must also reach more effectively the young adults for whom family problems have become matters of practical urgency and who may be expected to respond to opportunities for study and discussion of those problems. These are some of the means by which, on the long-term view, we may hope to produce a better generation of parents, if we can manage to survive the rot that now seems to have set in.

Nobody's education ought to end at sixteen or even eighteen. The education of the young adult will become increasingly important. That does not mean that universities should be in-

1. The work of Evening Institutes provides welcome evidence that, in spite of the prevalence of mass-produced entertainment, many young people will take the trouble to attend classes where they can make boats or skis for use on their holidays.

definitely enlarged and multiplied. What a university offers will never be suitable for more than a minority of the population. But, in one way or another, there should be available, for people in their twenties, a variety of educational opportunities ranging from formal studies in technical or art colleges or classes run by university extra-mural departments to informal activities of the kind organized by Women's Institutes or local dramatic clubs. The Scandinavian Folk High Schools, although they would not transplant to this country, have a good deal to teach us. And it should be remembered that many people are ready to learn in their twenties or thirties who successfully resisted education at an earlier age. The responsibilities of marriage and parenthood can awaken all kinds of interests which involve learning – the bringing-up of children, the efficient running of a home, a hundred-and-one do-it-yourself household skills, the improvement of one's technical equipment in order to get a better job, the development of crafts by which extra money can be made on the side. It is in very few people's natures to pursue truth or beauty for its own sake. But most people can respond to the practical challenges which family life presents, provided that the right opportunities are open to them.

Two aspects of education are too important to be dealt with incidentally in this chapter, and will be discussed in the following two chapters. They are the education of feeling and the education of thinking. It is perhaps worth pointing out that, although the traditional emphasis in our formal education has been on the education of thinking, there is quite as much need to educate feeling as to educate thinking. In modern times a great deal has been done to redress the balance. But even today we still attach too little importance to the education of feeling, and we certainly know too little about it.

CHAPTER 9

The Education of Feeling

SIR JAMES ROBERTSON, in his presidential address to the Education Section of the British Association (September 1959), spoke of 'an educational smugness which fixes its gaze on the well-ordered plot it cultivates and ignores the wilderness beyond. ... With the exception of our enlightened infant departments, there is no part of our educational system of which our present complacency is justified and little in our current practice which does not call for a close and critical scrutiny.'

We may doubt whether many people actually working in the educational field today are in fact complacent about the educational system. But we should agree with Sir James Robertson about the seriousness and urgency of the problems of organization within the system, and we should want to point to the important, though embarrassing, fact that our educational responsibility is more and more spreading beyond the schools into society at large. Less and less can we think about and discuss the work of the schools without extended reference to what happens to young people when they leave school and how the general public spend their increasing leisure.

Most of our practical educational problems can be seen in the context of the general problem of developing personal responsibility in a world that makes personal responsibility difficult. In this context such various matters as the size of classes, the organizational pattern of secondary education, the relation between school and home, the ancillary work of Educational Welfare and Attendance Departments, the shift of emphasis from school to further and adult education, and the Youth Service all fall into place.

As was indicated at the end of the last chapter, there are two aspects of education at all levels which are worth special attention because they are both closely related to problems already referred to – the rediscovery of a coherent view of life, the conditions of effective communication, and the promotion of voluntary activity within the highly organized society. These two aspects of education are the education of feeling and the education of thinking.

There is as much need for the education of feeling as for the education of thinking. The one cannot be left to chance any more than the other. And, although the general emphasis in educational practice is by no means so preponderantly intellectual as it was fifty years ago, it is open to question whether we have yet appreciated all that the education of feeling involves. There is little doubt that the rather narrowly academic channel of the grammar school and the university still achieves intellectual distinction at the price of neglecting the education of feeling. For those who go from the sixth forms of grammar schools to training colleges the balance is to a large extent redressed; most training colleges give an excellent all-round education.

It would be a great mistake to think of the education of feeling as a distinct area or department of education which can be promoted or neglected independently of the rest of the educational process. A human being is, or ought to be, a whole organism; and what affects one part affects the rest also. It is the business of education to foster the growth of balanced, whole persons. If education is deficient on the side of feeling, it is bound to be defective on the intellectual side; the resulting intellectual life will tend to be arid – it will, so to speak, lack body. Those who have studied the origins of music and drama in the primitive forms of dance know that the dance is a mainspring of human activity, a basic means of communication and inspiration. African tribal dances preparatory to a hunting expedition are not mere rituals; they are vital means of evoking and expressing the excitement and zest of the chase, with an elemental power far beyond anything that could be released by a deliberative assembly or even impassioned oratory. Although there is no analogy between tribal dances and the folk-dancing that is practised in our modern society (for the latter has lost any concrete connexions it may once have had with practical social needs), it is nevertheless found that folk-dancing has a valuable contribution to make, not only to the physical and aesthetic education of boys and girls, but to their whole growth as people, including their capacity for sensitive and considerate social relations and also for lively intellectual response.

An essential part of our job as educators is to help people to achieve depth and sincerity of feeling. There is an emotional shallowness which, in those who have never been deeply stirred in their personal experience, often goes with intellectual shallowness; and is fostered by habitual exposure to the second-hand feeling of mass entertainment. But there is also an emotional shallowness of the intellectual who, through a fear of being swept off his precarious intellectual balance, fastidiously withdraws himself from the current of popular sentiment and the sources of group loyalty. He finds a sophisticated compromise by making light of occasions which stir public feeling (for example, a coronation); by adopting a patronizing attitude towards popular sentiment he can sterilize emotion. In this way some of the most highly educated and gifted individuals may be cut off from participating in the emotional life of the people, and thus unfitted to be leaders. For it is quite certain that no one can be a public leader who cannot enter into the feelings of the people at large. A leader should certainly be able to see beyond, and think beyond, the range of ordinary people. But, unless he can feel with ordinary people, he cannot interpret them to themselves or set before them a vision that they can understand. He must be able to talk their language; and language is rooted in feeling.

For the health and wholeness of personality it is as important that people should feel their own feelings as think their own thoughts. That is to say, wholeness of personality involves authenticity, integrity, and depth of feeling. Failure of genuine, deep feeling may be due to the fact that deep feeling has never been awakened in personal experience; the individual has been able to float along the surface of life. It may be due to emotional inhibition, especially by fear; the individual is for some reason unable to face life as it is and contrives to substitute counterfeit situations for real experience. Or it may be a loss of capacity resulting from the abuse of feeling; if the mere sensation of emotional situations is indulged in for its own sake, genuine feeling may become impossible. A girl who had flirted indiscriminately said : 'I couldn't think of marriage until I can really feel deeply again.'

For convenience of discussion, aesthetic and moral feeling may be distinguished. But this distinction must not be taken to imply any real separation, any more than there is any ultimate separation between feeling and thinking. We function as whole beings.

(a) *Aesthetic feeling.* In the next chapter there will be some discussion of the nature of truth and of the ways of approaching truth. For the present purpose it is enough to remind ourselves that truth has to be lived into, not only thought into. To talk about experience is not the same thing as to undergo experience; in fact, talking about experience can be a way of keeping experience at arm's length. Our education is still inadequate from the point of view of creating opportunity for genuine experience. We all know the literature lessons which, especially under pressure of examinations, consist of biographical and critical notes by means of which the pupil can be forearmed against the examiner. He has the information for which he may be asked, and he knows what he ought to think about the literature prescribed for study. But what direct and genuine impact has the literature made upon the pupil, and what authentic response has he made to it? Undergoing experience is a different thing from memorizing facts; and we tend to forget that an opinion becomes a fact when it is someone else's opinion.

Some simple practical principles may be suggested for the education of aesthetic feeling.

(i) The principle of Do-it-yourself. Children should be given the opportunity to try their hands at a variety of arts and crafts – woodwork, pottery, dance, music, drama. The purpose of this kind of experience is not necessarily to achieve a high

degree of skill. The achievement of something like mastery of
at least one art or craft is of great value in building up the
personality. But there is another value in trying one's hand at
a wide variety of skills. Practical experience, however limited
and unsuccessful, gives an insight into what a particular art
or craft involves which cannot be obtained in any other way.
No amount of academic study of works of art, valuable as it
may be, can take the place of practical experience. One may,
for example, be an authority on pottery and one may have
watched the deceptively easy operations of a skilled potter at
his wheel and seen a pot apparently shape itself when charmed
into existence by his fingers. But half-an-hour's inept struggles
with a wheel and a lump of clay will teach one more of what
the potter's craft means than years of observation and study.
A day spent, under supervision, helping to excavate the site of
a Roman villa will teach one more about the way in which an
archaeologist goes about his work than all the books and
photographs one can lay hands on. To try one's own hand at
playing a musical instrument or at painting will give one a
healthy respect for these arts which one will never get from
listening and looking. It is part of education to watch a skill
really well performed (be it painting, skating, or juggling);
but it is also part of education – and a chastening part – to
try one's own incompetent hand at it.

(ii) Children should be given the opportunity to know the
best that has been done in an art or craft – to see really good
painting (in the original), hear good music really well played,
or see a Shakespeare play really well staged and acted. Only so
can they have good standards. There is a use for reproductions
of paintings; but reproductions are misleading unless one knows
how to make allowance for the difference between reproduc-
tion and original. Children, who will one day have to furnish
their homes, should have a chance to see well-designed furniture and china, compare good design with bad, and realize
that the most expensive things are not necessarily the best
designed. The trouble with many people whose taste is bad is
that they have never really encountered the best things, or
encountered them well done. It is foolishly optimistic to expect

that people will necessarily love the highest when they see it. But, if they do not see it, they cannot love it; while, if they see it, there is at least a sporting chance.

(iii) The wise teacher does not get between the child and the experience. He lets the experience sink in. He lets the music or the picture or the poem speak for itself. He knows the value of silence. There is a place and a time for critical analysis and discussion; and our enjoyment of any artistic experience is enhanced by an intelligent understanding of what we are enjoying and why we enjoy it. But before analysis of experience can be profitable there must be some experience to analyse. When music has been played or poetry spoken, it is inexpedient to fall upon it instantly with a dissecting knife or butcher's cleaver. The over-anxious teacher's desire to interpret may result only in stifling the pupil's authentic response and substituting a manufactured response. Children themselves become so accustomed to giving the answers which they think the teacher expects that it may be hard work to convince them that their own sincere response is far more important than what the teacher thinks or what the book says. Some years ago a colleague of mine strove throughout the greater part of a poetry lesson with a junior class to get from the children what they really thought of the poem. At long last a child put up her hand and asked, in excited half-belief : 'Oh! Miss, do you *want* what we *think*?' If children are to respond honestly to experience, experience must not be immediately pulled to pieces by the teacher, as one might catch a butterfly and pull its wings off. After many years I still remember the simple but impressive spectacle of a group of children, aged perhaps seven or eight, in a P.N.E.U. school, who listened to a piece of music on a gramophone. When the music stopped the children, like Sherlock Holmes's dog in the night, did nothing. They remained seated quietly on the floor, for a few moments of silence, that rare commodity in the traffic of education.

In discussing the education of feeling and of thinking it should be emphasized that there can be no question of dividing the curriculum into subjects that have to be 'felt' and others that have to be 'thought'. The business of redressing the balance of the curriculum is not simply a matter of putting more art, music, and 'movement' into the timetable. In all learning there is room for feeling and for thinking. The enjoyment of art is greater if it is intelligently critical. And there is room for emotion in science and mathematics; beauty and wonder properly belong to scientific inquiry. Not only is wonder a spur to thought; it is also a governor of thought, promoting a spirit of reverence rather than of exploitation. Thought and feeling nourish one another.

(b) *Moral feeling*. The health and growth of personality require that the person should be responsible for his behaviour. Conduct which is merely conditioned by the social environment has no more moral significance than a reflex movement. If we consider what should be the basic motive of responsible moral behaviour, we have to remind ourselves that the ground of all morality is respect of person for person. It is an important part of moral education to help those who are being educated to see how moral codes are rooted in respect for personality and do not consist merely of arbitrary rules. The breakdown of traditional moral authorities makes it all the more important in education to help young people to grasp the principles that underlie codes of conduct. Only by doing so can they learn to distinguish between those rules of conduct which can and should change with changing circumstances (that is, which are relative), and those principles which, if true at all, are true always and everywhere. If a caveman drags off his neighbour's wife by the hair, the outraged husband is morally entitled to pick up his club and take what measures may be necessary to correct his rival's behaviour. A different code is required in a highly organized society with an efficient legal system. But in both cases the ultimate purpose of the action taken is to obtain justice – to secure a state of affairs in which a proper respect of person for person is safeguarded. Again, in the kind of society to which most of us are accustomed, the practice of monogamy is held to maintain personal values at the highest level. My wife would consider that I was treating her with less than proper respect and esteem if I were to take several others at the same time; even if I assured her that she would have the status of chief wife, she would still feel insulted. In another kind of society, however, where eligible women cannot move about freely and safely without protection, monogamy may not be the best way of maintaining personal values, and polygamy may in fact preserve these values better.

Failure to distinguish between underlying, abiding principles and the changing expressions of those principles is a mark of limited minds which, to escape the difficulty of thinking things out, ascribe absolute value to precepts or customs which have only a relative validity. The same attitude of mind, which does not distinguish between relative and changing codes and ultimate and abiding principles, is also liable to confuse morals and manners. Thus a schoolboy may not see much difference of kind between a failure to tell the truth and a failure to wear his cap at the right angle or to leave the right button of his jacket unbuttoned.

No doubt there are people whose natural limitations make them incapable of a rational morality, and who can never advance beyond a state in which they are conditioned to do certain things and not to do certain other things. However that may be, it is the business of education to develop as fully as possible whatever capacity people have for an intelligent approach to moral problems. Every individual must pass through the stages of prior morality – response to physical pleasure and pain and response to social praise and blame – before reaching the mature stage of doing or not doing things because he has thought the problems out and made up his mind that he ought to act in this way or that – and, having made up his mind, is willing to be held responsible for his choices. The educator's business is to help boys and girls to grow – gradually, and often unevenly – into this third and mature stage of morality.

Moral education cannot be done by precept merely. In the last resort it can be done only through experience of the right kind of community life – by living in a community which is educative because the prevailing values and relations are good. In a school or family, a heavy share of responsibility for upholding the right values rests upon the adult members. If a teacher is to educate personal integrity and respect for the personality of others, he must himself possess these things in sufficient measure. He must also have humility, recognizing that education is a relationship of persons in which both teacher and pupil learn and are changed. One of the first things for a teacher to get into his head is that, if he is not learning, he is not teaching.

The question is sometimes asked whether a teacher ought to indoctrinate or to leave the pupil free to make up his own mind. Put in this way the question confuses the issue and cannot be answered, for the antithesis which it implies is false. The truth is that the good teacher can (and indeed must) reveal his opinions on matters of moment, but also can and should cherish the pupil's freedom to do his own thinking about what is offered to him.

Ralph Harper, in *Modern Philosophies and Education*, writes: 'A passionless teacher is a bad teacher. But there are passions that are better left out of the classroom, especially the passion to display one's self. Another is a passion for a system or an idea or point of view that discourages reflection. Two normal passions remain: (a) a passion for the truth of any question that arises or ought to arise in the development of a subject-matter, the truth no matter how strictly one is forced to review one's previous judgements; and (b) a passion for the end of teaching, the autonomous functioning of the pupil's mind and habitual exercise by him of a character that is free, charitable, and self-moving.' That is to say, there are two passions which must not be allowed to frustrate or neutralize one another: a passion for truth, at whatever cost to one's previous opinions; and a passion for the proper autonomy and freedom of the pupil's mind. It is far more important that the pupil should do his own thinking (provided he is sincerely seeking the truth) than that he should think the 'right' things (the 'right' things being the things the teacher would like him to think).

The teacher should not try to be neutral. In any case an attempt to appear neutral is unlikely to be successful. But, apart from the impossibility of concealing opinions, the teacher has an obligation to give his pupils the security which comes from being with people of firm beliefs and opinions, who know their own minds. A boy may reject his father's or his teacher's religious or political opinions; but he will have gained something from associating with someone whose character is rooted in firm belief which could never be gained from a person of uncertain mind.

The teacher, then, ought to be a real person with positive attitudes, not a mere transmitting medium. He should put his cards on the table and at the same time give his pupils the means of evaluating the different points of view that he will encounter. The pupil cannot make up his own mind if his mind remains empty; he must be fed with knowledge and exercised by meeting points of view. The teacher must be patient with his pupils' groping and tolerant of their brashness. But there is an important distinction between the tolerance that springs from charity and the tolerance that is only another name for indifference. It is the teacher's business to combat everything that disintegrates human personality, undermines the value set upon persons as such, or reduces human life to sub-human terms. He must vigilantly reckon with all those influences in modern life which numb the sense of responsibility, invite escape from responsibility, including those interpretations of human behaviour which sanction, or appear to sanction, the view that we cannot help being what we are.

Moral education is not easy in a world of shifting and confused values. The traditional, prudential basis of morality is an insecure educational foundation in an age when the traditional virtues are no longer supported by obvious expediency. It is unfortunate that moral education ever was based on prudential considerations; for, now that the prudential foundations of morality have to a large extent collapsed, or appear to have collapsed, we are left wondering what we can base our moral education upon.

If we do not appeal to prudential motives, we must appeal to the motives which in fact inspire all the best and most admirable human enterprise – the spirit of adventure, the idealism which puts the cause before personal safety and convenience, the sense of dedication in which self is swallowed up in something more than self. Kenneth Grahame spoke of 'the demand of youth for long odds'. Much delinquency is due to the best qualities gone wrong. Often the adolescent's urge to see himself in an admired character needs only a touch one way or the other to tip the scales of his admiration from criminal to saint.

The late Dr McAllister Brew said that young people need three things above all :

(i) Freedom to experiment and adventure. They need challenging experiences such as Outward Bound courses offer.[1]

(ii) Security to depend upon – especially the security of dependable personal relations.

(iii) A faith – something to believe in which can take them out of themselves.

There are certain practical things that we can do – or try to do – to help young people in their moral development.

(i) We can set before them the inspiring examples of people who, in all kinds of ways, found something more worthwhile than their own comfort and safety – who lost themselves to find their true selves. Example is worth a great deal more than precept, and biography offers an almost unlimited range of example. The great adventures of the human spirit are the heritage of our children, and they have a right to enter into it. We can show them explorers, like Nansen or Edward Wilson; scientists, like Faraday or the Curies; fighters, like Douglas Bader or Richard Hilary; workers to relieve human suffering, like Florence Nightingale, Kagawa, or Gladys Aylward. In presenting the lives of heroic characters, we should avoid the mistake of idealizing them. Their common humanity with ourselves is important. What they have done we might be able to

1. Young offenders have taken part in Outward Bound courses and in the Duke of Edinburgh's Award Scheme, and been treated like any others taking part. In November 1960, the first 'adventure' course for delinquent youths was arranged by the London Police Court Mission, which hopes to establish its own centre where suitable boys can go direct from the courts.

do. The school teachers of Norway, who made such a magnificent stand against the Quisling government during the German occupation – a resistance in which they were splendidly supported by their pupils – were ordinary people like ourselves, raised to a higher power by the challenge of events.

(ii) We can set before our pupils the obligation to make one's own choice, and not take refuge behind public opinion or prevailing fashion. It is not easy for the young to take their own line in matters of principle, and to do what they honestly believe to be right because it is right, not to do what other people do because other people do it. What other people do may be right; and the young have to learn not to be rebels for the sake of rebelling as well as not to conform for the sake of conforming. But if what others do is right, it is not right *because* they do it. Boys and girls need a great deal of help, given with sympathetic understanding, in learning to stand on their own feet. Their contemporaries are neither understanding nor tolerant, and can be more exacting and tyrannical than any grown-ups. When one is fifty, one's contemporaries are blandly tolerant of one's nonconformities. When one is fifteen one may have to face persecution for trifling deviations.

The great lesson of the Existentialists is their insistence on inescapable personal responsibility. Even the pessimistic, atheistic writers refuse to take refuge in the illusion that we cannot help being what we are. Sartre, looking despair in the face, says: 'We do not do what we want, and yet we are responsible for what we are.' If the cynicism of this spirit makes some appeal to contemporary youth, so also should its courage.

(iii) Most important of all, we should do all we can to give young people opportunity to experience, in the right kind of social group, the meaning of fellowship. What kind of community the school is matters far more than what kind of instruction is given there. The school ought to offer both the security of a group loyalty which transcends individual likes and dislikes, and also the challenge of situations that demand some courage and resource. It should offer a prevailing atmosphere of wholesome values, especially the proper appreciation of those things which money cannot buy, such as friendship, good conversation, and the satisfaction of achievement.

The school in these days is no self-contained community. The revolution in school architecture during the last half-century symbolizes a change of outlook. We no longer surround our schools with high walls and locked gates to prevent those within from getting out and those without from getting in. And we no longer set the windows so high that no one can look in or out. The modern school building, often graciously surrounded by gardens, is open to the world and suggests that education is one of the social activities in which the neighbourhood is engaged. Parents are welcome and are encouraged to discuss their problems. The school plays its part in promoting good family relations. Through the youth employment service the school helps to pass on its boys and girls into adult life. Many schools, although administered by local authorities, are in active relation with neighbouring churches. In one way or another the school, as we now think of it in this country, is an educative community in which young people can grow as persons; but not an insulated community. The school rather is a community where social relations of many kinds have their origin. The danger in these days is not that the school will be merely a place of academic instruction, but rather that its social connexions will proliferate, and its general responsibilities multiply, to such an extent that no body of teachers can be expected to cope with all that has to be done.

CHAPTER 10

The Education of Thinking

THE purpose of this chapter is to discuss two topics. One is the process of arriving at knowledge; and the thesis put forward is that this process is essentially the same in the different areas of human thought: scientific truth and poetic truth (for example) are not pursued by quite separate paths. The other topic is the education of clear thinking; and the main theme is that boys and girls should learn (as Lord Morley put it) to know when a thing is proved and when it is not, and should study the deceptions that can be practised on the human mind, and by the mind on itself, and so be forewarned against the arts of propaganda and advertisement. The two topics are connected inasmuch as both involve an inquiry into the mind's response to experience; both are concerned with the ways in which we think.

(a) *The search for truth*. Pasternak makes a character in *Dr Zhivago* say: 'Facts do not exist until man has put into them something of his own.' To that proposition must be added the important rider that what man puts in of his own is not optional, arbitrary, or capricious, if he wants to arrive at the truth; but rather is the recognition of something which is already 'there' in external reality. Knowledge is the response of the truth within to the truth without. This response is primarily and ultimately intuitional, though the explicit formulation of rational systems greatly helps us to extend our grasp of experience, and provides *points d'appui* from which successive intuitional flights can take off.

If this general proposition is sound, it means that the process of arriving at knowledge is essentially the same in different

areas of human thought – that scientific thought is not something different in kind from historical or theological thought.
This conclusion has an obvious bearing on the problem of
achieving a coherent view of life. Unity of thought and knowledge should be stressed in education.

Historically an erroneous belief has grown up that some
departments of knowledge have superior authority over others
by reason of the alleged objective certainty of the results
achieved. Thus the physical sciences, and to a less extent the
biological sciences, and to a lesser extent again the human
sciences of anthropology, sociology, and psychology, have acquired a prestige which, in our time is usually denied to, say,
theology, ethics, aesthetics, or metaphysics. For many people in
these days, scientific truth has become the only truth. At the
popular level we can observe how often the word 'scientifically', in such a phrase as : 'It is scientifically proved that . . .',
is used simply as an intensive. Advertisers know the value of
introducing the word 'scientific' into their descriptions of everything from cultivators to cosmetics.

The modern prestige value of science is obviously the result
of the enormous growth of scientific knowledge in the last
century and a half, and, even more, of the tremendous success
with which scientific knowledge has been applied to practical
life. Nothing succeeds like success; and the modern popular
reverence for science is sometimes mystical rather than realistic. At the time of the first Russian sputnik, a humorous
weekly published a cartoon of two Russian peasants, standing
amidst the squalor and dilapidation of their cottage and farm
buildings, their gaze fixed religiously upon the new celestial
portent.

In my book, *Mystery of Man*,[1] I have distinguished two ways
of knowing. One I called 'inward' or existential, and the other
'outward' or conceptual. Inward or existential knowledge is
the intimate, direct encounter with experience in which we are
personally involved. We 'know' a familiar face, though we
may not be able to describe the features. Our recognition of
such a familiar person is an immediate, total perception, not a

1. Chapter 3.

calculated checking and addition of items. Again we 'know' our way from one familiar place to another, kinaesthetically, not in terms of the map or street names; and, if we try to direct someone else, we may find ourselves helplessly making abortive gestures which represent a sort of condensed version of our movements in making the journey, but which we cannot communicate explicitly without some intellectual effort. This kind of knowledge we share with the animals, and we depend upon it for all original experience and for the stimulus that experience brings.

Conceptual knowing, which appears to be peculiar to man, depends on the power to abstract items from experience and arrange them in a sort of map. All such conceptual patterns are made up of symbols of one kind or another, and they vary without limit in complexity. As a simple example we may think of the docketing of particulars about an individual person so that he could be identified by the police. As a complex example we might think of the systematized body of knowledge that constitutes a whole science such as physics. The value of such maps and plans is that, by means of them, we can greatly increase our grasp of experience.

These two ways of knowing are not alternative and mutually exclusive, but supplementary and mutually necessary. Science does not rely on conceptual thinking only, but has its own intuitional elements which justify the use of words like 'mystery' and 'imagination' in connexion with scientific thought. Nor are religious, ethical, and aesthetic thinking purely intuitional; they require conceptual 'map-making' which is as rigorous, in its own terms, as scientific reasoning. The conclusion is that every logical and/or scientific system ultimately rests upon bases which cannot themselves be logically or scientifically proved, and depends for its extension upon fresh imaginative or intuitional adventures which are not prescribed by the logical or scientific system so far constructed. All knowledge involves an element of revelation, if that word may be permitted.

In this connexion it is profitable to consider Professor Michael Polanyi's argument in *The Study of Man*. Since he is a physical scientist, there is the more significance in his holding the views he does about the nature of human knowledge.

He distinguishes between 'tacit' and 'explicit' knowledge,[1] and argues that tacit knowing is the dominant principle of all knowledge, and that its rejection (as unscientific or illogical) would automatically involve the rejection of any knowledge whatever.

As an illustration Polanyi compares the making and use of a map with the intuitional method of learning one's way by trial and error which man shares with the animals. The map, however useful, cannot of itself speak to us unless we can interpret it; and interpretation involves drawing upon the tacit knowledge – the 'feel' of the situation – from which the map is abstracted. The purpose of the map is to enable us to extend our experience. It was derived from direct experience, and it is useless to us unless we can bring it to life by relating it to our resources of direct experience.

We do not always remember that maps, and even pictures, are conventions which – far from being self-evident – can tell us nothing unless we know how to understand them by referring them to the direct experience from which they were derived. My father was once sketching in China when a peasant came and watched the operation with great curiosity. The peasant followed my father's gaze as he looked first at the landscape and then at his paper, again and again. But it was quite apparent that the peasant could make neither head nor tail of what my father was doing. After some time he had an inspiration and put his hands together to form a tunnel or tube through which he looked at the sketch in such a way as to isolate it from the surrounding objects. The effect was as if he was looking out of a window; and his delight showed clearly that he had for the first time grasped the pictorial convention.

The next step in Polanyi's argument is to recognize that the interpretation of symbols (the reference back of explicit knowledge to tacit knowledge) involves personal participation. He poses the question whether personal participation in our scien-

1. These terms appear to correspond closely with my use of 'existential' and 'conceptual' knowing.

tific account of the universe is to be regarded as a residual flaw which ought if possible to be eliminated. His answer is: No. Indeed, he maintains that fundamental novelty can be discovered only by the same tacit powers which rats use in learning a maze. He uses the term 'understanding' to describe the operation of reorganizing an experience to gain intellectual control over it, and argues that understanding depends on our tacit powers, explicit knowledge being a valuable instrument, but no more. What applies to maps and pictures applies also to words and symbols. 'Neither words nor symbols nor maps can be said to communicate an understanding of themselves.'

He goes on to expand the meaning of 'understanding' to include intention and purpose. (It is of the nature of thought to issue in action, even if the action consists of further thought.) This active quality of understanding again implies the participation of a person.

Polanyi then proposes that our ideal of knowledge should be revised so as to recognize the participation of the knower in shaping his knowledge – this participation being regarded not as a flaw but as the true guide and master of our cognitive powers. Knowledge indeed is essentially personal.[1] This proposition, if true at all, is as true for science as for aesthetics or ethics. In a vivid phrase he says: 'The shaping of knowledge is achieved by pouring ourselves into new forms of existence.'

To say that all knowledge is personal, however, is not to say that it is idiosyncratic or capricious. When we discover truth, we can only discover truth that was already there to be discovered. We can fabricate; but we cannot fabricate truth. If we consider the invention of a machine, it might appear that something novel has been created. But Polanyi reminds us that it is only the knowledge of the invention that is new, not its possibility.

Not only is all discovery the discovery of something already there to be discovered, but – and here is a fresh emphasis on the personal character of knowledge – the act of discovery and the will to discover depend on belief. There must be (in another

1. The title of Polanyi's larger book on this subject is *Personal Knowledge*.

vivid phrase) 'conviction of the hidden presence'. It is when we
hit on the right question that we know we have struck a real
problem. And Polanyi reminds us that painters as well as physi-
cists speak of 'solving a problem'.

The end of the inquiry is in this sense determined: the
searcher must indeed guess, but he will achieve success only if
he guesses right. 'The sense of a pre-existent task makes the
shaping of knowledge a responsible act, free from selective
predilection.' Truth will yield only truth.

Finally, Polanyi argues that there is *a continuum* from observation to valuation. There is not one kind of thinking which is
empirical and objective and another which is intuitive and sub-
jective. There is no gulf between the scientist and the moralist.
Even physics, though based on observation, relies heavily on a
sense of intellectual beauty. When he comes to consider pure
mathematics, he says: 'Whoever does not love and admire
mathematics for its own internal splendours, knows nothing
whatever about it.' 'Mathematics is conceptual music – music
is sensuous mathematics.' He concludes this part of his study
with the peroration: 'Thus our acknowledgement of understanding as a valid form of knowledge foreshadows the promised transition from the study of nature to a confrontation with
man acting responsibly, under an over-arching firmament of
universal ideals.'

The contention is, then, that the process of achieving knowledge is made up of the same essential elements, though not
necessarily in the same proportions, whatever field of knowledge we may be exploring. If we can get young people to understand that this is so, we shall have helped them through an
important part of their intellectual education.

There will always be observation and inference, though it
may not be physical things that we observe. Physical science
may be *set out* as a systematic piece of induction. And ethics
may be *set out* as the deductive application of principles. But
in neither case does the human mind work in that way. Scientific discovery involves intuitive jumps, guesses, or inspirations
which have to be checked. Moral judgements are always made,
as direct apprehensions, in particular situations, though generali-

zations can be made by inference and, once made, can help to illuminate future situations.

If it is true that the process of achieving knowledge is fundamentally the same whatever field of knowledge may be explored, it must follow that no branch of knowledge (such as physical science) can claim priority of authority over another *by reason of its method*.

We must acknowledge, however, that systems of thought and knowledge differ. The physicist's account of a rainbow and the poet's account of a rainbow are different; though we must observe (i) that physics has its own poetry and (ii) poetry is not improved by scientific ignorance. The theologian's account of man, the anthropologist's account, and the physiologist's account of man are likely to be different; but, here again, none of these three will be improved by blunders in the others' territories.

What, then, distinguishes one of these systems of thought and knowledge from another? The essential difference, surely, is one not of method but of purpose. The theologian, the anthropologist, and the physiologist are not necessarily using different methods, nor are they using different material; but they have different jobs to do – they are pursuing different aims because they are trying to answer different sets of questions. They can work harmoniously alongside one another *unless* (and this is where things so often go wrong) any one of them denies the validity of his neighbour's operations and claims that his own truth is the only truth.

If I say: 'The first chapter of Genesis is wrong', that statement is meaningless until 'wrong' has been defined. And 'wrong' in this sentence can be defined only in terms of the purpose of the information conveyed in the first chapter of Genesis. If we take the purpose of Genesis I to be the presentation of a factually accurate account (accurate, that is, by the accepted modern scientific standards) of the way in which the physical universe came into existence, we should say that it is – in certain respects at all events – 'wrong'. But if we take the purpose of Genesis I to be the communication of the splendour and majesty of the Creator-God, in contrast with the unedifying polytheistic squabbles of the Babylonian creation myths, we shall give a different answer.

In any construction of thought and knowledge, our terms of reference not only give point and direction, but also impose limitations. It is of the greatest importance that we should not forget the limitations. A study of the influence of the natural and social environment upon individual behaviour is valuable because it reminds us of the extent to which we are conditioned by our environment. But such a study does not answer questions of moral responsibility; still less does it entitle us to say that there is no such thing as moral responsibility. On the other hand, a study of the conditioning of behaviour provides evidence which we ought not to neglect if our handling of problems of moral responsibility is to be realistic.

The final lesson perhaps is that our knowledge of truth is always 'open', in the sense that we can never possess it all. In order to answer certain kinds of question, we must adopt certain categories of interpretation. But these categories impose limitations because it is their business to exclude what is not relevant. The greatest – and the commonest – mistake we can make is to assume that what is excluded does not exist. That mistake is at the root of most misunderstandings – and lack of understanding – between different fields of human thought; notably it is at the root of the unnecessary and unedifying conflict between science and religion which began with Galileo and entered its most disastrous phase with Darwin.

We can approach the sacred mountain of Truth from many sides. What, in the natural limitation of our faculties, we cannot do is to see all sides at once. There is only one point from which we could do that, and no one has yet been there.

(b) *Straight and twisted thinking.* If one of the aims of education is to help people to do their own thinking, we must consider what we mean by independence or freedom of thought. Freedom of thought, as Robert Maynard Hutchens put it, does not mean freedom from thinking. It does not imply a right to be obstinately opinionated about something which one has not taken the trouble to study. The right to an opinion has to be *earned* by studying the subject. This is something easily forgotten in these days of popularized, easily accessible know-ledge, which destroys intellectual standards, deprives us of the wisdom of Socrates who knew that he did not know, and seems to sanction the disastrous notion that anybody is entitled to air his opinions on any subject. Profound problems of religion, economics, and so on, are lightly disposed of on the grounds that 'I've got a right to my opinion'. Democracy, whatever it may be, is not the right to talk nonsense about things one does not understand.

This principle – that the right to an opinion has to be earned – does not mean that teachers speak with authority and pupils do not. Boys and girls are often real authorities on something they have studied.

Nor – as was argued in the last chapter – is freedom of thought a principle which requires the teacher to occupy a permanent position on the fence, under pretext of 'leaving the child free to make up his own mind'. The teacher should be fair, but that does not mean that he ought to be neutral. It does mean that he should do everything to help the pupils form real opinions of their own, and refrain from anything that coerces or deceives his pupils into accepting opinions secondhand. But the teacher ought not to conceal his own convictions. The pupils' mental digestive system must have something to work on. Truth is not found in a vacuum.

Although logic and psychology should not appear as such on school timetables, at least below the sixth form, there should be opportunity to study the process of thinking. At quite a young age children are capable of reasoning; and their under-standing is limited by lack of experience rather than by in-ability to reason.

For our part, while circumstances often make it necessary for us to say what is incomplete, we must do our best not to say what is incorrect and has to be unlearnt. If a young child asks where babies come from, it is not necessary to say all that would be said to an adolescent. But one should not tell them stories about storks or gooseberries. The story is told of a child, brought up on the gooseberry-bush myth and subsequently told the facts, who rejected the truth with: 'Go on! You don't expect me to believe that nonsense!' That may be an old-fashioned story. In these days many children of five know as much as the doctor could tell them.

There is no better discipline for the adult than that of explaining things and words to young children; for it makes one think what one means to say and then find clear and simple ways of saying it. One can use words loosely with grown-ups and get away with it; but one cannot get away with it with children.

We meet the problem at different levels 'Daddy, what's science?' 'What's a bazaar?' 'Can we go to America this afternoon?' 'Why can't I have a cheque book and get as much money as I like out of the bank?' 'Why do people have wars?' 'Why should I save money?' 'What's the harm in ... (getting tight, necking, etc.)?'

The discipline of tackling questions from the young consists in our not being able to take anything for granted. We have to do our own fundamental thinking over again. 'Explanations' to children are very tricky, and we must beware of getting into deeper water than we know. It is wise to look before leaping, as the following example shows:

'Mummy, why does the sun move?'

'It doesn't, dear. We move. The world spins round.'

'Why don't we fall off?'

'There's an arrangement deep down in the earth which pulls us so that we can't.'

'I should like to go down and see it!'

'You can't, dear. Nobody has.'

'Then how do you know it's there?'

Syllabuses should be reviewed from the point of view of their suitability as material for children to think about. If we are compelled to teach the Renaissance and Reformation to children of ten, it is not surprising if teacher (and textbook, for that matter) resort to inanities like: 'About that time Europe began to wake up.'

Children should be enabled to see how thought can be assisted or frustrated by the way in which questions are posed. Many intellectual difficulties arise from asking the wrong question.

For example, the question often asked about telepathy is : 'How can an idea pass out of one mind into another?' This question assumes that minds are separate receptacles, and there is no answer to the question in that form. But, if we assume a common subterranean mental content, comparable with the common content that connects a system of volcanoes, the fact of telepathy is no longer perplexing; and the right question to ask is : 'Why is not telepathy going on all the time?' That is to say, the problem is to account for the progressive insulation of minds at the higher levels of development. From that point of view it might appear that the price paid for being human is the sacrifice of a great deal of the primitive *rapport* between individuals which can be observed among animals.

The study of thought must go along with a study of language. Children must appreciate that thinking never goes on without feeling; and words and phrases are flavoured by feeling. This emotional loading of language cannot be eliminated, but it can be understood. It is the source of all that is best and worst in human communication – of poetry and propaganda. When feeling and meaning match, there is poetry. When emotion does not match meaning, but is used to disguise and twist meaning, there is propaganda.

Newspapers, advertisements, radio and TV talks, can usefully be studied from the point of view of clear and confused thinking, honest and dishonest expression. The power of the headline is easily illustrated. *Three Objections to Women Priests,*[1] as the heading of a report of a meeting, would at first sight suggest that the scales of debate were tipped against the ordination of women. In fact the meeting was of an Anglican Group for the Ordination of Women, and everyone present was in favour. The logic of election speeches can be examined. 'The government of the country must be established on a wise and firm foundation. *That is why* all men and women of good sense will vote for ...' This formula may be used by any political party. The following is another example of hitch-hiking on a false premiss. A question in *Any Questions* not long ago ran : 'It is generally agreed that fruit and vegetables no longer have

1. *Birmingham Post,* August 1959.

the flavour they used to have. In the opinion of the team, is this due to the use of poison-sprays and chemical manures?'

Boys and girls can see how words are emotionally toned, and can find their own examples. 'Propaganda' itself is a word which began life in the most respectable manner and has now become disreputable. 'Democratic', 'British', 'Progressive', are all heavily emotion-loaded. Those of us who were born at the beginning of this century can remember when 'Radical' was a term of abuse, much as 'Bolshie' was just after the First World War; we have quite recently, after the defeat of Labour at the last general election, observed Mr Jo Grimond try to bring back 'Radical' as a prestige term. Pairs of words are often instructive. When compulsory national service was introduced in 1938, the term 'militiaman' was coined to avoid the unattractive associations of the word 'conscript'. Fox-hunting is a 'field sport' to the people who do it; but a 'blood sport' to the people who do not like it. There is no falser proverb than 'What's in a name?' Something more than a terminological revision was accomplished by Mr Winston Churchill when, in one of his memorable broadcasts, he rechristened the Local Defence Volunteers (a title that could only have come out of a government department) the Home Guard. It is also useful to study the tied epithet, which hangs the dog that has been given a bad name. Thus capitalists are (or, rather, were) 'bloated'.

Not only are words and phrases coloured emotionally, but whole situations can be so coloured. Herein is a large part of the art of advertisement, which depends to a great extent on the exploitation of irrelevant appeal. Several kinds of irrelevant appeal are worth illustrating.

(i) *The scientific appeal.* 'Science proves that ...' This bare assertion softens up the ordinary reader's mind so that he or she is ready to accept almost any nonsense. The statement may be accompanied by, for example, a graph on squared paper which in fact means nothing at all. Or statistics may be misused. Soon after the last general election, for example, there was correspondence in the press about the fact that the average age of Conservative M.P.s was lower than that of Labour M.P.s. Attempts were made to use this fact to prove the greater vitality of the Conservative party and present them as having a stronger appeal to youth. The truth seems to be that the lower average age was merely the result of the normal practice of putting the younger and less experienced candidates to contest marginal constituencies. Advertisers of cosmetics are fond of the pseudo-scientific approach. 'To keep your skin looking young, any moisturizer must do two things: it must *penetrate* and it must *hold* moisture within your skin. Penetration is the biggest half of the job. Because if moisture doesn't get into your skin – how can you possibly hold it there? Now many moisturizers contain grease which actually *interferes* with moisture penetration. . . .'

(ii) *The snob appeal.* 'Discriminating hostesses always choose . . .' The caption belongs to a picture of a sophisticated lady surrounded by Jacobean cut glass and polished mahogany who presumably cannot wait to open her next tin of baked beans. One interesting feature of the snob appeal is its suggestion that, by doing what everyone is being urged to do, you will somehow demonstrate your exclusiveness. Everybody can be 'different' by doing the same thing.

(iii) *The glamour appeal.* 'Give HER . . .' somebody's chocolates. Or, if the advertisement is aimed at the fair sex, there may be a picture of champagne on ice, candles, glasses, and a caption: 'When music plays softly, when the evening is spangled with promise, you will say to yourself: "Thank you, darling Goya, for Black Rose – the most successful perfume I've ever worn!"' The operative word is, of course, 'successful'. Or there is a picture of a beautiful girl going to bed in a forest, and the caption: 'Here is enchantment. . . . The enchanted garden keeps its silence but you shall know our secret – that we make the loveliest candlewick bedspreads and dressing gowns in the world. . . .'

(iv) *The heroic appeal.* A good example is the recent series of Bass advertisements, of which the first was perhaps the best – two brawny forearms aiming a sporting gun, and the simple caption: 'Bass for MEN'. The suggestion is a double one: first, that beer-drinking is virile, and secondly, that you are more likely to hit what you are aiming at if you have had some beer.

One might venture to offer, as an alternative caption : 'He never misses – his Bass'.

(v) *The humorous appeal*, the object of which is to evoke goodwill. Examples are the series of Fougasse drawings at one time used by Austin Reed, the rather cosy facetiousness of the Accles and Pollock advertisements, the rib-digging dialogues published by I.C.I., or the Guinness rhymes adapted from Lewis Carroll. There is also the comparatively modern technique of disparagement; all the resources of eulogy having been exhausted, there is nothing left but to turn the whole thing upside down and begin at the other end, in the hope that the customer will think *either* : 'This must be good if they can afford to say such things about it', *or* : 'Well, at least, it's honest'. Thus a well-known house-agent uses a formula something like this : 'Faintly feudal, rat-infested, this property must be seen to be believed.'

In general, we can help our pupils not to take what they see or hear at its face-value, and always ask what is the speaker's or writer's motive or purpose, and also what is his individual or social standpoint. On the positive side, we can help them to know how to get reliable information about goods advertised (there are two non-profit-making periodicals devoted to giving the consumer dependable information and advice); for it has to be appreciated that penetration of the technique of advertisement does not of itself make us immune to the appeal. We may know exactly how it is done, and yet we may go on falling for it, unless we have some positive knowledge to set against it.

In recommending exercises of this sort, a note of caution needs to be struck. Because propaganda and advertisement are dramatic examples of the necessity for critical thinking, they afford useful exercises for boys and girls in school. But the same kind of critical approach must be cultivated in *all* areas of school work. It would be a great mistake to present the analysis of propaganda to children as if it were a separate group of tricks. Nor can we assume that children who have successfully analysed examples of propaganda and advertisement will automatically transfer this skill to other fields of thinking. The skill and habit of critical thought can be learnt only by thinking critically in all the various situations which demand such thinking.

More broadly, we must do what we can to help our pupils to appreciate the qualities of sound and critical scholarship, including the unspectacular virtue of suspended judgement – a virtue which the young, with their impatient desire for certainty, find it very hard to acquire.

Methods of study have much to contribute to the formation of right ways of thinking. Books should be used as sources of information, not as texts to be memorized. Pupils should read in order to find answers to questions, and so learn to use books selectively. And they must have access to a variety of books. Even if a class library is not available, it is possible to requisition eight copies of five different books rather than forty copies of the same book. Nothing is so deadening as to have a single prescribed textbook in, say, history, which imposes on the child only a task of memorization and not of critical selection. Pictures, too, should be used as documentary material by means of which questions can be answered, not merely as decorations to relieve the monotony of a page of text.

The unit of organization for learning should be considered. There is a place for the individual working by himself, and for the class taught as a whole. But the most valuable unit of organization is probably the small group (of three or four), which lends itself both to cooperation and to methods by which there can be real contribution to the common pool of knowledge. What kills so much school teaching is the asking of questions merely to see whether the children know the answers, and the writing of exercises only to be marked out of ten. Where the small group is the unit, there can be real contribution to a common pool (the full class lesson is the means of gathering and ordering these contributions), and there can also be division of labour within the group so that individuals have their own jobs for which they are responsible.

It is unfortunately not unknown for boys and girls to come to the university with very little notion of how to use a library, make their own notes, and generally fend for themselves. The right methods of study should not have to be learnt at the university, or even in the sixth form. An active and responsible approach to study can be learnt quite early in life, if the right means and opportunities are given. Sound foundations can be laid in the primary school.

Epilogue

RELIGION

CHAPTER II

The Relevance of Christianity

THE term 'personal values' has been used in this book as a shorthand reference to a group of related assumptions which belong to the Greek-Jewish-Christian tradition of what we loosely call Western civilization.

We assume, to begin with, that it is the true nature of a human being to behave in a responsible (that is, rational and moral) manner; the mature person takes responsibility for what he does, says, and is. The next assumption is that the proper relation between human beings is one of mutual respect – we should respect the personality of others, not because they are rich, important, or clever, but because they are human beings. It follows that we are most fully ourselves when our relations with others are fully personal; human life is impoverished when human relations are less than personal. It is worth observing that the sacredness of human personality is the basis of all morality; lying and stealing are wrong because they involve using other people as means to our own ends (that is, using them as *things*, instead of treating them as ends in themselves). Another relevant observation is that the sacredness of human personality implies, not only that each should respect his fellow, but that each should also respect himself, seek to fulfil his own true nature, and not misuse himself.

Behind this group of assumptions there is the further implication that, in our obligation to others and to our own selves, we are responsible to an ulterior authority – a law of our being – which we can recognize but do not create. We are free to violate that law, but not to change it; we cannot decree that today's evil shall be tomorrow's good, or today's truth tomorrow's falsehood. Where the ultimate nature of things is concerned (including the nature of our own selves) there is something 'given', not of our own making.

This reference to an ulterior authority was noticed in two connexions in earlier chapters. In a discussion of democracy it was pointed out that good government recognizes ultimate values to which both governors and governed are answerable; only so can democracy be saved from the tyranny of majorities on the one hand or of parties-in-power on the other. In discussing the search for truth, reference was made to what Michael Polanyi calls the 'conviction of the hidden presence'. There must be something 'there' to be discovered. 'The sense of a pre-existent task makes the shaping of knowledge a responsible act, free from selective predilection.'

The main theme of this book is the danger that, in our present age, threatens personal values in the sense described above. Looked at externally, the great danger to our civilization is perhaps of physical destruction. Inwardly, however, the greatest danger is of the destruction of those values which alone make human relations spiritually productive and any civilization worthwhile. The future of our civilization depends on the extent to which we can rescue and maintain those values.

The threat to personal values was broken down into three distinguishable but related factors which discourage personal initiative and responsibility and encourage the treatment of people as things. First, the world becomes increasingly complex and therefore more and more difficult to understand. Secondly, our sense of values is confused; technical development changes the form in which moral problems present themselves; the stock answers no longer fit, and we are no longer sure what is right and wrong. Thirdly, our popular culture is increasingly standardized. The ease with which human beings can be 'processed' by the powerful mass media of communication has made possible the manufacture of a mass culture which obliterates frontiers of class and race.

Paradoxically, the threat to personal values comes at a time when, not only has there never been more opportunity for the exercise of responsible choice (owing to the development of political democracy and universal education), but also the need for intelligent, responsible people (to operate our technological civilization) has never been greater. It is indeed a question whether man will be able to keep the mastery of the machines that he has made; the machines are becoming more formidably intelligent and, in some respects at all events, human beings are becoming more like machines.

Before turning to a discussion of the relevance of Christianity to the main thesis of this book it is worth drawing attention to one other implication of that thesis – namely that the contradictoriness of our world and our situation has its source in the contradictoriness of man's very nature. Man is distinguished from the lower animals not so much by his success as by his failure. Man is at odds with his environment and with himself. He wants, and attempts, the impossible. He is never – or hardly ever – comfortably adjusted to his circumstances. From man's eternal restlessness and deep unease spring all the distinctively human activities – scientific inquiry, artistic creation, philosophical speculation. To understand man's predicament in this or any age we must ask the ultimate questions about the nature of man, the questions that from ancient times have exercised the deepest thinkers – the Hebrew prophets, Gautama Buddha and his followers, the Greek philosophers and dramatists, the early Christian teachers like St Paul and the author of the Fourth Gospel. All these, in their various ways, understood the inner contradiction of man's nature and knew that man's salvation lies in losing himself in something greater than himself.

There is no coercive proof of a total view of life, and therefore no view of life can claim exclusive validity. History shows that people have found satisfaction and strength in various answers to the problems of existence. Their views deserve respect in proportion to their proven adequacy.

This is a personal book. And this chapter is written explicitly from a Christian point of view. A writer with that standpoint is entitled – is perhaps obliged – to say why he thinks the Christian view of life meets the problems of existence with full adequacy.

It is not the purpose of this chapter to attempt a general

apologia for the Christian faith, or to make converts. Rather it is an attempt to discuss the relevance of Christianity to the main thesis of the book – to show how, for those who accept a Christian view of life, their religious beliefs accent and under-line the discussion of personal values and the influences that threaten them. It is important to emphasize that belief in the sacredness of human beings as such, which is basic to the whole thesis of the book, is common ground between Christians and people of many other beliefs. It would defeat the purpose of this book (and be unchristian into the bargain) if a Christian interpretation were presented in a manner which seemed to cold-shoulder those who, though not calling themselves Christians, share this common ground of belief in personal values. The relation between love of God and love of neigh-bour can be approached from either direction. The Christian has authority for believing that his relation with his fellow men is held within, and sanctified by, the love of God for all His chil-dren. 'If God so loved us, we ought also to love one another.'[1] Yet we must never forget that response to the love of God is implicit in our response to our neighbour's needs. It was Jesus Himself who said that the test of worthiness for the Kingdom is feeding the hungry, clothing the naked, and sheltering the homeless. 'As you did it to one of the least of these my breth-ren, you did it to me. ... As you did it not ... you did it not unto me.'[2] We have no right to say, of one who loves his fellow men, that he does not know God, even though he may deny any religious allegiance. 'He who loves is born of God and knows God.'[3]

Any attempt to state the relevance of Christianity to our con-temporary world must reckon with the mistakes that organized religion has made during the past century or two; that is to say, we must not confuse the Christian gospel with its imper-fect interpretation by the churches.

At the risk of labouring the obvious, it is worth insisting on the distinction between the Christian Gospel and its very in-adequate embodiment and expression in the lives of Christian people and Christian communities. It is very difficult to be a

1. I John iv, 11.   2. Matt. xxv, 40.   3. I John iv, 7.

good Christian. Most Christians are poor advertisements for their religion. The measure of Christianity is Christ, not Christians. That is not an argument against Christianity, but a reminder of the fact of our human imperfection which the Christian revelation comes to illuminate and redeem.

The man in the street's belief that the Church 'is out of touch' or 'has failed' is partly the consequence of two major mistakes which have done much harm to organized religion, in spite of such revivals as Methodism and the Oxford Movement. In the first place, the Church became involved, quite unnecessarily, in a controversy with science. It was Archbishop Temple who pointed out most clearly the folly of this alleged conflict between religion and science. Once the Church made the mistake of allowing the supernatural to be identified with the *un*-natural – of allowing the finger of God to be detected in those events for which no natural explanation was forthcoming – the Church had committed herself to a hopeless rearguard action. The further science extended her frontiers, the less room was left for God. Archbishop Temple reminds us that the Founder of Christianity, so far from looking for evidence of God's activity in the chinks of His universe, saw the hand of God in the rising and setting of the sun, the changing of the seasons with their rhythm of seed-time and harvest, and the whole wonder of Nature. Today the Church realizes that she has no quarrel with science as such. And the best scientists know that science does not exclude religion. Meanwhile a good deal of damage has been done in the public mind.

The other mistake which the Church made was its failure to assimilate the new importance of social, as distinct from personal, morality. Personal, or private, morality is no less important than it ever was; it is no less wrong than it was a hundred years ago to steal or commit adultery. But the enormous growth in modern times of the organized state and the closer dependence of groups and countries on one another have brought into a new prominence the importance of social, or public, morality. The Church, which has a clear message about private morality, has nothing of comparable clarity to say about the social implications of financial speculation, unofficial strikes, international economic relations, or the development of self-government among subject peoples. It is small wonder if the man in the street, finding the churches silent or confused in their utterance about matters which affect the lives of thousands or millions, is inclined to pay less attention to injunctions about conjugal fidelity. In fairness to the churches it must be acknowledged that the field of public morality is a far more difficult one in which to find one's way than that of private morality, and we can scarcely blame the clergy (who are not usually economists or sociologists) for not having ready solutions of our problems of economic relations. The layman who complains that the Church gives no clear lead in these matters might reflect that he is himself part of the Church, which does not consist only of clergy, who are overworked and underpaid anyway.

If it is important to observe the distinction between the Christian Gospel and the Christian churches, which as human historical institutions are at best imperfect mirrors of their Founder, so also it is important to distinguish between the Christian Gospel (which concerns God's power to remake man) and that kind of ethical humanism which assumes man's power to remake himself. Although it is Greek and not Hebrew in origin, humanism has both influenced and been influenced by historic Christianity, as modern writers such as Jacques Maritain make plain. The Greek humanistic tradition has always supplied a corrective to Christian thought which, if disproportionately preoccupied with the implications of the Fall (in, for example, the Barthian emphasis on the abysmal separation of man from God), needs to be reminded that man is, after all, made in God's image. Nevertheless, although Christian thought is under a great debt to the humanist tradition, Christians believe that their religion has insights which are denied to enlightened humanism. Unless Christianity adds something to humanism – unless it resolves some problem which humanism cannot resolve, or goes beyond a point at which humanism sticks – it is obviously confusing to bring religion into the discussion at all; it would be clearer and more honest to talk the language of enlightened humanism.

To the question whether man can perfect himself, or needs a power beyond himself to rescue him from his predicament, there are, apart from despair, two kinds of answer. One answer is to affirm our faith in human reason and virtue. Notwithstanding the failures of history, we can point to the tremendous growth of human knowledge and the development of political and economic democracy. Never has humanity's potential for progress been so great as it today. The next fifty or a hundred years, if they do not bring the total destruction of civilization, could bring the millennium. The darkest hour is before the dawn. Either way, it is up to us. That view has courage and deserves respect.

Christianity offers a different answer to the problem, starting from the affirmation that there is no solution of the human problem in terms of human effort alone. The trouble about a belief that man can perfect himself is that the longer the imperfections of human society continue, the harder it is to believe that man has the power to put the world right. A review of human history impels us to ask whether there is some flaw, some self-contradiction, in man's nature that dooms him to the lot of Sisyphus when he tries to achieve his aspirations by his unaided human efforts. Outbreaks of brutality in civilized society force us to ask deep questions about the nature of man. Discussing the Eichmann trial, Dr James Parkes writes: 'Ordinary men did and watched these things, and then went home to supper, played with their children, listened to music, while their victims went to death. ... The evidence gave me a new respect for my Christian forefathers, who proclaimed continuously the sinfulness of man and his need for grace and redemption. This thing is in us as human beings; and it can dominate and lead us into acts of cruelty and obscenity which have reduced men and women throughout the world to tears. ... What the Nazis did was not to create a new type of sub-men, but to remove the inhibitions of civilization and the controls of religion from people like ourselves, and allow the result full scope for its expression.'[1]

The Kingdom of Heaven can come on earth only as an act of God – an act which we can frustrate or facilitate, but which

1. *Birmingham Post*, 26 May 1961.

we cannot of ourselves accomplish. Christian living is not a matter of human achievement, for which we can pat ourselves on the back, but essentially a matter of divine grace, which we may be granted but do not deserve. So long as we persist in looking for some human substitute for the grace of God, we shall go on stumbling in the darkness of our own making. That is not to say that we are to despise techniques. The grace of God is no more a convenient substitute for human effort than human ingenuity is a substitute for the grace of God. Of ourselves we can do nothing. But, if the spirit of God is working in us, we shall make more, not less, effort, and be satisfied with nothing less than the best techniques.

The Christian answer demands a humility which is never easy, least of all in this age of technological achievement. The Christian apologist would insist that, beneath the particular obstacles to faith which distinguish the different stages of historical development, there is the greatest, unchanging obstacle – the reluctance of man to recognize his human defects, to give up worshipping the magnified image of man, and to humble himself before his God, whose created image it is man's dubious privilege perpetually to deface.

If we take our stand in the Hebrew-Christian tradition, we can fairly claim to reckon realistically with the failure of human history and the evil in the heart of man. But we must also admit that we do so by making assumptions which are as enormous as they are, in the ordinary sense of the term, unverifiable. We must also admit that these assumptions can have little or no meaning to those who limit themselves to intellectual scrutiny and hold back from commitment at the level of feeling and action. 'To the Greeks, foolishness.' We are asking people to take a leap in the dark. To this objection we can reply, however, that religious truth is not the only kind of truth that has to be personally experienced before it means anything, and that it can be maintained that all truth is personal in the sense in which that view was summarized in Chapter 10.[1]

1. With reference to Michael Polanyi's *Personal Knowledge* and Louis Arnaud Reid's *Ways of Knowledge and Experience*.

With these preliminary observations, we may go on to consider the bearings of Christianity on the problems discussed in this book.

There are perhaps four main claims that can be made for the Christian interpretation of life in relation to problems that have been discussed in earlier chapters.

The first is that Christianity is a faith for living. The Christian faith has something which no purely humanistic outlook possesses : it is realistic in its assessment of the human predicament and at the same time finally optimistic. A humanistic faith can be optimistic if it assumes the power of man to perfect himself and society; but this assumption seems unrealistic when set against the evidence of history, which shows man evolving ever more complicated ways of making a mess of his destiny. History testifies to the increase of human means for both good and evil, but scarcely to any general trend in either direction. If, on the other hand, the humanist recognizes the self-contradiction in the very nature of man, there is no ultimate position but despair, albeit the noble despair of the tragic hero. Christianity, in its doctrines of Original Sin and Salvation, combines a realistic recognition of human imperfection with a belief in the possibility of human remaking by the grace of God. In the Christian view the redemption of communities, even of the whole world order, is not excluded. But, so long as the historical process remains unredeemed, it is still possible for the Kingdom of God to come into being here or there, gleaming in an obscure world, wherever love and compassion prevail in personal relations. And, since death does not ring down the curtain on the drama of human destiny, there are possibilities out of time which no mundane evil can defeat.

The Christian faith, it may be claimed, makes sense of history by going beyond history. It is questionable whether any purely mundane view of human destiny makes sense of the endless struggle of the human spirit, and the endless frustration of human hopes. On the purely mundane view, human destiny seems a pretty bitter joke. If man can create the perfect society, if he can make even a tolerable working success of society, why

is he after six thousand years of civilization apparently as far
from it as ever? But, if we do not limit human destiny within
the framework of time, and do not demand that human hope
and human effort shall be vindicated within history, our whole
perspective changes, and even the *failure* of history takes on a
positive meaning, since it proclaims the perpetual fate of man
when, in the pride of his own achievements, he tries to do with
his own powers and resources what can be done only by offering himself as the humble vehicle of divine power. The Greeks,
whose understanding of the meaning of existence was considerable, knew that *nemesis* follows *hubris*.

From the Christian standpoint the failure of history not only
becomes intelligible; it becomes necessary. It is what has to be
expected. 'The most obvious meaning of history', wrote Dr
Reinhold Niebuhr, 'is that every nation, culture, and civilization
brings destruction upon itself by exceeding the bounds of
creatureliness which God has set upon all human enterprises.'[1]
There is nothing surprising in the fact that, in an age of enormous technological development, personal values are under-
mined – that human life takes on the image of the machine. We
become like what we worship. Nevertheless, in the Christian
view, the prospect is never hopeless. Although the full meaning
of history and the full redemption of mankind lie beyond this
world, the redemptive power of love is active all the time in the
world. The point was well put by A. J. Toynbee, writing of the
'Kingdom of God which is not in time ... but in a different
spiritual dimension' and, he added, 'just by virtue of this difference of dimension is able to penetrate our mundane life and
transfigure it'.[2]

Not only does Christianity reckon realistically with history;
it also takes seriously man's responsibilities in this world. The
true Christian is certainly 'other-worldly' in one important
sense. Since no mundane power can destroy the things that
matter to him most, he does not fear what man can do to him;
he does not fear the world, and is therefore beyond its power.
But Christ's teaching gives no sanction whatever for the other-

1. *The Nature and Destiny of Man*, Vol. 1, p. 150.
2. *A Study of History* (abridged edition), p. 128.

worldliness which means retreating from the claims of this world and seeking a perfection of mystical contemplation. The founder of Christianity left his followers in no doubt at all about their duty to feed the hungry and shelter the homeless.[1]

The first claim that can be made for Christianity, then, is that it is a faith for living which is both realistic in its attitude to daily life and human history and at the same time ultimately optimistic. It is a faith that gives meaning and purpose to life in this world and beyond it. Quite simply, the Kingdom of God is Love in action – the response of human love evoked by the Love of God which broke into history in Christ, and to the image of that Love in other human beings. The essence of the Christian revelation is that it is not a *statement* merely, but an *act*. God in Christ entered the world's pain, ignorance, and evil and, by undergoing that evil, defeated it in the only way in which evil can be defeated. In the long run evil cannot be defeated with its own weapons. The only power greater than evil is love which is prepared to give itself unconditionally. Christ shows what God is and what man could be. 'God was in Christ, reconciling the world to Himself.' The Cross means spiritual victory through mundane defeat – victory which issues in the power of the Resurrection. 'This hath God done.'

In the second place it may be claimed that Christian theology gives added meaning to personal relations and to the morality that proceeds from respect of person for person. Belief in the sacredness of human personality, and in morality based upon that sacredness, are not indeed limited to Christians. But if the

1. On 23 July 1961 (*Daily Telegraph*, 24 July 1961) the Rev. Joseph Williamson, vicar of St Paul's, Dock Street, Stepney, preaching in St Paul's Cathedral, said that hundreds of girls were in slavery in the Stepney district under threat of razor and gun by men who lived on their immoral earnings. The higher clergy knew little about these conditions and the Church did little about it. The churches ought to protect and rescue these girls and urge the government to demolish the slums that housed vice. 'The Church authorities are set too far away from the scenes of hell and degradation; too far from the life which drags down and claims too great a number of our young people. ... Literally our hands are too clean.'

agnostic humanist is asked *why* human personality is sacred, and *why* I should not use my fellow men as means to my own ends if I can get away with it, there is no very clear answer. To say that human personality is *per se* sacred is to beg the question.

Christianity gives us a clear reason why human personality is sacred, and why we should treat others as ends in themselves, and not use them as means to our own ends. Men are brothers because sons of God. I may not *like* my neighbour. But, if I believe that God cares for me and for my neighbour too, that Christ came for the sake of my neighbour as well as for me, then I may find myself *loving* my neighbour. If I do not, I know that I am casting God's love back in His face.

We cannot of our own power love one another as we ought. But the grace of God comes into human life through the relations between persons; these are the growing-points of the spiritual life. And our imperfect love for one another, brought into the radiance of His perfect love for us, can be consecrated and transformed nearer to the pattern of Christ.

In his discussion of personal knowledge, Professor L. A. Reid [1] observes that in the best human relations there is an inescapable tension or frustration arising from the fact that friends or lovers long to break down the separateness between them which, in the nature of the case, cannot be broken down, and the breaking-down of which (if it were possible) would destroy the relationship, since the maintenance of individual identity is part of the meaning of love. At this point the Christian faith is relevant. Professor Reid suggests that the frustrating 'externality' of each to the other may be transcended by the realization that both are one in God. In this setting the externality of I and Thou is transformed. But, for the Christian, the recognition of the transcendence of separateness in God also lays an authority upon the human persons; their friendship or love must be consecrated to what is of God.

Thirdly, the Christian faith is, in proportion as it is sincerely held, a source of power for coping with the practical problems of life. St Paul put no trust in himself ('The good that I would

1. *Ways of Knowledge and Experience.*

I do not, and the evil that I would not, that I do'); but he put his whole trust in Christ ('I can do all things through Christ which strengtheneth me.' 'Not I, but Christ who worketh in me'). While the Christian faith insists on the importance of our obligation to live as well as we can in this world, it does not limit our destiny to this world. For this reason Christianity can carry us over worldly disappointment, failure, suffering, as no purely this-worldly faith can do. Given loyalty to Christ (which is something much more momentous than an academic proposition, as the lives of all great Christians show), nothing else really matters. Liberated from ultimate involvement in the things of this world, the true Christian is for that very reason more effective in dealing with the affairs of this world, because he will not be inhibited by fears about comfort, safety, or reputation. Like the psalmist he can say: 'The Lord is my defence: my God is the rock of my refuge.' 'I will not fear what man can do unto me.' In the last resort he can go to the extreme of Job's: 'Though He slay me, yet will I trust in Him.'

That is not to say that this liberation and power will be available for all who, in the manner of most of us who call ourselves Christians, concede lukewarm acceptance of Christian truth and offer conditional loyalty to Christ. It has been said that 'there is no disloyalty to Christ more heinous than a discipleship pared down to the limits of convenience'. That phrase fits many of us, for most of us are bad Christians. Yet the example of the great Christian spirits, from St Paul onwards, shows what is the spiritual reward of total acceptance and unconditional loyalty. And the means are there, if we will use them, for making our own faith less feeble and our discipleship less unworthy. The way is long, and most of us slip at least one step back for every two steps forward.

In the fourth place Christian faith and practice provide a framework of common shared experience, with shared modes of expression, which can bind together in fellowship people who are separated from one another in other ways – by social status, occupation, and so on. Christianity is not a religion of solitude. It is significant that, from one end of the Bible to the other, salvation is social. The Old Testament prophets proclaimed the redemption of Israel, and the message of the New Testament is of redemption into the New Israel of the Church. The foundation of the Christian Church was the group of intimate followers whom Jesus gathered round him; and, when he parted from them, he promised that 'where two or three are gathered together in my name, there I will be in the midst of them'.

Membership of the Christian community, where people have some chance of meeting with their defences down, can do a good deal to overcome not only the contemporary fragmentation of thought, but also the actual fragmentation of society. Christian communities, provided they appreciate their outgoing obligations to society at large and are not merely withdrawn escape-groups, can be microcosms where, in a phrase of the late Lord Lindsay's, the game can be played better than the rules and so, in a measure, the rules can be improved. The Christian community, by stimulating active fellowship, can do much to offset the general trend towards passivity and uniformity in modern society, and, by the essentially personal character of the relations cultivated within it, may help to rescue us from the dehumanizing effects of large-scale organization and mass-culture.

It may be convenient to sum up this chapter by referring to the discussion, in Part II, of the conditions for the promotion and maintenance of personal values in the modern world, and noting the relevance of Christianity to each of these conditions.

It was suggested, to begin with, that we need a coherent view of life, not only formulated as an academic exercise, but held as a faith that can supply inspiration for living. Christianity offers both a coherent interpretation of existence (individual and historical) and a faith for action; a purpose which goes beyond mere social conformity and beyond the bounds of this mortal world. The central promise of the Christian Gospel is that, in the power of Christ, we can accomplish what of our own selves we could not do. In Him we can be more than conquerors because we can be set free from fear (the real and eternal enemy of love) and find that peace which is not a sedative but a serene concentration of effort.

Secondly, it was argued that we need more effective communication, both in the sense of having something worth communicating and also in the sense of having intelligible means of communicating it. It was also claimed that the basis of true communication is the establishment of person-to-person relations. Christianity insists that human relations should never be less than personal, and that each individual is a person in his own right. Moreover, in Christian doctrine and worship, there is a long tradition, changing but continuous, which provides both the content and the means of communication about the essential meaning of life. It must be emphasized that the Church's communication is not a dead but a living thing, responsive to changes in social and intellectual climate. At the present time the various Christian denominations are very much alive to the need for constantly reviewing their traditional statements in the light of changing conditions. At no time since the Reformation has so much attention been given to biblical translation and to liturgical study.

Thirdly, it was urged that, if modern society is to be healthy, there must be plenty of opportunity within the structure of the social-service State for voluntary activity – voluntary in the sense that it is the result of private initiative and is not undertaken and ordered by public authority. Such voluntary activity may take place alongside, and in addition to, public services; or it may be (in the distinctively English tradition) integrated into the organization of the public services themselves, so that the amateur giving his services works together with the professional, as in local educational administration. In a world which both invites passivity at the receiving end of a laid-on system of services and entertainments, and also, for that very reason, instigates young people to pathologically violent excitements, Christianity is relevant for at least three reasons. (a) Christianity insists on the irreducible responsibility of each individual to use his gifts constructively. (b) It insists that we are members one of another. The Christian life is essentially corporate. The individual in a world of mass-culture is small, helpless, frightened, sometimes rebellious. The social collective is more and more irresistible, and perhaps most irresistible when killing by kindness. In a world that does little to encourage fellowship, and where neither conformity nor rebellion is liberating, Christian fellowship offers the service that is freedom. (c) In a world that offers too few natural and healthy opportunities for adventure, Christianity demands unlimited courage, moral and in some circumstances physical. The Christian life is never dull.

Lest, however, we should think of Christianity as a kind of magic which is at our command if we know the right incantations, or a sort of spiritual Pelmanism which we can 'take up' by filling in a coupon and paying an instalment, we must remember that we cannot bargain with Christ. The gifts of the Spirit are available only through unconditional discipleship. There is a terrible realism in Christ's teaching which is disquieting to those of us who are this side of fully committed discipleship. 'My peace I give to you. Not as the world gives do I give to you.' [1] 'The hour is coming, indeed it has come, when you will be scattered ... and will leave me alone; yet I am not alone, for the Father is with me. I have said this to you, that in me you may have peace. In the world you have tribulation; but be of good cheer, I have overcome the world.' [2]

1. John xiv, 27.   2. ibid., xvi, 32–3.